The Redemption of Isobel Farrar

ALAN ROBERT CLARK

Fairlight Books

First published by Fairlight Books 2023

Fairlight Books
Summertown Pavilion, 18–24 Middle Way, Oxford, OX2 7LG

A CIP catalogue record for this book is available from the
British Library

1 2 3 4 5 6 7 8 9 10

ISBN 978-1-914148-44-6

www.fairlightbooks.com

Printed and bound in Great Britain

Designed by Rebecca Fish

In memory of Robert Palmer, from whose loving encouragement every word flows.

I

In the summer of 1926, calm followed the storm of the great strike. The dark clouds having passed, the sky was now as blue as before; the birds still sang and the cows still munched in the fields of England's green and pleasant land. God was in His heaven and had He glanced down at the slim folds of the Surrey Hills on the second Sunday in July, He would have spotted a man on a bicycle.

Like most people on that afternoon, the man was a little too hot for comfort, especially since his journey had been a long one. He'd taken his bike on the train to the small country station, then cycled the rest of the way. It was a challenging ride, but the weather was perfect and he was, as he liked to say, fit as a fiddle. Besides, he loved that bike, often speaking to it as if it were human, exhorting it to carry him up the steepest hills and bear him safely around treacherous bends. For the bicycle was his passport from the world in which he existed to that in which he yearned to be and, almost every Sunday, it would transport him loyally from one into the other.

In the saddlebag was an Ordnance Survey map, meticulously studied before he set off. He couldn't be certain of the exact spot he wanted to find, though the houses in these parts were so widely scattered it shouldn't be that difficult. Anyway, a glimpse of it from a distance was really all he sought. It wasn't in his nature to think to ask for more.

He was a tall, slim man, somewhere in that hazy borderland between being young and middle-aged. From a distance, he could easily pass for the former; only close up might an observer suspect the latter. But it was beyond doubt that he was handsome – almost beautiful indeed, if one should ever use that word of a man. He himself would have rejected it with distaste. Vanity had never been part of his upbringing. Praise had rarely come his way.

Despite the heat, the man on the bicycle had dressed formally. A summer suit, a cap of dark blue linen, a shirt and tie. In reversal of the usual logic, he had left the city without the collar and tie and only put them on when he reached the countryside. A land that was not his own and in which he wanted to look his best.

The village he'd expected to find was hardly more than a hamlet. Beyond it, the route was uphill and, fit as he was, he sweated hard inside his summer suit. The lane was like a tunnel bored by some sapper into the woodland. High above his head, the tops of tall firs swayed imperceptibly, blotting out the sun. Lower down, banks of sweet-scented broom crowded in on him from the edges of the road. It was now that the sense of being an intruder began to creep over him. He had guessed that it might.

Suddenly, the land levelled out and the woods peeled away. Now he found himself on the crest of a low hill looking out across the open countryside. An undulating patchwork of green fields, small clumps of forest, a sprinkling of rooftops, a steeple or two. And in the far distance, like some fortification around this paradise, the hazy crinkle of the distant downs. He stopped and breathed in the air, heavy with the scents of summer.

For weeks now, he'd imagined this day. It had taken him that long to decide to make the journey. So many times, he'd told himself it could only be a pointless one and called himself a fool. Yet in the end he'd been quite unable to resist it. Never had he expected to get this close. Never in a hundred years. He freewheeled downhill between ranks of wild poppies, the rush of air drying the sweat on his brow and the back of his neck. He stopped to consult the map. In a farmyard, a young woman was throwing feed to a flock of geese.

'Lost?' she called.

'Not exactly. Are you Blount's Farm?'

'That's us.'

'Pardon me, miss, but is the Farrar house near here?' he asked, as if it were of little matter.

'You an architect? Folk looking for it usually are.'

'Not me, miss. Nothing half so posh.'

'Just round the next bend. Up on the little hill. But it's not the Farrar house anymore. They sold it a few years back and went to Canada.'

He knew that last fact already. Still, it was hard to hear it articulated, shouted out indeed. As if this unknown woman somehow knew why he had come. As if she too was calling him a fool. But her smile was welcoming enough. A fresh, pretty girl, her face not embalmed in powder and paint like most city women, though marked by a scar down one side of her eye.

'Who owns it these days, then?'

'Some old lord who lives in the south of France most of the time. It's all shuttered up now. Nobody there.'

The man raised his cap and pedalled off. He banked around the gentle bend and sure enough there it was, up on a low escarpment. The farm woman had said it would be, but he hadn't quite believed her. Daft, of course. Why should it not exist? Why should this place, which had been constructed so solidly in his imagination, not also be real?

But what he found now was unlike anything he had seen before. The houses he knew were squat toads of soot-blackened brick, squashed together in ill-tempered rows lining streets that led to nowhere you'd want to go. But this house was a creature of the light and the air. Facing south towards the downs, it seemed to drink in the sunbeams that washed against its high, wide windows. A gossamer house, whose presence on the low hill was no diminution of the beauty of its surroundings but an embellishment to it. With as much right to be there as the trees, the grass and the flowers. Evidence that humankind, if it tried, could give nature a run for its money.

For many minutes, the man stood just looking, his bike propped against a fence. The map told him of a narrow right of way across the field that stretched up towards the foot of the low hill. Finding the little gate that led onto it, he pushed his bike into waves of corn, so high and thick that he felt like a swimmer battling a tide. He ran his free hand over the tops of the corn, his fingertips caressing the pregnant husks. On the far side of the field, the land dipped slightly into a little coppice of larch and beech. Here the public path veered off in another direction and a sign reading *Private please* was nailed to a tree. Yet the sign was a paltry thing, roughly painted on a sliver of wood, less of a prohibition than a request tinged with apology. He wondered if well-bred people felt little need of sterner defences, expecting obedience as their right, their worst imaginable misdemeanour being one against good manners.

Glad of the shade of the trees, the man drank some water from the flask in his saddlebag. He took off his jacket, cap and bicycle clips and wiped his brow with his handkerchief. A squirrel watched him from its branch, then dashed away, having found him of little interest. For a moment, he had the absurd notion that it was off to alert someone to this trespasser, this person who had no business there. Someone not well-bred, but a child of the mean streets.

The house on the hill was hidden now by the trellis of trees. He found an odd relief in that because, for a moment, his courage had failed him. It would be so easy to retreat across the corn, through the hamlet, back to the little station and to the place he called home. Apart from the woman in the farmyard – and she would hardly care – nobody would ever know he'd been there. Yet again, he asked himself what was to be gained from this. Not much, of course, but surely better than nothing. A moment or two of connection. He rolled a cigarette and told himself he was a coward, though he was hardly a man without courage. Christ, he thought, he'd served in the trenches, gone over the top and lived to tell the tale. Why did this seem so much harder? Nor was this a tale he'd ever need to tell anyone. Come on, Corporal, pull yourself together.

He stubbed out the cigarette and put the fag-end in the saddlebag. He put his jacket and cap back on, straightened his tie again and hid the bike among the bushes. On the far side of the coppice, beyond steeply sloping lawns of unmown grass, the house rose on its escarpment. So much closer now, the sun still blazing off its windows. In that moment, his hands shading his eyes, all doubts left him. He'd done right to come. His heart had been racing, but now it had calmed itself and he was infused with that sense of stillness for which he had searched all his life. Seldom had he found it, and it was nearly always the natural world which brought it to him. Only once had it ever come to him from another human being. The person who, that morning, had asked if he was going anywhere special. But even that, he knew, was not the complete fulfilment for which he longed. He was grateful for it nevertheless.

He climbed the slope of the neglected lawn, sprinkled like sugar with daisies and buttercups. Over to one side stood a crumbling loggia, its bones hardly visible beneath a thick shawl of white roses, unpruned and blowsy with summer. And off in the distance, he now saw the silvery ribbon of a narrow river that wound its way around the lower reaches of the hill. The singularity of the house struck him anew. It was not especially large: a simple rectangle of two storeys with a pair of shorter wings jutting out, its lines straight and clean, without embellishment or affectation, even its chimneys hardly visible. Nor was it remotely grand, having no need for grandeur as, by not trying to draw attention to itself, it achieved just that. He had no means of knowing how old it was, how long it had stood on its hill, for he hadn't the learning that might have helped him to judge. In any case, that judgement seemed of no importance.

He wondered about the man who had first imagined this place. He marvelled at the possession of such genius and, knowing that you possessed it, wondered how that knowledge might make you feel. At this reflection, a low sigh escaped his lips. For he considered himself to have no distinction whatsoever, let alone genius. In that belief he was quite wrong, but it was nevertheless the one he felt the world had made of him, and he had accepted it, as he accepted most things, without demur. Know your place, they'd always told him. Know your place. Don't give yourself big ideas, son.

There was no sign at all of human life. He walked up towards the broad terrace which ran along the length of the garden front. Christ, it was hot, but still he kept his jacket on and his tie straight. You could fry eggs on those flagstones today, he thought, except you wouldn't because they were covered by dirt, dead leaves and the mess of birds. The wicker legs of stacked garden chairs peeked out from under the skirts of a grubby tarpaulin. Two wrought-iron tables, scurvied with rust, stood on either side of high glass doors. But the doors were curtained, as were all the windows. What a shame, he thought, that the house could not look out on this glorious day. Those great doors should be open, people coming and going, sitting on the terrace reading books, drinking tea or wine, having clever conversation about whatever people like them might talk about.

Bees and wasps crawled across the window frames as if trying to peep in between some gap in the curtains. He tried the same thing himself but had no more luck. He went around the house to the other side. Here there was no vista at all. Beyond a gravelled carriage circle, a high wall of hydrangeas, blue as a summer sea, kept out the world. A padlock and chain, distressing in their ugliness, secured the broad front door – a reminder that this was a place of value as well as beauty. Here too, drifts of desiccated leaves had accumulated in the porch. A chimney was crowned with an abandoned bird's nest, tilted at an angle like a battered hat. A fractured drainpipe reeled drunkenly off a wall; a barrel overflowed with fetid water. Away to one side, a small stable block, its doors wide open, still held the faint odour of horse manure, and among the piles of dirty straw, rats woke up at the sound of his footsteps and buried themselves even deeper inside their tunnels. On the stable block's little clock tower, time stood still.

Yet somehow the house on the hill rose above the scars of its desolation. Back in the garden, he found a decrepit chair, half-buried in the long grass under a big old oak. Dusting it off, for he worried about his suit, he rolled a cigarette and, for an hour or more, sat quite motionless. He wished he were poetic and could write all this down when he got home. Capture it so that it would never be lost to him. But expression had never been his strength. At an early age, he had learned the wisdom of silence – the comfort of it too. Was that why, instead, he seemed to feel everything so strongly?

Yet he didn't lack imagination, a fact he usually kept to himself, and now he peopled the lawns with those who might once have lived in this garden. As he'd been acquainted with none of them, they could be no more than ghostly figures, minor characters from a story in which he had played no part. Only one figure was more substantial than the rest. Only one had a clear shape and form as she strolled through the daisies and buttercups in a long white gown, holding a parasol against the sunlight, batting away the bees and the wasps with a languid hand. Even though he had never met her, he had known her all his life. And now, in this place and in this moment, in the depth of the drowning stillness, he had never felt closer to her, as if he might even reach out and touch her. And that, after all, was what had brought him here. For that moment of connection. And it had happened.

He closed his eyes on the image and told himself again not to be a bloody fool. Still, he'd done it, hadn't he? He'd come. He'd seen it and now he could go away, back to the life he knew. And that was fine. He had no right to ask for more. Walking away down the grassy slope towards the coppice, he allowed himself one last glance back at the house on the hill. He would never forget it, but he would never return.

He took off his jacket and folded it neatly into the saddlebag. He loosened his tie and rolled up his shirt sleeves. He pushed his bike along the path through the corn and, at the gate on to the lane, he mounted and pedalled back the way he had come.

When the young woman at Blount's Farm happened to look out of her kitchen window just then, she saw a man on a bicycle weeping like a child.

2

The wooden footbridge that spanned the tracks hadn't yet collapsed, as had been prophesised for many a year. The same garish posters which, for as long as she remembered, had encouraged trips to Brighton and Eastbourne still did so. The machine in the ticket-hall that dispensed Fry's Chocolate, so adored by her son in childhood, still swallowed infant sixpences. Isobel felt the faintest irritation that the little railway station was quite unchanged by the desertion of the Farrars.

The old stationmaster had helped her down from the train, bowing as if she were Queen Mary. His face was flushed as always; it was whispered that he drank.

'A thousand welcomes, Lady Farrar,' he said. 'We heard you were coming. I feel quite emotional, dear lady. Quite emotional.'

'How very nice to see you, Mr Travers,' she replied. 'I find you in good health?'

'Thank you, yes. And you, dear lady – not looking one week older.'

'Nonsense, Mr Travers. It's five long years. Time must mark us all.'

But the old stationmaster was not far wrong. In her sixty-third year, Isobel Farrar was still beautiful. The rich golden hair of her youth, that strange contrast to those deep dark eyes, had charitably turned into a casque of soft, shining silver, none the less striking. The skin of her face and neck remained firm and pale as the moon, though there was no denying the tiny lines fanned out around the corners of her eyes and mouth. Not that she herself would ever have denied them or taken much trouble to hide them. And despite a taste for *pain au chocolat*, her figure retained both the shape of her prime and the odd swaying gait she had always possessed, as if her body were fragile as a butterfly and she feared the very air might blow her away.

Some people, before they first got to know her, found Isobel Farrar remote. Her first husband, unable to get to know her at all, had once shouted that she was an infernal mystery and slammed the door behind him. Yet when she met a kindred spirit, someone with whom she might speak of music or art or literature, she was gregarious enough in her way. Then those great dark eyes would shed their glaze of indifference. The full lips, at which so many men had found themselves gazing, would suddenly become animated. But kindred spirits had rarely been found in the gilded drawing rooms of Park Lane or Belgravia. In the glittering crowd, she had always felt alone.

That mystery of hers had been a misfortune because it was, in truth, an illusion. If ever a girl had been born to be loved, it was the child christened as Isobel Leigh. Twice in her life, it had been her good fortune to know an all-consuming devotion. For a genteel, troubled professor of music and a rollicking, impecunious architect: her father and her lover. To neither of these men had she been any sort of mystery. With neither had she needed any such defence. Without hesitation, she had opened herself to them entirely. Yet both had been cruelly taken from her, both in a matter of moments. Each time, the loss of being loved, merciless in its finality, had crept into her body and soul. Bad enough for anyone, but for Isobel a deprivation scarcely to be borne. And on this November morning, on the pavement outside the little country station, she recognised that feeling again now. Coming her way. No less merciless than before.

From the taxi, she remembered every twist and turn of the lane. How the midday sun would filter through the tops of the firs and litter the ground with a thousand fragments of light. How the trees briefly parted to give a glimpse of the picture-postcard view towards the downs, which her son, obsessed with the cinema, always called 'a preview of coming attractions'. At another spot, as the lane turned a sharp corner, the camber became uneven, which in the old days could alarm the horses and require a carriage-driver of some skill.

The first snows of the year had fallen in the night. No courteous sprinkling to ease people gently towards the notion of winter, but a full-blown deluge of merciless white. The lane, though partly cleared, was still treacherous. At the uneven camber, the taxi slithered and the driver cursed, making no attempt to apologise. A middle-aged man without much charm but with a limp which might excuse that fact. Outside the station, he'd taken her suitcases and half thrown them in the boot, leaving her to open the passenger door herself – something she couldn't recall ever having done before.

Such manners shocked Lady Farrar, widow of an ambassador. Goodness, what else might have altered in England since she'd been gone? From what she'd read in the Canadian newspapers, it seemed to have changed and she knew that she herself had not. Yet the new world hadn't suited her either. It had been her son who, offered his first junior posting in an embassy, had begged her to go with him. A new start for both of them, Johnnie had said. After the death of Octavius Farrar. Dad would have cheered us on, don't you think, Mum? But Ottawa had seemed a dull, provincial town to a woman used to the capitals of Europe. The Farrar title had opened doors, of course – even faster perhaps than in England – but the doors rarely led to anywhere she felt inclined to go. And the new world was a nosey place. It reached out for you, pushy and insistent, wanting to pull you in and to know your secrets. Mystery wasn't something that interested it, unless it was safely between the pages of a novel or on the flickering screen of the cinematograph. Lady Farrar was not its cup of coffee and vice versa.

And then, as had to happen, Johnnie met a girl and married her. A girl from the Rocky Mountains, all teeth and smiles. A girl quite unable to relate to, and certainly unable to handle, the nuances of a reserved Englishwoman. It was time, Isobel decided, to go home, wherever that might now be. At the pier in Halifax, Johnnie being Johnnie had wept and, holding her tightly in his arms, had begged her for the hundredth time to think again. At the ship's rail, seeing the waving figure of her child shrink away, she almost changed her mind and wondered if she could call for a tugboat to take her back to shore. Then came the awful emptiness in the pit of her stomach. She knew it at once. The loss of being loved.

'It's here! Turn here, young man,' she had to call out now from the back of the taxi.

The modest signpost that carried the name of the house was lost under a drift. The driver braked too hard and the taxi slithered again. It was clear that the drive was largely blocked. The man refused to go further, bleating that he'd never get the car out again, unless she'd be happy to pay for a new axle. He'd carry her cases, though, if it wasn't too far. How far exactly was it?

And so Isobel Farrar was forced to return to the house that had once been hers, and now was again, by creeping carefully along its half-buried drive as if she were trying to surprise it. Not a sound reached her ears except the scrunching of her shoes in the snow and the mutterings of the man trudging behind her. For a moment, she even wondered if the house would still be there or if, when she turned that last bend, there might be one vast empty space on the low hill that looked out towards the downs. No evidence left of the place that had figured so vividly in her history, its memories bred into her bone.

But no, there it was. The snow draped like dust sheets over the gently sloping roofs. A figure hurried towards her from the porch. A young woman, her face vaguely familiar, pulling a coat on top of an apron and rolled-up sleeves.

'Lady Farrar, I wasn't expecting you quite so early,' she said. 'Goodness me, come away in or you'll catch your death. Such weather! Careful now, mind you don't fall.'

The young woman slipped her arm through Isobel's. This sort of thing was happening more often of late. The statement by the young, kindly meant but carelessly insulting, that one was no longer young oneself.

'Thank you, my dear. And you are?'

'I'm Letty,' the young woman said, as if it were an obvious fact. 'From Blount's Farm. I'm to look after you. Till you're settled at least.'

'Oh yes, my dear. Of course – I recognise you now.'

'I bet you didn't,' replied Letty. 'Time stands still for no man and certainly no woman. Look at me, I'm the living proof of that one.'

Letty Blount laughed, but it was true. The girl whom Isobel only half-remembered was indeed different. A scar down the side of her left eye, from her temple to her jaw, the eye itself milky and unfocused. She must be more than thirty now.

'I'm the only one Mr Saunders, the agent, could find at short notice,' said Letty, 'but I'll do my best for you if you want me.'

'I'm sure I'll be very pleased to have you, Letty.'

The young woman threw open the big front door and stood aside to let her pass. For a moment, Isobel stopped in the porch to catch her breath.

'Welcome home, Lady Farrar.'

She stood now on the exact spot to which Octavius, his arm through hers, had led her so long ago, in the last years of the old century.

'I do so want to show you my place in Surrey,' he'd said over supper at Rules, after they'd been to the show at the Gaiety. 'Might next Sunday suit you?'

She'd enjoyed being romanced again after so many years of being on her own.

'Next Sunday would be fine.'

It had been from here in the lobby that she had first gazed into the heart of the house – a large covered court, two storeys high, lit by a vast skylight. On the upper level, it was surrounded by a gallery off which led the bedrooms and bathrooms. But it was always the light you noticed, even on a desolate day. It was a house of light and air. A house in which, apart from the human requirement for warmth and shelter, there would be minimal separation between its occupants and the natural world that surrounded and embraced them.

'Quite something, isn't it?' Octavius had said that day, his chest puffed out a little in that funny way she found endearing – like a schoolboy showing off an especially fine conker or a tadpole in a jar.

'It's wonderful,' she had replied.

Then Octavius had casually spoken the words that would bind her to this house forever.

'Designed by a young architect and landscape gardener called Hugh Pasco. A minor genius. Died young in an accident. Such a shame. He'd have gone far, I shouldn't wonder.'

She'd felt her heart stop. Octavius had only spoken vaguely of his house in the country, never giving it a name. But this was Halcyon Hill. The near legendary Halcyon, which she had never seen before, on which the posthumous reputation of Hugh Pasco largely rested. Dear God. And when, a week later, after *The Barber of Seville*, Sir Octavius Farrar apologised for being so much older than her, but wondered nevertheless if she might consent to marrying a lonely retired diplomat and sometime amateur artist, she had agreed. Knowing, as he kissed her and slid an engagement ring onto her finger, that she was marrying not just Octavius Farrar, but a connection to the golden moment of her life.

Now, dragging her back across the years, the voice of Letty Blount broke into Isobel's consciousness.

'I'm sorry it's still nippy in here,' she said. 'Mr Saunders's man only came yesterday to tinker with the heating system and the old place hasn't warmed up yet. I've lit the stove, though, so you just sit yourself down beside it and I'll make some tea. You must be dog tired, Lady Farrar.'

A bowl of flowering shrubs stood on a small table by the big window. Blue and white cyclamen, aconite, artemisia. The chilly blossoms of approaching winter.

'Such lovely flowers, Letty,' she said when the girl returned with the tea tray.

'Lord Marchwood sent them yesterday,' replied Letty.

'How kind. How is he these days?'

'Still an old devil. The last wife ran off with a commercial traveller. Had you heard? They say he's on the lookout for a new one. Better watch out, Lady Farrar.'

Letty poured out the tea and looked across the snowbound garden.

'It's a glorious view, isn't it?' she said. 'I'd never been up here before the other week.'

'You hadn't?'

'I'm a bottom of the hill sort of person, Lady Farrar. I know my place.'

Letty Blount laughed and when she did, the long scar disappeared into the folds of her cheek and she was almost pretty. She was a broad, buxom woman, flaxen-haired, the epitome of a farmer's daughter. But there was a quality about her, Isobel thought, which suggested that, if Letty did indeed know her place, she would give it little heed.

'The things you put into storage are arriving tomorrow if the road is clear,' said Letty. 'You'll soon feel like you've never been gone.'

'Oh, my dear, it will take a while before I can ever feel that.'

Yet the house was far from bare. Most of its furniture, designed to fit this place and no other, had been part of the sale five years ago and had now been part of its repurchase. Only Isobel's most personal items had been covered in dust sheets or placed in cardboard boxes and ferreted away in a warehouse in Kingston.

The restoration of Halcyon to Isobel Farrar had been a matter of the purest chance. Waiting in Halifax to take the ship back to England, she had caught the flu and delayed her passage by a week. But for that, the telegram that reached her hotel would have missed her. Even in its staccato brevity, she could hear the voice of Miss Maud Farrar, the sister of Octavius.

Darling, can't wait to see you. Will be at Southampton. Quelle surprise, your dear old home is for sale again. Oh, do say you'll buy it back!

And after pacing her hotel bedroom for half the night, staring out at the lights of the harbour without seeing them, Isobel had dispatched her own telegrams to a dusty lawyer's office in Chancery Lane and enquired about doing just that. The repurchase had gone so fast and easily that Isobel soon persuaded herself fate had applauded her decision. The ancient vendor, hopelessly addicted to the roulette tables of Monte, had sold it back if not exactly for a song, then for a lot less than it was worth. Now, as she sat sipping her tea by the great window, she felt as if this stranger had scarcely existed in her house. As if, apart from the pockmarks of his neglect, it had somehow ignored his brief intrusion.

And yet, unlike the little station and the twists and turns of the lane that led from it, the house that had been hers wasn't quite the same. Ridiculous to think it could ever be. The gloomy season, the entombment under the snow, those pockmarks of neglect – she knew that all of these would alter when time had passed. What began to trouble her was the feeling that, in its abandonment, the pulse of the house, like the clock on the stables, had stopped. Could there still be meaning for her on this hilltop, beyond the sustenance of her memories? And, without meaning, what was the point? But her husband was dead, her son on another continent. Where was she to find meaning now?

Letty Blount came and removed the tea things. She was wearing a coat, a woolly hat and a scarf so long it nearly touched the ground. She had changed her indoor shoes for wellington boots that carried a faint whiff of the farmyard.

'I've made a casserole for your supper,' she said. 'You just need to warm it in the oven. And there's a pan of broth on the stove. Same with that. And bread and milk and eggs and cheese in the larder. You'll not starve. Anyway, I'll be back by eight in the morning to get your breakfast. I must get home now and see to my father.'

'Are you on foot, my dear?'

'Just down the garden and across the field to the lane. Ten minutes. No more.'

'Well, hurry, then, before the light has completely gone.'

'Will you be all right tonight, Lady Farrar?'

'I've slept alone in this house a hundred times. I'm not afraid.'

She watched the beam of Letty's torch as the young woman crossed the whitened garden, waving up to the window as she passed. The beam narrowed, grew fainter, then was swallowed into the darkness of the late afternoon.

The big bedroom, in which Isobel had slept with her husband and given birth to her son, was not yet ready and Letty had prepared one of the smaller rooms. Much cosier anyway, she'd said. Isobel unpacked the necessary night things from her suitcases. Letty had been quite right; she was exhausted. She would go to bed early.

In the bathroom mirror, she studied her face for a moment – a thing she rarely did. Unlike many beauties, Isobel Farrar had always been free of vanity, treating her gift carelessly, easily accepting the passage of time because it had hardly bothered to mark her. Yet when she had last glanced into this self-same glass, it had been a younger woman who had stared back. There was no denying that. Nor the fact that she had begun to feel the breath of mortality on her neck: something that might not have troubled her had she not felt the past at her heels, still unresolved, still pushing its way into the present.

For a while, she wandered the rooms of the house, feeling the strangeness of familiarity. She heated the casserole and found a bottle of red wine in the larder. One glass, no more. Just to warm the blood on a night like this. She ate at the kitchen table then carried the wine glass back to the covered court. Despite the cold, she didn't draw the tall curtains; whatever the season, they had rarely ever been closed. Octavius always said it was sacrilege to cover that view, either by day or night. Besides, the moon had lanced through the cloudscape and the sight of it made Isobel's heart quicken. In the lobby, she found her coat and the necessary key from the neatly labelled regiment which Letty had left on a shelf. She unlocked the high glass doors and stepped out onto the terrace. The moonlight washed over the gardens of Halcyon Hill and the landscape that rolled away beyond. It lit up the trees down in the coppice, the frozen circle of the pond and the ribbon of the little river far off to one side.

The night was dead still, as if the air was so cold it couldn't bear to move. A dog was barking somewhere over by Blount's Farm, but otherwise all she could hear was the sound of her own breathing and the voices of beloved ghosts calling up to her from the garden.

She had lied to Letty Blount. It wasn't true to say she was not afraid. But it was not of the darkness, nor of the half-empty rooms and silent staircases. Nor was it of her beloved ghosts. It was the feeling that she herself might slowly, before her time and perhaps without noticing, sink into becoming one of them.

3

I didn't know if you were alive or dead! the letter complained. *I'm now in the latter category... or bloody near it. I have something to tell you and it can't wait. Neither can I, so you must come urgently, my duck. I'll try to look my best, though I doubt my effort will impress you much.*

The signature was not prefaced by *yours sincerely, best wishes* or even *with love*. The writer of the letter assumed that such assurances were not required, that the recipient would take them all for granted. And the sender was quite right in this. All that was necessary was to read the name, flying in big letters across the page as if something were chasing it.

Alice.

*

If she was not to join that company of ghosts who inhabited Halcyon Hill, then she had better let people know that she was indeed still alive.

In the days after her return, as Letty Blount bustled around sorting things out, Isobel had written a sheaf of letters. Somewhat against her nature, she had reached out towards the whist drives, the charity bazaars, the vicar, Lord Marchwood and her other half-remembered friendships in the neighbourhood. And politely, with varying degrees of interest, her letters had been answered.

Small white cards of invitation, stiff with pomposity, their lettering embossed, began to line up on the shelf above the big stove which did duty as a mantelpiece.

But some of these old friendships, though a handful only, were far from half-remembered and were deeply engraved upon her heart, their markings made by memories both happy and sad or by some mixture of the two. Into this category came Alice Godsal.

At the sight of the familiar handwriting, Isobel had felt a throb of guilt. In her years in Canada, she had grown neglectful of those few souls of importance whom she'd left behind. Yet, since such carelessness was unlike her, it had probably gone deeper than that; the determination to look forward now and not back. For a while, too, she and her son had moved around the awesome spaces of their new homeland and she had lost the discipline of communicating each new address. Arguably, her most egregious omission had been towards the writer of the letter she now held in her hand.

Alice. Dear Alice. She must go at once.

The next day, before the sun had risen, Isobel sat at her dressing table preparing to go up to town. She had sent a telegram to say she would arrive by mid-morning. Conscious for once of wanting to look her best, she took extra care with her hair and used a little more make-up than she normally did. Alice had always delighted in Isobel's beauty, quite without a trace of the envy which often curdles such compliments from women who are themselves not beautiful.

'If it hadn't been for this nose,' Alice had often laughed, 'I might have done better than old Billy Godsal. Who knows, the Prince of Wales even. I might have become Mrs Keppel.'

Yet Alice had done remarkably well out of old Billy. These days, she was the widow of William Godsal Esquire of Goldhurst Terrace, West Hampstead, NW. A lady of respectable means, which had been gained respectably too. Old Billy, when he was young Billy, had started life as a simple carpenter with big ambitions and had become one of the most successful house-builders in north London. By serving the middle classes, he had achieved the image of being one of them and passed that achievement on to Alice, who had solicited him in the gallery of the Alhambra and whom he had grown to love enough to save from the streets, whether or not she thought she needed saving.

A young maid, small as a dormouse, answered the door of Goldhurst Terrace. In the lobby she hung up Isobel's coat and hat with such care that Isobel sensed the action was not a frequent one, that perhaps visitors did not come often. She looked around her, waiting for some inner door to be flung open to reveal Alice standing there, her arms outstretched, waiting for a kiss on both rouged cheeks. Instead, there was only silence in the lobby, apart from the heavy tick of a grandfather clock and the low purr of a cat that had wrapped itself around her ankles.

'Mrs Godsal is not well, I understand,' said Isobel.

'No, madam, not well at all,' replied the girl. 'The doctor has not long gone. He's had to give her another injection, so you might find her a bit woozy, madam.'

'Oh dear. Have I come on a bad day?'

'She wasn't too poorly yesterday, madam. Looking forward to your visit. But she was took a bit bad in the night.'

'Mrs Godsal's letter asked me to come urgently,' replied Isobel, lowering her voice. 'Does that mean what I suspect it means?'

'It does, madam,' said the tiny maid, her face tense and pinched, her voice cracking as she spoke. 'Pardon me, but are you an old friend?'

'Yes, very.'

'Then you will do her good, madam. When she's not in pain, she loves to talk about the old days. The stories she's told me! I blush sometimes and that's the truth. You'd never believe it, madam.'

'Oh my dear, I would.'

The girl opened the door into a sitting room bright with wintry sun. Shielding her eyes against it, she saw the hazy outline of a figure lying on a chaise longue beside the window. The prism of the sunlight through the stained glass cast patches of iridescent colour over the figure, covering her in a shifting quilt of flickering light. But as Isobel approached, the sun tripped behind a cloud. In an instant, all the colour drained out of the room and from the body stretched out upon the chaise. And there lay Alice, her eyes closed. The thick red hair now white and sparse. The fine skin mottled and sunk beneath her cheekbones. The nose she hated now larger than ever. The skull already there and waiting for its moment.

Isobel sat on a hard chair beside the chaise and spoke her friend's name. When the eyes opened and stared into hers, she saw no recognition, only confusion and even, for a moment, a hint of fright. Now Isobel spoke her own name and took the hand in hers, choking down the sadness that had risen in her throat. She said her name again; twice, three times, four. Now, the eyes focused and registered. A smile lifted the sunken skin of the face.

'Christ almighty, why couldn't you crumble like the rest of us?' asked Alice.

'Oh, but I have,' replied Isobel. 'A little powder works wonders.'

'Well, not in this case, my duck, as you can see.'

'I still see my dear old friend.'

The hand, feather light, tightened around Isobel's.

The tiny maid brought tea and then knelt down by the chaise, cradling Alice's head in the crook of her arm and raising the cup to her mistress's lips.

'Might I do that, please?' asked Isobel. Suddenly, it seemed the most important thing in the world. But when Alice's head leaned against her, she smelled, beneath the scent of lavender water, the faint odour of decay.

'Where have you been?' asked Alice between the sips of the tea.

'Been?'

'I haven't seen you in ages. Have I?'

'I've been in Canada. For five years. Don't you remember?'

'Ah yes, that was it,' said Alice. 'Canada. That was it.'

Isobel returned to the hard chair and took the feather hand again. The women looked at each other in the way they had always done: with affection and understanding, without barriers or dissembling. At least, Isobel thought, all that was intact. There was no loss there, no fading away of what they had once meant to one another. With the cat purring at Alice's feet, they spoke of that past. Of places and of people. Of the gallery of the Alhambra. Of the little room under the eaves. Of Octavius in his grave at Highgate. Of Billy Godsal in his, entombed in the rusted wreck of the *Lusitania*, though not, as Alice had always been fond of saying, before she'd finally got the old sod to make his will.

Not once had Isobel Farrar ever tried to bury the significance of Alice in her life. She had told her husband the tale of that night on the Embankment and of the stranger who had come to her out of the fog and pulled her back. Octavius, the most sentimental of men, had wept on hearing it. But the reasons for the relationship between his wife and Alice Godsal were even more complex than he had ever been told. To Octavius and their son Johnnie, and to those very few others whom, down the years, she had allowed to know of it, the tragedy of the young Isobel had lain in the offence once committed against her. What only Alice knew was that Isobel's true desolation was something else entirely. An offence which Isobel herself had committed and which Alice had aided and abetted.

Yet today, their aimless wanderings into the past were disjointed, shifting quickly from one scene to another. As if Alice's memory had become a kaleidoscope – a picture forming for a short time then, in a sudden twist of her mind, that picture dissolving and another, quite different, taking shape in her consciousness.

And then, without warning, no more pictures came. Alice winced and gave a quiet cry, her teeth biting into dried-out lips.

Her hand rose shakily to her armpit and held it there. Yet the invasion of the pain seemed to clear her head. What the maid called wooziness vanished from her eyes. They became larger, brighter. The doctor's injection hadn't lasted long. Its veil had lifted.

'But I asked you to come for a reason, didn't I? In my letter?'

'You said it was urgent.'

'I've got a piece of news for you,' replied Alice. 'I've been keeping it now for, God knows, maybe six months. But I didn't know where you were or how to find you. Oh, the sleepless nights it's given me. Punishment for my sins, no doubt, but at least the dear Lord let you get here before it was too late.'

'Goodness, Alice. I can't imagine what it might be.'

'I bet you can't. Not in half a lifetime anyway.'

Alice became restless now, her breathing more rapid, her body shifting constantly on the chaise. Her movements woke the cat, which stretched itself then snuggled up closer to her, as if the creature knew when its comfort was needed. The feather hand reached out to take Isobel's, gripping it with unexpected force even though it trembled too.

'Alice, dear, do calm yourself. Tell me.'

Still Alice did not speak or meet Isobel's eye. But then the sun reappeared and repeated its trick with the stained glass, bathing her in the quilt of coloured light. And it seemed to bring some peace back into the woman on the chaise. Alice tilted her face towards the sun and closed her eyes for a moment. Isobel heard her take a deep breath. Alice turned back to her and opened her eyes as wide as she could manage.

'He has come looking for you,' she said.

The only sounds in the room were the purring of the cat and the banging of Isobel's heart. Alice thought Isobel hadn't understood and repeated herself.

'The boy,' she said. 'The boy has come looking for you.'

4

It had been back in May, he thought. Yes, probably May, because the old woman had been in the front garden with a trug on her arm, cutting the last of her overblown tulips.

It was an ugly house. A dumpy box of brazen redbrick squatting in a row of identical boxes. As if unaware of its ugliness, it had pretensions to splendour, decorating itself with tall brick pillars at the gate, a garden path tiled in black and white diamonds, fancy fretwork in the porch and stained glass in the doors and windows.

He'd worn his summer suit, his collar, shirt and tie. As soon as he'd reached the street, he'd spotted the old woman, but had cycled to and fro past the house until he'd told himself to stop being so stupid. Sensing a presence, she had looked up and there he was, standing at the gate watching her. She'd started back a little, as if he'd frightened her. He said he was sorry, as was his habit, even when there was nothing to say sorry for. Then he saw that it wasn't fear which suffused the face but curiosity, swiftly followed by some kind of fragile recognition. She put her trug down on a green-painted bench and stared.

He asked if she was Mrs Alice Godsal. He'd been given her name, he explained, by the man he had once called his father. That simple statement had been enough. The old woman had covered her mouth with her hand and sat down on the bench beside her tulips.

'Dear God in heaven,' she said. 'Oh, dear God.'

'Then you know who I am?' he asked.

'Oh yes. Yes. You could be nobody else,' she said.

She pulled a handkerchief from her sleeve. She dabbed her eyes, then blew her nose, then twisted the fabric between her fingers. He stood outside the gate, still holding his handlebars, not knowing what to say next. In the garden, the bees buzzed in and out of a white magnolia. A telephone rang somewhere behind an open window. A milk cart went past on the street, the churns clanging gently together as it moved.

'Would you talk to me, then, Mrs Godsal?' he asked at last. 'I'd be ever so grateful.'

Alice Godsal stood up slowly and opened the gate. He asked if he could bring in his bicycle in case it was stolen from the pavement. She invited him to sit on the green-painted bench, then went to the open door of her house, calling inside for her maid to bring tea and biscuits. An unexpected visitor. When the maid came, a tiny little thing, the girl looked at him suspiciously and asked if Mrs Godsal was all right. The old woman answered that she was, though the hand that still held the trowel shook a little.

In the face of such enormity, small talk was required at once. Alice asked if he had come far. No, she didn't know Hammersmith well, though she had a friend in Shepherd's Bush. She admired his bicycle, saying she had once loved cycling. Taken to it like a duck to water she had, back in the nineties when it first came in. Quite daring for a woman then, but she'd not cared a fig about that. Too old for it now, she said. Bloody arthritis. It was all she could do to hold the watering-can. Getting old was a bugger, she said.

When the tea tray came and was placed on a small garden table, he felt his own hand tremble as he raised the cup and saw that she noticed it. The tears and the handkerchief returned to her eyes. He said he was sorry he'd upset her. He'd not meant to.

'So, what's your name?' the old woman asked.

'Francis,' he replied. 'Well, Frank. Frank Brodie.'

'Oh, that's nice,' she replied. 'They kept your Christian name at least. That's nice.'

'So you do know who I am?' he repeated.

'You're the image of her,' replied Alice.

'Of my mother?'

'Yes. Is that why you've come?'

'I just want to know who she is,' he said.

'But I don't have her permission to tell you. She's lived in Canada for years now, or was it America? Anyway, I've lost touch with her. My letters aren't answered.'

Frank Brodie looked down at his shoes. He'd polished them as best he could, but they'd seen better days.

'And I hate to say it,' said Alice, 'but it's even possible she might be dead and buried by now. I just don't know.'

He leaned back against the bench and rubbed his hands across his eyes.

'They never hid it from me, you see. The people who brought me up. I've always known I wasn't theirs.'

'Who were they?' said Alice.

'You don't know?'

'I didn't want to know. It seemed best at the time.'

'Then who are *you* exactly?' he asked. 'Why was it you I've been sent to?'

'I was your mother's friend, that's all,' said Alice. 'Have a biscuit. They're very good. Come on, you're thin as a whippet.'

The old woman poured him more tea, as if tea and biscuits might sustain him through what he needed to hear.

She explained that it had been her late husband Mr Godsal who had arranged it all. It was before they were married; they were just walking out together then. Mr Godsal had known of a couple who might take in the child of her unfortunate friend. This couple's own boy had died and the wife could carry no more. He'd fix it all up, Mr Godsal had said. Alice didn't need to know anything more about it. If she knew nothing then she could never tell her friend where the baby had gone, should her friend ever want to find out. Far better all round, especially for the child, if only Mr Godsal knew the details. And he had taken those to the bottom of the Irish Sea. God rest his soul.

So, Frank had gone to a Scotch butcher and his wife? In Tufnell Park? Well, well. The Scotch were good solid people as a rule, Alice said, though sometimes a bit hard to understand. And Tufnell Park was quite nice, wasn't it? She hoped he'd been happy there. But Frank Brodie did not reply and his silence hung in the late spring air as the bees still buzzed in the white magnolia.

'I've always thought about her,' he said at last. 'In France even. In the war. It seemed wrong that I might die without even knowing her name. You understand?'

'Of course,' sighed Alice.

'Yet it's still taken me this long to do anything about it. Bloody daft, really.'

'No, not daft,' replied Alice. 'Not bloody daft at all.'

'The Brodies retired years ago and went back to Scotland. I'd not been in touch since long before the war, but I had an old address so I wrote and it got passed on. She's dead now and he seems a bit gaga, but he still remembered your husband's name. And here I am.'

As he spoke, he saw something shift in the old woman's face. He could not know that it was three months now since her pain had started; just a week since the clever doctors at the Royal Free had told her the game was up. And since Alice reckoned she'd played a pretty good game, she took it on the chin as she'd always taken everything. No operation of any use, they'd said. Well, why not do a good deed while she still could? What could it matter now anyway? So, she took a deep breath and revealed the secret she'd expected to take to her grave and very nearly had.

'Your mother's name is Isobel Farrar,' she said to the man on the bicycle.

He repeated the name back to her, then asked for it to be spelled out so that he'd got it right. And then he said it again, softly this time. Afraid that, if he spoke it too loudly, he might frighten it away and lose it again.

'She was a good woman who had tragedy in her life,' said Alice. 'It happens to the best of us.'

'What was her tragedy?'

'That's not my story to reveal,' replied Alice. 'Her name must be enough for you.'

'And my father?'

'Your father was an unkind man. Your mother fled from his house long before you were born. Before she even knew she was carrying you.'

'He was her husband, then? So I'm not a...?'

'No, you're not that.'

'Is he still alive?'

'I couldn't tell you,' replied Alice. 'I never met him. But please, no more questions. I've said too much already.'

'Did she want to give me up?'

'It was hard for her.'

'But did she want to give me up?'

He watched the old woman shift in her seat and knew he was not going to get an answer. He saw something behind her eyes – something that belied the image of the old lady picking tulips with a trug on her arm. Something harder, something more complicated.

'These things aren't simple,' she said, as if she had read his thoughts and wanted to confirm them. 'Never ever simple. I know that as well as anyone.'

'I don't understand,' he said, 'why such a thing shouldn't be simple.'

'Ha!' replied Alice. 'Men!'

She poured more tea and asked him about himself. He worked in a big shop, he said, in the West End. It was steady enough. He lodged in Hammersmith. No, he wasn't married, nor did he have children. He told her all this in the space of under a minute, as if it wasn't worth mentioning.

He commented on her garden, told her why her *pieris japonica* weren't doing well in their current position and the exact spot to which they should be moved. Gardening was his hobby, he said. And then, almost as quickly as he'd arrived, he decided to go. He put on his bicycle clips, shook her hand, thanked her for the tea and wheeled the bike towards the gate.

'Your name,' she said. 'Francis. It was her father's name. She wanted you to have it. Something of her to take with you, she said. I remember that.'

In getting up from the green-painted bench, the old woman stumbled on a loose flagstone on the path. He dropped the bike and caught her in his arms, their faces only inches apart. For a moment he thought she looked almost scared of him. But then she raised her hand to his cheek and stroked it softly, almost as if she still thought he couldn't be real, that he was some sort of phantom. Against his skin, her hand felt cold and dry as dust.

'I held you in my arms once,' said Alice. 'And now you hold me.'

He guided her back to the bench and sat her down. She reached up for his hand and clasped it fiercely to her.

'Do you want to give me your address, Frank?' she asked. 'If your mother is still alive, if I ever hear from her, I can get in touch.'

He drew his eyes away and stared up at the spring sky. The need to give an answer, and give it right now, pulled him in two directions. So easy to say yes, so hard to say no. But then he felt the anger rise up in the way it did and the anger won.

'No, it's fine,' he replied at last. 'If she didn't want me back then, she's not likely to want me now, is she?'

'I didn't say that, Frank. I never said that. I just said that it was hard for her,' said Alice. 'So very hard for her. In those days. A woman on her own...'

He raised his cap to her and pushed the bike out through the gate. Then, as no more than an afterthought, he turned and asked where his mother had lived in England. And Alice saw no harm in telling him. Again she thought, what could it matter now?

'A house called Halcyon Hill in Surrey. I forget the name of the village,' she replied. 'Isobel Farrar of Halcyon Hill.'

When he'd gone, Alice sat for a long time on the green-painted bench. On the day when the clever doctors had told her the game was up, she'd held herself together. She'd been as tough as old boots all her life and proud of the fact. And that was the way she wanted to die. Yet there, among the tulips, the white magnolia and the *pieris japonica*, she began to weep for the man on the bicycle.

'A sad boy,' she said aloud to the birds and the bees. 'Such a sad boy.'

5

It was such a clever little box. Made of satinwood, inlaid with marquetry and lined with moss-green silk. One couldn't help but admire its ingenious craftsmanship. Yet there had always been something mildly shameful in its function as an enabler of secrecy and deceit. Such an object should surely belong in the possession of a Catherine de Medici or Mata Hari, not a respectable matron living in the Surrey countryside. But even now, in this brave new world, what the jewel box concealed would not have been considered by many as entirely *comme il faut*.

When Isobel returned home after her visit to the ugly house in Goldhurst Terrace, Letty Blount had frowned at the sight of her.

'Are you not well, Lady Farrar? You look done in.'

'I'm fine, my dear. Just tired.'

'Why not go up and take a little nap?'

It was only now that Isobel registered the heaviness of her body, its crushing need for sleep. She'd just go up for half an hour, she said, and lie on top of the quilt. Instead, she went to her dressing table, unlocked the drawer and took out the box. Emptying it of rings and brooches, she pressed the point on the false floor which gave entry to a hidden compartment.

It was all she had ever possessed of him. One photograph. As a rule, which she had imposed strictly on herself, she only opened the compartment once a year. On the anniversary of the day when she had given birth to him in a tiny room under the eaves, with Alice Godsal watching over her, mopping her brow and promising that it would soon be over.

To perform this annual ritual, she had always found some quiet place to go. In the early years, after the scandalous divorce from her first husband and before the marriage to her second, she had lived alone and so it had been easy. She'd just sat quietly in her small rented flat in Pimlico or, if the weather was fine, walked over the bridge to Battersea Park, to a corner of the rose garden, where something in the depth of her stillness deterred any stranger from approaching too close to where she sat. When, on the cusp of the new century, she had married Octavius, moved to the country and given birth to Johnnie, it had become more difficult. A husband who treasured every moment of her company. A baby who didn't only cry when it was convenient. A servant asking for instructions. There was always somebody wanting her for something. But still, by planning or chance, by hook or by crook, she somehow always managed it. Her remembrance, secret and silent, of the birthday of the first child. Remembrance was the word she always used to herself. Celebration hardly seemed appropriate. The trauma had been, and remained, too great for that. But remembrance was surely his due. She owed him that at least.

Alice had taken the photograph with the new camera given to her by Billy Godsal – the latest expensive token of his courtship. It had been the day before the boy was to be given up. Wrapped in Alice's shawl, the child cradled in her arms, Isobel lay in bed in the room under the eaves. It wasn't a very good photograph; the light was poor and Isobel, still exhausted, was white as the pillows. But even so, she could see the fear in her own eyes. Fear of what she had done, fear of what she was about to do. And oh, how young she looked: not yet twenty-five.

Still, the poor photograph was all she had possessed. So, on that one day of the year, she allowed herself to rescue it from the darkness of the jewel box, then close her eyes and say a silent prayer. Though born a Catholic, she was not a notably religious woman; her experience of life had taken care of that. Yet there was still enough of some God inside her for her to follow the convention. And she had prayed for the happiness of her child, wherever he was, whoever he was now, not knowing the answer to either of those questions. In the first years after his birth, she'd even prayed a little for herself, though without feeling that she deserved to be listened to. Not after what she'd done. Once, in the rose garden at Battersea, a delinquent dog had dashed up and snatched the photograph from between her fingers. To her own astonishment, and that of those around her, she had screamed hysterically until its owner had cuffed the creature and restored the picture to her, slobbery from its jowls but otherwise undamaged.

'Am I not to be left with even this?' she'd heard herself shouting before she hurried from the park.

In the years that followed, if she'd ever thought that the birth of another child would obliterate the absent presence of the first, she had been quite wrong. If anything, the reverse had been true. As Johnnie sucked on her breast, the hungry face of the other son would superimpose itself. As Johnnie toddled his first steps across the terrace, the other son would be there, walking in his small, eager shadow. As Johnnie's adolescent chin sprouted its first pimples, then its first whiskers, so did the unformed face of his secret sibling. In the family at Halcyon Hill, there were two boys.

But whatever sketchy pictures Isobel had formed of her future would have to be rubbed out and begun again. There could be no mistake about that. The alteration in her life was irreversible. From today, everything was different.

She tried to imagine him with Alice in the front garden. Alice's memory, so moth-eaten now, had failed to describe him much. Was he dark or fair? Tall and sturdy or some more delicate being? Visualising this child was nothing new to her; she'd been doing that for nearly forty years. At least now, though, she had some scraps of fact. He worked in some big shop and lived in Hammersmith. He wasn't married and she wondered why that was so. But it lifted her heart that the name she had bequeathed to him was still his, an indelible birthmark connecting them across the years of separation. Francis was still Francis. And he had come looking for her.

She'd sometimes asked herself if such a day might ever come and this had been it. Yet that had always seemed so unlikely. It was all so long ago. Why had the child waited this long to try to find her? Surely, he must hate or at least despise her? So, was that it? Did he now want to express his hatred? Had he come to condemn and vilify her? She couldn't bear to think of it when, for thirty-eight years, she had done that to herself.

Now, as a haze of twilight snow began to fall past her bedroom window, Isobel decided that her lost child would never return to the darkness of the jewel box. She propped the photograph against the dressing table mirror. She would have it framed, then place it on the table by her bed. The place where the boy called Frank Brodie rightfully belonged.

Then at last, sleep did come to overwhelm Isobel Farrar. She slipped off her shoes and lay down on the quilt, but before she surrendered to it, she heard again those words of Alice Godsal's. Words that had perched in Isobel's mind with the tightest of claws.

'He seemed a sad boy. Such a sad boy.'

She must find him. Nothing else now mattered more. She must find Frank Brodie and expiate the sins she had committed against him.

6

In the small kitchen of a house in Hammersmith, Arthur Collins was making supper as he did every evening. He liked cooking, even though he would be the first to admit that he was not Escoffier. His menus were basic – good plain English fare and none the worse for that, as he liked to say. Tonight, he would serve lentil broth followed by boiled beef, cauliflower and a few spuds. If either of them was still hungry, there was some trifle left from the weekend, though that was looking a bit sad around the edges. Once quite vain, Arthur no longer worried about getting a little portly. What man didn't fill out a bit as the years piled up? Didn't people often see it as a mark of distinction?

Through the window out into the yard, he could see the beam of the torch jigging around. It was nearly December – what on earth could anyone find to do out there at this time of year? Surely, sod all could be growing. But it was always the same. And he had come to realise that he wouldn't have it any other way and he was grateful for that feeling because he had never expected to experience it.

Arthur Collins was an optimist as a rule, perhaps excessively so. In younger days, he had fully expected to become a major star of the music halls like his old pal Marie and had never understood why that hadn't quite come to pass. At the outbreak of the war, he'd been one of those who said it'd be over by Christmas and had been personally affronted when that was not the case. Life is what you make it, Arthur always said. The show must go on. And so, with a smile, and often with a song, Arthur had sailed onwards into late middle age, treating it with the contempt it deserved. Keeping his pecker up. Keeping the home fires burning. Waving his Union Jack like 'Burlington Bertie from Bow'.

But even Arthur Collins was troubled tonight. He knew that something was up. He wondered if their quiet lives were somehow going to change and what the outcome of that might be. Perhaps nothing much. Perhaps everything.

'Frank, supper's ready,' he called out into the yard.

'My hebe's not looking good,' said Frank Brodie when he came inside. 'The big one by the dustbin. There should be far more flowers on it by now. I'd better look up one of my books.'

It was the longest sentence Frank had spoken since Arthur had got home from the shop in which they both worked and found him there already. A stomach upset, Frank had said. Really bad. He'd had to leave work early.

'I know,' Arthur had replied. 'Wilf Jones told me. He wasn't best pleased. A busy day apparently.'

'I'll make it up to him,' Frank had replied. 'I'll do an extra shift.'

Then, wrapping up in a pullover and scarf, he had gone out into the yard to be among his pots. The hebes and the cyclamen, the hellebores and the aconites. Frank's 'babies', Arthur called them.

At supper in the small dining room that led off the kitchen, Frank said little. But Arthur was used to that and often skimmed the evening paper as he ate. He liked to read the theatre page, especially the musicals and revues. He liked to keep in touch with the world that had once been his.

'You made short work of that beef, sonny boy,' Arthur said now. 'Your tum seems to have recovered sharpish.'

'Fine now, thanks,' replied Frank, dunking his last potato into the gravy.

Arthur Collins rolled his napkin and slid it back inside its wooden ring. He pushed back his chair and stood up.

'Tell you what,' he said. 'D'you fancy a beer? I'd quite fancy a gin.'

'But it's only Thursday,' said Frank, surprised.

Arthur liked to keep up a pretence that he only consumed the demon drink on Saturday evenings when there was no work the next day.

'What the hell,' he said. 'You're only young once.'

Frank got a beer from the larder and followed him into the parlour. Arthur was mixing his gin on the silver-plated tray that stood on a two-tiered mahogany trolley. The trolley stood in the centre of the front window so that the neighbours could see it and decide that Number 74 Pitt Street was owned by a man of greater sophistication than was customary in their simple street. Arthur was proud of this tray, a family heirloom, and kept it well-stocked with gin, whisky, brandy and all the other necessaries. He had recently purchased something called a cocktail shaker and was teaching himself the intricacies of this new art. The tray was kept ready in case somebody dropped by, though that had become rarer in recent years. There had been the war, of course, and especially the flu of 1918, which had polished off more than a few of the old timers with whom Arthur had once trodden the boards.

But there was another reason too of which Arthur was well aware. People had come round less in the years since the arrival of the lodger; the young man from Arthur's shop, who would only mutter a shy hello before vanishing upstairs or out into the yard at the back. Arthur was hurt by this, though he'd made his peace with it. There was a price for everything, he always said, and this price he willingly paid. Nevertheless, the sunlight still shone on the tray in the front window, glancing off the coloured bottles, the crystal glasses and the cocktail shaker. You never knew when somebody might knock.

But the image of sophistication at Number 74 was undermined somewhat by the faded chintz that covered the armchairs, by the wallpaper that was coming away in the corners, by the chipped tiles around the fireplace and the permanent patina of dust on the harmonium that had belonged to Arthur's sainted mother. Like Arthur himself, his little house had seen better days, though he firmly refused to see the decline in either.

In the parlour of an evening, Arthur would usually turn on the wireless. He loved the concerts from the Queen's Hall and had the irritating habit of humming along to what he called 'the tunes'. Tonight, though, the wireless stayed silent.

Arthur put his glass of gin on the table beside his armchair, but left it untouched, which was unusual since he normally gulped the first one quickly before pouring himself another. Frank sat down opposite on the other side of the chipped fireplace, taking out his tobacco and cigarette papers and rolling one up. Without the wireless on, the stillness of the parlour oppressed Arthur. The only sound was the crackle of the fire and the occasional bus going past. But something needed to be said. Bugger this. Enough was enough.

'You didn't have an upset tum at all, did you?' he asked. 'What's up, Frank? You going to tell me?'

'Nothing's up,' replied Frank.

'For the past few weeks, you've had a face like a wet Monday in Bognor,' said Arthur. 'And you're not a million laughs at the best of times. Come on, spill the beans, as the Yanks say.'

'I said there's nothing wrong.'

'Wilf Jones tells me you're a right old misery guts at work as well. People don't like that, you know. Better watch your step, sonny boy.'

Frank had been staring into the fire, puffing on his roll-up, but now he looked up at Arthur and fixed him in the steely gaze which could sometimes transform the beautiful face into something much darker.

'Oh, leave me be, Arthur.'

And that was what Arthur Collins usually did. What many people still did with the lads of Frank's generation. Make allowances for men who had seen things nobody should see and suffered more than anybody should suffer. Turn a blind eye to bad behaviour. Frank claimed never to have had shellshock. He wasn't one of those poor souls who still shook if a motor car backfired. And in contrast to those mutilated beyond recognition, there wasn't a scratch on that beautiful face. Not one.

But Arthur Collins wasn't fooled. In the cold, small hours, he had heard the cries and shouts coming from the back bedroom as the tumult of the nightmare reached out for Frank again. It would start gradually then build to a crescendo that made the hairs stand up on Arthur's neck. Then there would be silence for a few minutes, followed by footsteps on the landing, the light on the stairs and the distant hiss of the old copper kettle from below.

'Why have you stopped going out on your bike on Sundays?' he asked now, trying to make it sound like an innocuous question.

'It's getting a lot parkier, isn't it?'

'That's never stopped you before.'

'What's the problem? You're always going on about how I'm never here.'

'Just curious. Just wondering what's got you down lately. You can always tell me, you know.'

'I know that,' said Frank, the darkness on his features lifting a little. 'I know that, Arthur.'

'And so?'

Frank threw the end of the cigarette into the flames.

'I'm all right, Arthur. Honest I am,' he said. 'I'll try to snap out of it. Sorry.'

'You can always tell me,' Arthur said again, 'if it would help.'

Frank stood up. He'd have an early night he said. He'd do the supper dishes first thing and try not to be a misery tomorrow. As he went past Arthur's armchair, he patted his shoulder.

'Maybe we could go to the pictures on Saturday night. There's a new Ivor Novello. You like him, don't you?'

But Arthur, who would usually have loved to do such a thing, did not reply. Over the years, he had discovered as much as he could about the life of the quiet young man who had been his lodger since before the war. It had come out tortuously, bit by bit, like the extraction of a broken tooth, its roots tenacious and unyielding, shrinking back from the light. And Arthur, wielder of the pliers, had felt every stab of that pain himself, every stab of the emptiness that infected Frank Brodie.

Tonight, as Arthur went to the scullery and began to wash the dishes himself, he felt sure of one thing. That inside Frank, some new emptiness had taken hold. And how much more emptiness could there be in a person before there was nothing left but a shell?

7

'Good morning, Lady Farrar,' called the old stationmaster. 'Not going up to town again, surely? That's three mornings in a row, if I'm not wrong. You'll exhaust yourself, dear lady.'

'I'm stronger than I look, Mr Travers.' Isobel smiled.

'I keep a half bottle of brandy in the office,' he said, with a theatrical wink. 'So, if you need a drop when you get back...'

But the old stationmaster was wrong. It was in fact the fourth morning that she had risen in the dark, bathed and got her own breakfast before Letty Blount had arrived to make it for her. By the time the girl entered the kitchen, Isobel had her hat and coat on. Letty had made no comment, as it wasn't her business to do so. But today, she had delivered the same remark that the stationmaster would shortly make. Lady Farrar would tire herself out. You'd not catch *her* going into London at this time of year.

This early in the day, the suburban train was always busy with office workers. Now, though, they had been joined by middle-class ladies on that same mission upon which Mr Travers had assumed Lady Farrar to be embarked. The closer the train got to Waterloo, the worse the squash, even in first class where the noisy rustle of a newspaper was usually considered bad form. From Clapham Common to the terminus, a small dog sat with its head resting on her shoes, gazing up at her, longing for some open field. Brown and white and woolly, it was the same breed as the dog named Gladstone which had once belonged to Octavius and been so loved by him. Gladstone who had been by his side as Octavius had taken his last breath beneath the old oak tree on an August afternoon in the year the war ended. No retainer ever more faithful.

As the dog stared sadly up at her, she wondered what Octavius would think of the journey she was making on this December morning, in a direction he would never have imagined possible. Dear Octavius, an oddity in the eyes of the grand world in which he had been raised and on which he had ultimately turned his back and struck out along his own road. The ambassador, the man of pomp and circumstance, who had turned himself into a painter of landscapes because, he said, he needed to explore different ones before his time was up. A spirit as pure as any she had known, she could still hear his voice in her head, light and eager as a boy's until the day he died. How easily she could picture him leaning towards her, taking her hands in that way he'd always had, as if they were the most fragile things he had encountered on this earth.

'But why?' he would have said, 'why did you never tell me? We could perhaps have put things right.'

And so many times, she had come close to it. So many moments when something triggered a sudden, overwhelming impulse to lighten the load she carried. Often, that trigger would relate to the late-life child they had together. The sight of Johnnie playing with his toys. Johnnie tearful and wanting to be cuddled. Johnnie going off on his first day to school. At those moments, she had ached to simply turn to her husband and look him in the eye.

'Octavius, I have another child.'

But she never did. The happiness of that autumnal love, so unexpected and so precious, had somehow prevented her. Before they married, she had told him everything about her love for

Hugh Pasco. He was glad, Octavius had said, that she had experienced a transforming love in her life. Everyone ought to have at least one such. In his own case, it had been his housemaster's wife at Stowe, a heavy-breasted woman of thirty-five. He roared with laughter and that laughter had been his great gift to Isobel. There had been little enough of it in Isobel's life, but for the twenty years of their marriage, they'd hardly stopped.

Octavius had offered to sell Halcyon if the association with Hugh Pasco would distress her. Theirs must be a happy house, he said. Another place could easily be found. But her pre-nuptial confessions had not included a mention of Edwin Reed's child and his abandonment. Her error, she understood now, was to fear that her happiness with Octavius might be fragile when, in truth, it could have borne anything. In different ways, both had been through the flames of life; they were strong. It would have made no difference.

'We could perhaps have put things right,' she heard Octavius say again.

Was that what she was doing now? Isobel asked herself as the train curved into the platform at Waterloo. Putting things right? Or making them worse? Turning over the stone of the past and finding all sorts of things underneath, things best left undisturbed. And yet. And yet the child had come looking for her. Whether to embrace or to reject her, she did not know. It was the child who had offered up this second chance. How could she not take it?

Isobel opened her handbag and looked again at the list she'd made at the beginning of that week. A line was drawn through the seven or eight places she'd already visited; only three more remained for today. After that, she wouldn't know what to do. A private detective perhaps. She'd thought about that option from the start, but felt this was something she should do herself. Some sort of courtesy. If her feet hurt, if her head ached, if she caught a chill on the bitter streets, then so be it.

As the train jolted to a halt, the dog raised its head from her shoes and sprung to its feet, desperate to be off. It wagged its tail and licked her grey-gloved hand. And that gave an odd comfort, a fresh rush of resolve.

On the platform, her eyes smarted from the smoke that swirled inside the iron cavern of the station. All these trains, like fat slugs, regurgitating suburban folk from their insides, reinventing them as city people, requiring them to assume a slightly different self, perhaps less appealing than the gentler one they had left behind at their garden gates. As she was swallowed up by the throng, Isobel fancied she could see the transformation. Deep breaths being taken, shoulders squared, jaws set a little more firmly. And now she did the same. One last day of this. One last attempt to turn over the stone and face up to what was there. She would find him today. After thirty-eight years, she would find him today.

Isobel had always hated the stygian labyrinth of the Underground. It would be unbearable in these crowds, so she queued for a taxi. But the cabbie took the route that led across Waterloo Bridge and drove straight into a traffic jam. For fifteen minutes, she found herself trapped midway over the river. On one side, her view was of a fishmonger's lorry, on the other, the curve of the Embankment and the great Egyptian obelisk.

She remembered little of the night she had stood there, staring into the black water lapping against the river steps. Alice Godsal had always skirted over the circumstances of their meeting. *I found you lost by Cleopatra's Needle* was as much as Alice ever said; the unspeakable left unspoken. But Isobel's memory had not been entirely wiped clean. Still inside her was the recollection of her merciless need to follow where the man called Hugh Pasco had just gone before. And even in the later years of her happiness with Octavius and Johnnie, that need would still sometimes creep up and surprise her. It never entirely went away.

Captive now on Waterloo Bridge, she thought how close she had brought her other child to extinction. Not once but twice. The first time unaware that he was seeded within her, the second only too aware.

Dear God, how much was owed to the boy called Frank Brodie. Where on earth might she begin? But first, she must find him. And she would find him today. He had been lost too long.

*

The great shop seemed to shimmer as she walked towards it. The outlines of the huge plate glass windows, the pillared porticos of grey-white marble and the rotunda which crowned the roof were picked out in a hundred thousand tiny light bulbs, every colour of the rainbow, twinkling off and on so that the whole building looked alive, its usual solidity happily discarded for the few weeks of gay abandon.

Inside those different windows, Santa Claus flew in his sleigh over the dome of St Paul's, Snow White made breakfast for the seven dwarves and the handsome prince put the slipper on Cinderella's foot. But for the thousands who would enter its portals over Christmas, the emporium itself was the true fairy tale. From the deepest basement to the tip of the rotunda, floor after floor crammed with things, the possession of which would confirm who they were or who they desired to be. For those few weeks, it no longer mattered what boring Mr Baldwin might say in parliament or that Rudolph Valentino had died in Hollywood. And the damnable strike – in which they, the middle classes, had rallied round the flag, manned the buses, driven the food lorries and kept the show on the road – was now long over. The people like them had prevailed, as they had always known that they would. And now it was Christmas. The time for their reward. The vast department stores of London, those cathedrals to the still potent values of the high Victorians, echoed to the squeals of spoilt children and the carillon of cash registers.

Today, as she had done outside each of the shimmering shops, Isobel paused for a moment. Each time, she had stood on the opposite side of the street until she had imbibed enough courage to step across the road. On the first morning, outside the very first shop, that courage had quite failed her. She had retreated to a nearby tea room and sat there for an hour before it returned to her. Amazing the power of a pot of tea and a macaroon. In that first emporium, she had not found him. But the very crossing of the road had been something of moment. The first steps towards possibility.

And now, here was the second-to-last shop on her list. On the other side of the street, Isobel composed herself once again. Every morning this week, she had dressed as perfectly as she always did. On the crowded, uncaring pavements of the West End, some heads would still turn. And there was one addition to her usual appearance. In Ottawa, just before she left, she had gone to a chic milliner and purchased a miracle of a hat. Of dove-grey silk, broad-brimmed and with a white veil. This week, it had been the veil she'd needed most. How difficult it seemed that such a private matter must be pursued in such a public way. No delicate letter could be written. No telephone call made. She must make her solitary way into that uncaring crowd, her story still hidden deep inside her but ready at last to be told. The story he must hear, if and when she ever found him. At long last, the lifting of the veil.

*

She always tried to avoid the floorwalkers – those men who hovered just inside the pillared porticos, waiting to pounce upon you and guide you to the department you sought and to the others for which they judged you, with a practised eye, to be an appropriate customer. Their language was formal, their greeting effusive, as if one's arrival was comparable to that of The Queen of Sheba. But Isobel did not like effusiveness at the best of times and certainly not today. She wished to slip in amidst the throng, unnoticed in the dazzle of the twinkling lights and the bunting. Should this turn out to be the place, she flinched from the prospect of being led up to Frank Brodie and have him presented to her as if she were indeed The Queen of Sheba.

So, from behind the white veil, she would skirt the floorwalkers and softly approach some assistant who was not occupied. Were they acquainted with a member of staff called Francis Brodie? Or Frank, as they might know him? But the answers had always been negative. A department store is a big place, madam. Thousands of employees, madam. Quite impossible to know everyone, madam. Perhaps madam might wish to visit the offices on the top floor where the staff records were kept; they would be able to help her there. Or one of the floorwalkers might be aware of this Mr Brodie. And today, in the second-to-last shop, the girl behind the perfume counter had signalled across the floor before Isobel could melt away.

'If anyone will know, madam, it'll be Mr Collins. He's been here for many years and knows everyone.'

The man strutted across to the perfume counter. Shortish and solid, his chest puffed out like a pigeon, the straining waistcoat of his suit not concealing that he had gone to seed a little. In the heat of the shop, a nearly bald head shone, sprinkled with a rash of the colours reflected from the Christmas lights. He bowed from the waist.

'Francis Brodie, madam?' asked the man. His voice was loud and she detected surprise in it.

'Or Frank Brodie perhaps. I'm not certain of the name he might use.'

'Yes, indeed, madam. Mr Brodie is employed here in our ironmongery department. On the basement floor. The staircase down is just over there. Allow me to guide you.'

'Thank you, but I will find my way.'

'Our customers of the fairer sex rarely descend into the dark masculine realms of ironmongery.' The man smiled. 'It would be my pleasure to act as your escort.'

Isobel did not answer. Suddenly, she needed to sit down on the chair beside the perfume counter. The floorwalker asked if madam was all right. Did she want a glass of water? But after a moment, she stood up again. It was nothing, she said. The heat. So many people. A moment's giddiness. All gone now. She would, she said again, find her way. But the floorwalker insisted on accompanying her down the stairs to the basement. In case of another giddy moment. At the foot of the steps, he held open the big glass doors into the ironmongery.

'Thank you so much, Mr…' she said. 'You've been very kind.'

'Collins, madam. Arthur Collins. Delighted to have been of service.'

Now, in his smile, she noticed curiosity too. She walked a few yards and glanced back. Still the floorwalker was watching her. He bowed again, then was gone.

He had not been wrong in describing ironmongery as a dark realm. Between these bowels of the store and the frivolous, scented regions above, the contrast was stark. In this windowless subterranean cavern, there were no Christmas trees with fairy lights, just the cold drab beams of electric lamps hanging in rows high above the floor. As the floorwalker had said, this was a man's world. The customers here were quite different from those upstairs. Men in cloth caps, well-scuffed boots and shirts without collars. Men who looked like gardeners or below-stairs servants, to whom the fripperies of the shop above were as alien as the far side of the moon. The wares they sought were stored on countless rows of metal shelving, fifteen feet high or more, the upper regions reached by ladders that could be moved along on rollers. Huge as it was, the shelving seemed to fill the entire cavern, running straight for countless yards or intersecting with other rows coming at right angles. On top of the shelves were the tools of every trade. Here the gardener could find his spades, forks, hoes, shears, rakes, wheelbarrows. The builder his hammers, chisels and screwdrivers, his nails, nuts and bolts. The painter his pots of paint, brushes, turpentine. The below-stairs servant his brooms, brushes and buckets, his bottles of bleach and tins of wax polish. It was, Isobel thought, like arriving in the streets of some unfamiliar city without a map. Confusing, forbidding, somewhere in which you know you will lose your bearings. But still she entered in.

As the floorwalker had prophesied, the indigenous citizenry turned to look at the elegant figure in the white-veiled hat who had descended into their midst, roaming the narrow passages between the overweening shelves, turning this way and that, searching for they knew not what, leaving in her wake the gentle fragrance of the world above.

And then she turned a corner. And then she saw him. And, in him, saw herself. There was no doubt. There had been no mistake. Alice Godsal had recognised him at once and now so did the woman who had held him to her breast for such a very short time, so very long ago. In an overall of mud-coloured serge, he stood behind a broad wooden counter, measuring lengths of thin rope against a metal tape fixed onto the countertop. His customer was trying to make conversation, but he kept his head down over his task, only answering now and again.

In the shadow of the shelves, Isobel stood and watched. Now that the moment had come, her nervousness had left her. Her heart had stopped racing and a kind of calm had descended upon her. It felt simply right that she should stand here now, doing what she was about to do. Simply right and simply miraculous. She could not take her eyes off him. When the customer went, she would approach the counter. God knows what she would say, should say. She merely hoped that somehow the words would come out. But as soon as the man buying the rope moved off, another customer took his place and yet another queued behind him. It didn't matter. It had been thirty-eight years. She would wait here all day if she had to.

And then the customers had gone. She watched him stifle a yawn with the back of his hand and rub his eyes against the glare of the lights. Dear God, she recognised the yawn and the rubbing of the eyes. Then suddenly he saw her, half-hidden among the shelves.

'Good morning, madam – may I help you?' he asked. 'What is it you're looking for today?'

Isobel walked towards the counter. Suddenly it felt to her that the few yards of linoleumed floor between them had stretched into countless miles, a long hard journey across the years of separation.

'It is Frank, I think,' she heard herself say.

'It is, madam.'

'Then it is you I'm looking for today,' she said. 'Because I understand that you have been looking for *me*.'

Isobel lifted the white veil from her face. As she had seen herself mirrored in him, he now saw himself reflected in her. No doubt, no mistake. The tired eyes cleared of their torpor and stared into hers. She stretched out her grey-gloved hand.

He began to offer up his own to meet it, but it fell short of its destination and travelled instead to cover his mouth. She smiled now, hoping for one in return. But still he only stared. And then he took a step backwards. Then another and another, until his back was up against a wall. Yet still he stared. The smile began to falter on Isobel's lips; her outstretched hand did too.

'Frank, I only wanted to…'

'What's the hold-up here, son?' said a voice. 'Time is money.'

Two or three new customers had appeared at the other end of the long counter. Frank Brodie's eyes dragged themselves away from her now and fixed on a burly man in a cloth cap, drumming his fingers on the countertop. He crossed over to the man and asked what he wanted. 'Five dozen eight-inch nails? Yes, sir, please come with me. We have several sorts of the eight-inch variety just along here.'

Without looking at her again, he came out from behind the counter and vanished into the streets of shelving, followed by the burly man. Isobel called out his name, asking him to stop. Her stomach lurched and she had to hold on to the edge of the counter. Then she went after him, turning left and right and left again, up and down the narrow passages, but there was no trace of him. She moved quickly, her heart pounding in her ears, all calmness gone. Again, she called out his name, but her words only echoed back to her from the hammers and the chisels and the screwdrivers.

Lost and found. Found and lost.

8

Isobel would never remember the journey she had made from the house in Pelham Crescent to the river. Through the fog which had stifled the city for days, she must have traversed Knightsbridge, St James's Park, Trafalgar Square. She must have walked past hundreds of people and crossed streets perilous with half-blind hansom cabs and omnibuses. Yet though she recalled not one moment of it, her journey had not been haphazard. Propelled by hopelessness, her body had simply taken her where her heart had wanted to go. At least her body was young, for it seemed to her that, when she had been given news of the accident, her heart had grown old in a matter of moments.

Despite the late hour, despite the foul weather, there were still people on the Embankment. Folks no better than they should be, as her maid would have put it. All along the river tonight, sins of every colour would be committed with impunity, the foggy night concealing their purposes. The only eyes upon them the mustard-yellow light from the lamp standards, usually piercing but now softened by the mists, as if they no longer wished to illuminate such follies.

But Isobel was not aware of any of this. Tonight, she existed only inside her own reality and knew that she could take no more of it. When she could walk no further, she stopped beside Cleopatra's obelisk, its pinnacle lost in the gloom, the needle blunted. She was aware now of an aching tiredness, as if on the mindless walk every drop of blood had drained from her, every muscle suddenly wasted. And this place would do as well as any other. Better perhaps. All she had to do was descend the shallow steps and let the water take her. As she had always suspected her mother had done. Back then, she'd been too young to understand why anyone might do such a thing. But now, in that moment, she did understand. The question was not why, but why not? When hopelessness invades you and restoration seems impossible, why not? So gentle, so easy. Just let it go. One simple step, the lifting of one foot in front of the other. Just let it go.

She stood there, utterly still, and watched the black water slump against the lowest step. The opposite bank was quite invisible, as if there were nothing there at all. The river, made even more fluid by the fog, seemed to stretch forever, vast as an ocean. And it would surely carry her where she wanted to go.

She no longer heard the traffic on the road, the occasional shout or cackle of laughter. All she heard was the faint lapping of the river, at the same time close and far away. So it took a while for a new sound to reach her from the farthest reaches of her awareness.

'What are you doing there, my duck?'

And then, a touch, light as a feather, on her shoulder.

'Christ, you'll freeze down here. Why don't you come with me?'

Isobel did not turn round, did not answer, her eyes still fixed on the black water. Then a second hand, firmer now, touched her other shoulder and gently pulled her away.

'Come on, there a cabbie's shelter by the bridge. It ain't exactly The Ritz, but the tea's not bad. A nice hot cuppa, that's what you need. You just come with me.'

At first, she scarcely looked at the stranger who had come to her out of the dark, nor even registered whether it was a man or a woman. Yet she would always remember the sudden warmth of the arm which now encircled her and half-carried her along the pavement. For a while, the person with the warm arm said nothing, just gently rubbed between Isobel's shoulders now and then, as if to make sure that life was still there. Only when the cabbie's shelter took spectral shape before them, did the stranger speak.

'My name is Alice.'

*

It had been a tiny room, up under the eaves. One small window, sliced neatly into four panes, framed by short chintz curtains. The fireplace was in proportion, as if in a doll's house, but its glow never seemed to lessen by day or night. Not that Isobel was quite sure which was which, as the chintz curtains stayed closed. She had slept for nearly half a week, aware of nothing beyond this little space and the stranger who came and went. All she heard was the soft rush of the coal from the scuttle, the sound of something being poured into a cup or a glass. Then the warm arm would come again, raising her slightly off the pillows which smelled of violets, telling her to drink the broth because it would do her ever such a lot of good, it really would. And tomorrow, might she try to get a bit of bread and butter inside her? A biscuit or two even? A lovely young girl must take care of her looks. That's what the stranger's mother had always said.

Isobel had no idea how she'd reached the small brass bed in the room under the eaves. Now and again, gentle questions were asked of her, but her voice would not come.

'It's all right, my duck,' the stranger would say. 'You just rest easy.'

Isobel would let herself sink back into the violet-scented pillows. No dreams intruded upon her, as if her brain rejected pictures as well as words. As if some kindly deity had, for a while at least, wiped her mind of everything that had ever happened to her, good or bad, knowing that without such a cleansing this sorry creature stood little chance of resurrection.

Sometimes she'd drift back to half-consciousness and see the stranger sitting in a chair by the fire. The woman might be dozing herself, snoring softly then waking with a start and a yawn. Or reading a newspaper or a magazine. Or holding a hand mirror to arrange her hair or pluck her eyebrows. All this Isobel watched, burrowed in the bed under the eaves, the quilt drawn right up to her chin. She studied the woman's face, this saviour who'd come out of the fog and on whom she now depended. The woman was older than Isobel, by ten years or more, edging past her prime. She was not beautiful – her nose sharp as a scalpel and her eyes too close together – but her skin was fine and her reddish hair thick and lustrous, its curls alive against the firelight.

From time to time, she heard the whisper of silk as the woman came and went from the little room. Isobel didn't like her going, though she would usually return quite soon, with the broth or the biscuits or a little scrambled egg. Sometimes, though, the woman would be gone for longer and Isobel would hear hushed voices beyond the door. The voices of the woman and that of a man. Isobel wondered who the man might be until she realised that his voice was always different. But the voices never lasted long, no more than a minute at most, followed by the soft closing of some other door and Isobel would sink back under the bedclothes.

Once, though, she woke with a start to find the woman bending over the bed. The red hair was dishevelled; a thin wrap, only half-tied, failed to hide the nakedness underneath or to muffle the scent of sweat and other odours. The eyes awash with concern, the back of her hand stroking Isobel's cheek.

'What's wrong, my duck?' she asked. 'You were crying out again. Like a banshee you were. Go back to sleep now. I'm only in the room next door. I shan't be long and then we'll have our tea. Yes?'

But when she'd gone, Isobel lay awake. She heard the thumping of pigeons as they waddled across the slates above her head. At first, thinking they might be human intruders, the noise had frightened her. Would he try to hunt her down? Would he have gone to the police? Would the door suddenly burst open? Would they seize her and drag her back? But soon she'd come to find the pigeons an odd comfort, as if, like the woman, they too were her guardians. Cooing at her to sip the broth, eat the scrambled eggs, drift off again into the arms of Morpheus. She realised that she felt safe in this place, with this stranger and the chatter of the pigeons.

And as her memory, after its time of oblivion, returned to her on tiptoe, she realised too how long it had been since she had felt any such safety. On the pillows which smelled of violets, as the gossipy birds bustled above her head, she allowed herself to face her memories. At first, she had turned her cheek against their images, wishing them away but, as the hours and days passed, she let them come back. But, like visitors to any sickbed, she rationed their presence. Just one at a time and for a few minutes only. Maybe tomorrow, she might be strong enough to admit another one.

And then the day came when Isobel readmitted the chance of an existence beyond the little room under the eaves.

'Alice?' she asked, her voice feeble from disuse.

'You remembered!' The woman smiled as if Isobel's waking was a Christmas present come early. 'Have you travelled back to us?'

Alice opened the chintz curtains. Just a little. Not enough to frighten. Isobel blinked against the light, but she did not flinch from it or retreat beneath the bedclothes. With the warm arm around her again, and the smiling face beaming down, she allowed herself to be pulled up against the pillows and back into some sort of feeling.

9

What had he been supposed to do? She'd just turned up out of the
blue and lifted her veil. That old woman, that Alice Godsal, had
said she was in Canada and that she might even be dead. Since
then, he'd accustomed himself to that possibility, that final closing
of the door. It was the reason he had first made his pilgrimage
out to the house on the hill. A pilgrimage of both greeting and
farewell. But today, just a few hours ago, he'd found out that she
wasn't dead at all. Christ, there she'd stood, large as life, right up at
his counter, at the head of a queue wanting nails and screws. The
shock of it. His own face looking back at him. And what had she
expected? A touching reunion, an embrace, floods of tears? Like
something from a picture with Mary Pickford or Lillian Gish?
What had she wanted him to say? Very nice to meet you? How are
you? Or maybe, with a cheery smile, it's been a long time.

Arthur was making the supper as usual. Since Arthur had
arrived home, he'd not said much and Arthur usually had some
bit of gossip. A girl in the shop who'd got herself into trouble; an
old-timer from the halls who'd gone to what Arthur always called
'top billing in the clouds'. Later this evening, there would be a
concert on the wireless he'd been looking forward to. Elgar himself
conducting *The Dream of Gerontius*. One of Arthur's favourites.

Frank had gone out into the yard, the light from the scullery
window making it possible to check on his 'babies' after dark. Yet

more leaves had fallen from the neighbour's raggedy lime tree which overhung Frank's tiny kingdom. For the hundredth time since early October, he brushed them up from the flagstones and picked them carefully off his plants. He'd politely asked the ruffian next door to cut the tree back and been met with abuse. But Frank never rose to abuse anymore; he was too frightened of what he might do if he did.

He was still worried about his sickly hebe. He'd put its little pot on top of the coal bunker to give it more light, but was afraid he might have been too late. Plants and flowers, Frank firmly believed, were just like people. Each one different, even within the same species. Some strong, some weak. Some able to tolerate the shade, others desolate without the sun. There had been no rain for days, so he gave it a little water. He told it to cheer up and that he knew it was going to produce some beautiful blooms for him come January. For a moment, he pictured it in the earth at Halcyon, looking out over the garden down towards the pond, the winter sun from the south bringing it to glorious life. But then he pushed the picture away.

In the scullery, Arthur had been peeling potatoes.

'Wilf Jones is spitting blood,' he said, without looking up. 'He says you left work early again today. What was it this time? The trots?'

'Yeah, a bit of that,' replied Frank, washing his hands at the sink. 'You have a good day?'

'Except for one little drama.'

'Oh yes?'

'A woman fainted. Happens all the time, of course. Especially with the Christmas crush.'

'Oh dear.'

'It was the same woman who'd been asking for you a quarter hour earlier,' said Arthur. 'A lady in a big hat with a white veil. The woman I'd escorted myself down into ironmongery. But when she came back up, she got as far as the perfume counter and passed out. Legs just crumpled, but I managed to grab her. We got her into a chair and brought her some water.'

'Right,' said Frank.

'So she had to lift her veil to drink it.'

'Right,' said Frank again.

Arthur dropped the peeled potatoes into a saucepan and half-filled it from the tap. Then he put it down on the draining board and leaned back against the scullery wall.

'Is that all you can say?' asked Arthur. 'When she lifted the veil, you were staring back at me. I'm guessing who she might be, but I want you to tell me.'

Frank didn't know what to answer. He wasn't sure if he should use the two words of the obvious reply. Did people in his situation have the right to do that? And what about in reverse? What if, by most unlikely chance, someone she knew had been lurking in the ironmongery to purchase a wheelbarrow and had witnessed their encounter? What words would Isobel Farrar have used to introduce the youngish man in the overall? Someone she knew long ago? A distant relative? Would she too perhaps feel, as Frank did now, that the normal vocabulary was somehow barred to them both? So, he used the only phrase which seemed fitting.

'She's the woman who gave birth to me,' he said.

'And the meeting didn't go well?'

'It was the shock, Arthur. I wasn't certain she was even alive. I didn't know what to do.'

'Don't tell me you ran from her, Frank. Don't tell me you ran, like you always run from everything that makes you uncomfortable.'

Frank looked down at his hands and began to pick at the earth still lodged under his fingernails. Arthur sighed and carried the saucepan through to the kitchen.

'Well, you can't run this time, sonny boy,' said Arthur, putting the pan on the stove. 'You can't just hide in the yard, talking to your bloody plants. You're thirty-eight, Frank. It's time to grow up.'

Arthur turned on the gas under the potatoes, then turned it off again, spinning round to Frank.

'The woman is your *mother*,' shouted Arthur, who prided himself on never raising his voice except in song.

In that split second, Frank Brodie was transformed. From his deepest gut, he felt the poison rise up in the usual way. He stood facing Arthur, his fists clenched, his eyes blazing, the beautiful face contorted with that rage which, he and Arthur both knew, could sometimes erupt from him. When, at some trigger, the wounds which Frank bore were suddenly ripped open and the damage inside him was visible, red raw and bleeding.

'I have no mother,' Frank shouted back across the floor of the little kitchen. 'I have never had a mother. Not the bitch who raised me and certainly not this woman who did nothing more than carry me then walked away. I have no mother. I never will.'

He pushed past Arthur and clattered up the narrow staircase. A door was slammed. It was always the same 'turn', as Arthur liked to think of it.

He sighed. Frank would not reappear that evening. Arthur left the potatoes uncooked in the saucepan. He put the side of gammon back into the larder. He no longer felt hungry. He went into the parlour and built up the fire. He thought about having a gin, then decided he wouldn't. By the light of a single lamp, he sat by the fire for a time, letting the serenity to which his little house was accustomed, once more descend upon it. And when it was time for *The Dream of Gerontius*, the wireless was not switched on.

But Arthur knew that, come the morning, Frank would be himself again. By the time Arthur entered the kitchen, the tea and toast would be made, the porridge just ready on the stove. Frank would pass the butter and the marmalade without being asked, because he always kept an eye on even the smallest thing which Arthur might want or need. Then he'd push his bike out through the front door and head for work. They seldom bumped into each other in the shimmering shop, so he would wish Arthur a nice day and Arthur would know that he meant it. And to Arthur that knowledge was everything.

*

He hated it when the anger roared up inside him like that. He was ashamed of himself. He shouldn't have shouted at Arthur. Dear old Arthur. The best of friends, the best of men. He reminded himself to water down the gin bottle again, as he'd been doing for years now. The vaunted prohibition on drinking during the week was a myth. He'd known that since the time he'd gone into Arthur's wardrobe looking for a collar stud to borrow and found a second bottle, hidden behind a pile of socks. He'd been watering that one down too. If Arthur ever lost his job for being a tippler, they'd be really caught short. Frank's wages alone would never support them both.

But shouting at Arthur had been the least of it that day. In the back bedroom that overlooked the yard, Frank stayed sleepless into the small hours. And that thought which had first troubled him long before and which he so often pushed away, returned once again. The question of why he cared so passionately for that ailing hebe down in the yard, for all the green spaces of the city, for the neglected garden at Halcyon Hill. The unpalatable answer had never changed. That he wanted to earn the place on this earth that he'd never been able to feel he deserved. Every hebe nurtured, every rosebud fed and watered, every cutting taken and new life grown from it was a declaration. A plea perhaps. This is who Frank Brodie is. Look, he's not that bad, not that worthless, not a waste of space. He is somebody after all. For thirty-eight years, he had striven to believe that.

Even the little bedroom in which he now lay was a reflection of this struggle. Number 74 Pitt Street, faded though it may have been, was a cosy enough house. But this room was not. When Frank had arrived as the new lodger, Arthur had apologised for its bareness and encouraged him to decorate it. A few rugs, Arthur said, a few pictures, another table lamp. Nice curtains, instead of just the roller blind. They could get a decent staff discount at the shop. It wouldn't cost much. But Frank had said it was just fine as it was. No need to go to the expense. The narrow bed. The hard-backed chair. The little wardrobe. The bookcase filled with fat tomes on horticulture. That was all he needed. Indeed, it was better than the attic room he'd had as a child or the hostels to which, down on his luck, he'd sometimes found himself reduced. So that was how the back bedroom had always remained. If the man on the bicycle had gone under a bus in the morning, all trace of his presence could have been cleared by teatime.

When, at the age of thirty-eight, he had finally found the courage to search out Alice Godsal, it had been because of a lingering hope that knowing who he truly was might make all the difference. He might even be able to become that person instead of a blank canvas. And might this woman, this Isobel Farrar, so far above his station, offer him that sense of unapologetic existence which had so far eluded him? For a while, he'd believed that sense might come to him here in Pitt Street. But though he was grateful for the degree of comfort he'd found here, it had never been quite enough.

As he lay awake in the December night, Frank asked himself if that was what had been offered to him today, in the subterranean cavern of the ironmongery. When the white veil had been raised and he had seen himself in a mirror. Was that what Isobel Farrar had brought him and on which he had turned his back and run away? An unapologetic existence? A place in the world? That Holy Grail. That dream beyond imagining.

IO

Afterwards, she would tell herself it happened because everything had been so stirred up that day. Her thoughts in a tumble, her heart off its axis. She hadn't set out to do it. Heavens, no. Something she'd promised herself she would never do, a promise she had kept for more than half a lifetime.

When she'd felt well enough to leave the shop, she'd craved fresh air. Air not polluted with the scents of Chanel and Worth, emetically blended with the sweat of bustling bodies. She crossed over into the park, though scarcely noticing where she headed, one path no more meaningful than any other. It was only when she felt a stone in her shoe and sat on a bench to remove it that she registered being by the Victoria & Albert Museum and thus too close to a place she hadn't seen for nearly forty years.

For all that time, there had been a small dark hole in Isobel Farrar's mental map of the city. One precise corner of South Kensington that was simply no longer there, as if some tiny fragment of an asteroid had obliterated it. Over the years, this hole had led to minor inconvenience. When a social invitation was located a little too near, she had made some excuse. Harrods could no longer welcome her at its portals. Once, when compelled to attend a funeral at Brompton Oratory, she had been sick afterwards at the feet of a bishop in full purple. But somehow, on the whole, the eccentricity had been manageable. Her dreams, of course, had been another matter. Less amenable to annihilation. In her dreams she had gone there often.

But now, on the bench with her shoe in her hand, she realised what she was going to do. Despite the general turbulence of her mind, the thought came to her almost calmly. No voice in her head warned her off, nor did her pulse race or fear knot her stomach. For a moment, she thought how odd that was. Perhaps the place, so long unthinkable, had simply lost its power. Yet she knew that was not the reason. That reason was what had just happened in the big shop on the far side of the park. Time, place, character. It was all part of the same story, the same penny-dreadful.

At first glance, nothing much had changed in Pelham Crescent. It was still an oppressive place, scant sunlight able to penetrate the squash of the tall lean houses and the regiment of trees in the central garden. The trees, though leafless now, had grown taller, better allowing its denizens the privacy which their money had sought to purchase. No longer could the occupant of a bedroom on one side of the crescent see directly into someone else's on the opposite. The clip-clop of the hansoms and the broughams had long been replaced by the guttural chug of the motor car. Through an open window, a wireless blared out some dance music, a vulgarity which would never have been tolerated in her day. But still, in its entitled essence, Pelham Crescent was just the same. A fine address for men of property. Men who knew the value of possession.

And there it was. The house where she had once existed under the name of Mrs Edwin Reed. Standing at a distance, by the garden railings, Isobel had to turn away from her first sight of it. Only slowly, cautiously, was she able to raise her eyes from the pavement. The three steps up to the front door, framed by delicate wrought-iron arms holding up a lantern. The door itself, now painted a gaudier colour than the dark green which her first husband had thought acceptable, never wishing to do anything which might be cause for comment. On the ground floor, the morning room. On the *piano nobile*, the drawing room. Then, with a deep breath, she compelled her gaze to go higher. But that courage only lasted an instant, until her unwilling eyes shut themselves against the image. Yet it was a pointless stratagem because what lay, or rather had lain, behind the second-floor window of 32 Pelham Crescent was imprinted upon her forever. Not just on her retinas, but on all her senses. The colour and fabric of the heavy swagged curtains. How the carpets had felt beneath her bare feet. The squeaking doors of the satinwood wardrobe. The dressing table and exactly how her hairbrushes had been arranged upon it – the beautiful ivory-backed brushes her mother had left to her. And of course, those other sights, other sounds, other smells.

Again, Isobel wrenched her face away. For the second time that day, the view before her swayed and she had to grab hold of the railing. An elderly man raised his hat and asked if she was quite well. She answered that she was, but knew now that she had been quite wrong, that the house in Pelham Crescent had not lost its power after all. Why had she imagined she could look on it with any sort of equanimity? You stupid woman. When she was able to let go of the railing, its iron spearhead was impressed on the palm of her glove.

Suddenly, the gaudy door was flung open. A couple, smart and glossy, appeared with a young child. The couple grasped the child's arms and swung him down the three steps onto the pavement. Shrieks and laughter. Can we do it again, Daddy? Please, Daddy. More shrieks, more laughter. They jumped into a shiny Austin, the very same shade as the front door, and roared off towards Brompton Road. Isobel looked back at the empty doorway. Once, in another lifetime when she had first come to this house, she'd let herself imagine that such a pleasant scenario would befall her here. Something which would miraculously validate the choice she had made under such pressure, every fibre of her being screaming 'no'. But that was before the disillusionment she had always feared had indeed gripped her in its claws. Before she had admitted to herself that there would never be a cause for laughter at this address, let alone any deeper emotion. Except perhaps for hatred.

But now it seemed that happiness had finally come to the house and she was glad of it. In the dining room, where she and Edwin Reed had sat in endless silence, there might now be laughter. In the drawing room, parlour games, a gramophone and a wireless. And in that space on the second floor, tenderness would have taken its rightful place in the marriage bed. Isobel hoped too that nothing of her own misery had ever seeped into the walls. That the happy child had never been woken by the wind and heard in it the distant echo of her tears. And that the smart young wife, reading by the fire in the evening, had not been suddenly aware of something alien in the air around her, something amiss that she couldn't put her finger on before she shrugged it off and went back to her book.

By the railings of the gardens, Isobel's mood changed again. After the agitation, a deep grief bore into her. Because what had happened here, in that other lifetime, was what had led to the events of this very morning. Without it, she would never have found herself in the ironmongery of a department store. Or kept a faded photograph secreted in a jewel box. Or carried guilt and regret like a parasite inside her.

Everything, all of it, was the toxic legacy of a November night so very long ago. When a woman with a longing for love had been desecrated in body and in soul.

Before Isobel turned away, she stared for the last time at 32 Pelham Crescent. At the door through which, after five years of confinement, she had finally fled. At the window behind which, in blood and brutality, the man now called Frank Brodie had been given life.

I I

The worst of it was not understanding. Not knowing what he'd done to upset her.

The first time, Frank must have been four or five. He'd been in a corner of the parlour, playing with the toy one of the customers had given him. She'd come in so silently he'd not noticed her at once. For a minute or two, she'd just stared down at him, not saying a word. Then it was as if a storm had broken inside her. She'd grabbed his collar and dragged him by the scruff of the neck out of the room, along the dark hallway and downstairs into the butcher's shop.

The shop had not long closed for the day. The main door locked, the blinds down, the counters and chopping boards swabbed clean. As usual, Butcher Brodie had gone out to the Tufnell Park Tavern. He'd always felt uneasy when Brodie went out, leaving him alone with her. But until this winter evening, that was all it had been. A faint unease. But now, out of the blue, it had become something else entirely.

As she pulled him through the curtain into the back shop, he began to feel sick. He'd never liked the smell of the front shop, but the reek of what lay behind was even worse. On summer days, it would drift up through the open window of his stuffy little room in the attic. That faint fetid odour. The precursor of decay.

She reached for the fat ball of rough, hairy string that was used to wrap the parcels for delivery. She pulled his arms behind his back until he yelped in pain, then tied his wrists together. The string cut into his wrists. He told her how much it hurt. He asked what it was he'd done and, whatever it was, he was really sorry and would never ever do it again. But she wasn't listening. And suddenly he knew that what he so dreaded, the worst thing his little mind could imagine, was about to come to pass.

'No! Please! No!' he yelled. 'I'm sorry. I'll try to be better. Please, Mum, no!'

The woman spun him round to face her and cuffed him hard across the cheek. It seemed to him that her eyes were on fire, that some conflagration had ignited in her mind, only visible through the windows of those two blazing eyes. With his collar still gripped in one hand, she used the other to wrench open the heavy steel door of the cold chamber, fling him inside and slam it shut. If his hands had not been tied, he'd have battered on it with his tiny fists. But all he could do was to scream and beg for release. He screamed until no more screams would come.

He kept facing the door, afraid to look behind him because he knew well enough what was there. Hanging from big hooks bored into the ceiling, the carcasses of cows and sheep, newly slaughtered, awaiting their last humiliation from Butcher Brodie's knives and hacksaws.

It was almost dark in the cold chamber, except for a ventilation grille which let in a mean shard of light from the lamp in the alley behind the shop. But in truth, pitch blackness would have been more merciful. For when he did dare to glance behind him, the monsters on the hooks seemed even more frightful. In the winter air coming in through the vent, the carcasses swayed slightly, as if some semblance of life remained in them still.

He didn't know how long it was before he'd slid down onto the floor, unable to scream, unable to feel his bound hands anymore, unable to see for his tears. But then the mist cleared in his mind and it came to him what it was that he had done. The framed photograph on her special table in the window. He'd knocked it over with his elbow and left a tiny scuff on the frame. A mark so small you'd hardly see it. But it was the photograph she'd warned him never ever to touch, never even to go near. The one beside which a candle was lit every Sunday evening.

Nor did he know how long it was before the door was opened and he dimly saw Butcher Brodie's hobnail boots on the threshold.

'For Christ's sake, Morag, you been at the gin?' he shouted. 'Never do that again or you'll have the coppers on us.'

And she hadn't. At least not when there was any chance of Brodie returning soon. But when there wasn't – when the butcher had gone to the market or to play billiards all evening in the Tufnell Park Tavern – the child would feel once more the hand on his collar, the gin breath on his neck and his arms pulled behind him. In time, the primeval fear of the cold chamber would diminish a little. But the sadness that it brought never did, as he shivered in the corner, his knees up to his chest, listening to the creaking of the carcasses that swayed on the hooks. As the years passed, that posture of his body would also become the posture of his spirit. And somehow, the child would sense it and mourn that part of himself which had been lost.

If only he'd known what it was that he had done.

12

He wouldn't tell her all of it. When Arthur Collins sat down to write to Isobel Farrar, he chose his words carefully. Besides, he didn't feel it was his place to impart these things. Such sad confidences must come from Frank himself at some point in the future, when a relationship had been built between parent and child, strong enough in its foundations to bear such information without too much pain or indeed recrimination. It had now become Arthur's mission to make sure that relationship came about.

It was over a week since the evening of the day when the woman in the white veil had come to the shop. Nothing had been said the following morning, as Arthur had known it wouldn't be. Frank, the blaze of his rage dampened down, had retreated back into himself. Their daily routine resumed. The putting on of the bicycle clips, their separate journeys to the shop. The supper in the dining room, the wireless in the parlour. Something had to be done, Arthur told himself. But he didn't know what.

On the fourth day after the drama in the ironmongery, a letter had landed on the doormat. The envelope was rich and creamy, the handwriting that of someone who cared about such things. He knew at once what it was; nobody ever wrote to Frank. She must have got the address from the staff office. In the little kitchen, Arthur held it over the old copper kettle that had once been his mother's, until the posh envelope yielded to the steam.

The notepaper was headed with the title of the sender. 'Jesus,' said Arthur aloud. The content was short, just a few sentences. He read it once, then read it again. He re-sealed the envelope and waved it in the air to dry.

The second letter arrived a few days later. The steam revealed that the first missive had not received a reply and pleaded that this second one might fare better. The handwriting, Arthur noticed, was a little different this time. Less measured, more erratic. The words sloping so far forward they looked as if they might fall flat on their faces. A few wrongly spelled, crossed out and rewritten. It was still brief, though each sentence seemed to carry even greater urgency than before. How well Arthur remembered half-carrying the writer to the chair by the perfume counter and raising the veil to give her water. But his shock at the sight of that face had been twofold. Not just the instant revelation of who she must surely be, but the intensity of the pain branded on her features. Now, in the second letter, that same pain leapt off the page, lancing through the steam from the copper kettle.

For a day or two more, Arthur had waited. In the evenings, he'd played Sherlock Holmes, looking for clues that a reply was being written, watching to see if Frank shut himself away at the dining table after supper. At the best of times, Frank disliked writing anything. When something official came, they would sit together and Arthur would help him deal with it. But it was always a struggle. Words flowed no more easily from Frank's reluctant pen than they did from his mouth. When they had first met, all those years ago now, Arthur had wondered if, inside this strange, beautiful boy, there were perhaps no words at all, no story to tell, just some kind of void. Or was there a torrent of words just waiting to be released – words in their hundreds of thousands, words that would tumble over themselves in their rush to escape from confinement? That it was the latter had become obvious the first time Frank had flown into one of his tantrums. Arthur had dropped the coal shovel onto one of the plant pots in the yard and the explosion had been titanic. And yet, Arthur had been glad of it. He had yearned to know that there was no void after all, that there *was* a story to tell. And, in that moment, Arthur had determined to discover what it was.

He'd found the key by chance a month or two after Frank had moved into the back bedroom of 74 Pitt Street. He'd twisted Frank's arm into having a second bottle of beer and that had done the trick. For Frank couldn't hold his liquor. Something in his lean, fit body rejected its poison at once. The deep dark eyes became bleary, the cheeks flushed, the speech slurred. But the tongue untied itself. The words came, the tale was told. It had come in dribs and drabs over many months of evenings in the parlour, while the wireless, turned down low, relayed the concerts from the Queen's Hall. At times, Arthur had found it almost unbearable; the beauty of the music as an accompaniment to the ugliness of the chronicle that Frank spat out. Arthur felt guilty too, using this shameful method of finding out the truth. But the end, he told himself, justified the means. Only if he knew that truth, might he be able to help the boy who sold the hammers and chisels in the subterranean cavern beneath the big shop. More than anything in his life so far, that was what Arthur Collins wanted to do. Over the years, he'd tried his best, though he knew quite well that his successes, of which there had been more than a few, had only gone so far. And when Frank had returned from the war, that process had continued; only now there was so much more to be told and it was even harder to excavate than before.

But of all the wounds inside Frank Brodie, one had cut more sharply than any of the others. The healing of which, Arthur always felt, might magically heal all the others. Now, like some Christmas gift from God, the chance had come to do something about that. And Arthur would not let it go. He was getting on now, sixty next birthday, his health not good, though he tried to hide that from everyone, especially Frank. Who knew how long he'd last? So when, a few days after the second letter had come and he had found it, ripped in two, unopened and unanswered, among the potato peelings in the dustbin, Arthur decided to act. The woman in the white veil would get her reply from 74 Pitt Street.

And so he retreated to the front bedroom and the little escritoire which, like the copper kettle, had once belonged to his sainted mother. Arthur enjoyed writing letters as a rule. He still wrote to the old pals he'd made during his life on the halls – most of them retired now, of course, too old for the touring, as he himself had become. Many were on their uppers now, 'flat stony' as Arthur called it; he often sent a few quid to the worst off. He thanked his lucky stars that he'd managed to find a new job. The role of floorwalker had come quite easily to him, its chief prerequisite being to give a performance of sunny bonhomie. A chance to spread good cheer. For that was what had always motivated Arthur Collins. He simply liked making other people happy by whatever means he could. Once he'd done that with his singing and that had been a marvellous thing. God's gift to him. On top of the escritoire stood his proudest possession, the framed photograph of the queen of the halls. *To the Camden Caruso. Love from Marie.* That was what the old girl had always done, despite her own troubles. Making people happy. And that was what he was doing now as he picked up his pen to write to Lady Isobel Farrar.

But the difficulty that Frank Brodie had with words now descended upon Arthur Collins. What on earth to say? Where to begin? In this most private of matters, would she resent his intrusion? Would she reply angrily? Would she reply at all? But he somehow cobbled together some words of reassurance, of encouragement, of his willingness to help her if she would kindly allow him. He introduced himself as Frank's landlord, colleague and good friend. He told her a little of Frank's tale, but only a little. Nothing that might distress her.

Almost by return of post, another of the rich, creamy envelopes landed on the doormat, this time addressed to himself. He secreted it in his inner pocket and sent a swift reply. Yes, he would be glad to do what Lady Farrar proposed. He was at her service in every way possible. Arthur filled a tooth-mug from the bottle hidden behind his socks in the wardrobe, leaned back in the bedroom chair and raised a toast to the photograph of Marie Lloyd. Yes indeed, that was what a life well-lived was all about. The spreading of happiness. Dear old Marie, bless her, had known the truth of that one.

In his early days, the Camden Caruso had fancied himself not just as a singer, but as a writer of songs. A few of them had gone down well with the audiences, though he'd never quite hit the jackpot, never produced anything to make Ivor Novello quake in his boots. Ballads, most of them. Sweet, sad, sentimental songs that made the ladies dab their eyes. And it came to Arthur Collins that this was the lyric in which he now found himself. A sad, sentimental song. The story of a mother and child, separated by the cruel hand of fate. A real tear-jerker and no mistake. But now he would help to write the last verse in which all the clouds blew away and the sun came out. A happy ending. He went over to the wardrobe, refilled his glass from the gin bottle behind the socks and drank to that.

13

It was far too crowded. A flock of chattering, footsore women weighed down with Christmas packages. An elderly string quartet, raised on a dais, played popular tunes, though the weariness of their audience seemed reflected in the performance. At once, she'd regretted her choice of venue, but at least they had led her to a table exiled in a corner, half-hidden by a pillar and a large aspidistra. She had arrived early, wanting to be settled and calm before he arrived. As calm as possible that is, for a meeting with this stranger who had written to her, who had somehow known of her most intimate business.

But when Arthur Collins appeared from behind the aspidistra, she recognised him at once. That day in the shimmering shop, when her eyes had opened from her swoon, his face had been close to hers, holding the glass of water to her lips. She still recalled the sweat on his forehead, the shine of the brilliantine on his thinning hair and the faint whiff of drink on his breath.

There were few men in the tea room that day – reluctant escorts, numb with boredom, wishing to God they were anywhere else. But she noticed at once that Arthur Collins was quite at home. This was his world, after all. The world of perfumed ladies, perfectly wrapped packages and aching feet. Yet though he was immaculately dressed, he belonged to a different tribe from the other men here. He lacked their languor and their entitlement.

He sat on the edge of his seat when he spoke. He asked the waitress her name, which was Mildred, and complimented her on the neatness of her uniform. There was something more, though. Absurd as it seemed, she sensed that Arthur Collins the floorwalker cared for the waitress, recognising in her a member of his tribe. And she wondered if he might somehow care for her, Isobel Farrar, too; another woman quite unknown to him. Or why else would he be here?

'Since you knew my address, I presume you read my letters?' asked Isobel as soon as the waitress had gone.

'I apologise most sincerely for that,' he replied. 'But I found them discarded and unread and I knew they must be from you. Nobody else would be writing to Frank.'

'And you knew who I was? When you saw me in your shop? You knew who I was?'

'In an instant. When I had to raise your veil. You could have been nobody else but...'

'Does Frank know you know? Did you speak to him of it?'

'I tried, Lady Farrar,' replied Arthur Collins. 'But he wasn't listening. Frank only listens when he wants to.'

'Why, then, did he seek out my friend Mrs Godsal in the first place? Why try to find me if now he doesn't want to know me?'

'I'm what they call a floorwalker, Lady Farrar. For what they call a head-shrinker, you'll have to go to Harley Street. I'm a simple man, Lady Farrar, and Frank Brodie is anything but that. Still, I do my best.'

The waitress called Mildred reappeared with the pot of tea and plates of cucumber sandwiches. Silence fell on the table as the tea was poured into the cups and the first sips taken.

'Mrs Godsal thought he was not a happy person,' Isobel said. 'Is that true?'

She saw the man shift uncomfortably in his seat.

'He has some comforts in his life.' Arthur Collins smiled, brushing off the question and a fleck of dust from his sleeve. 'He loves plants and flowers. That's the main thing. Obsessed with them, he is. And he likes the countryside. Always pedalling off on his bicycle at the weekend. I've no idea where he goes.'

'We all find comforts to sustain us, Mr Collins,' replied Isobel, her eyes fixed on his. 'But my friend told me that Frank was a sad man. So I ask you again: is that true?'

The smile left Arthur's face. He looked away from those dark eyes and down at the cucumber sandwich on his plate.

'Frank has had a difficult time of it. There's no doubt of that.'

And so it was, in the tea room of Fortnum and Mason, on an afternoon not long before Christmas, that Isobel Farrar's own great comfort was snatched away from her. The comfort she had clung to so fiercely for so long. The possibility that the child of her body had had a good life. That the decision she had made had been the right one – a noble and a positive act. She had never forgotten the moment when the child had been torn from her arms. Now, in the words of this stranger, there was a second tearing, almost worse than the first. A difficult time of it, the man said. A life not blessed.

The waitress called Mildred returned with a triple-decked cake-stand which she presented with a fanfare of a smile, as if Santa Claus himself had taken a hand in the baking. Scones oozing jam and cream, iced sponges and sculpted French fancies piled high on the doilies. Arthur Collins requested two éclairs. Isobel asked for nothing, a sudden emptiness now filling the pit of her stomach. Instead, she steeled herself to ask those questions to which she dreaded the answers.

'Tell me, please. Tell me what you know.'

Arthur Collins no longer sat on the edge of his chair. Now he drew himself back, his lips tightening, his gaze cast down, his cake fork abandoned beside the éclairs.

'I don't know the whole story. Just a little.'

'Then tell me the little, Mr Collins.'

'Of course. You have the right, after all.'

'No, Mr Collins, I have no rights,' replied Isobel. 'None at all. But I should very much care to know.'

'The couple who were supposed to look after him didn't do so. They were unkind. Very unkind. Worse than that in fact.'

'But why? If they wanted a child...'

'The woman had had a son who died young and she couldn't have any more. The husband hoped that taking in another child would make her happy, but it didn't. The living boy was a constant reminder of the dead one and he was made to pay for that. In short, Lady Farrar, nobody really brought Frank up. Nobody. He was left to fend for himself. And that is what he's always done.'

'And there is no wife and children?'

'No.'

'A sweetheart? A girl to walk out with?'

'No one has been spoken of in the years he's lodged with me.'

'Friends, then? Surely he has friends?'

'No doubt some chums among the staff at the shop,' replied Arthur. 'And I think there were some mates in the war who didn't make it back, though he rarely talks about that. Still, he is polite to everyone, always considerate and kind. Nobody could ever take exception to our Frank.'

Isobel put down her teacup and looked hard at Arthur Collins. She was not fooled.

'But I believe you're telling me, Mr Collins, that my son has never been loved? Is that the gist of it?'

She posed the question so quietly that he had to ask her to repeat it. When she did, it came so loudly that he started back in his chair. She saw the sweat bead out on his brow and a flush come to his cheeks. Arthur Collins gave her no reply. She put her hand over her mouth to stifle the sound that rose up, uninvited, from her throat.

It seemed to Isobel that the room around her had somehow retreated, the faces of other people become blurred, the music of the quartet diminished to a distant echo. At the table behind the aspidistra, the two of them sat marooned in silence. My child has never been loved, she thought. That was the tale this stranger told. Never to have known love. Could any worse fate have befallen the boy she had held in her arms in Alice's tiny room under the eaves? For so short a time, so long ago. The pain of the knowledge cut into her, sharper than the unused cake knife on her plate.

'Yet it's not quite true, Mr Collins,' she said at last. 'Frank has been loved every day of his life. Every single day of those thirty-eight years. I can take no credit for it, Mr Collins, because I tried not to love him. You can have no notion of how hard I tried. Especially when I went on to have another child. But like those unkind people who took Frank in, my new child could never obliterate the memory of the old. Trying not to love Frank was useless. Quite useless. Wherever he has been, whatever he has lived through, he has been loved, though he never knew it and though it has done him no good.'

She took out the photograph and passed it over.

'This is all I have of him.'

As he stared at it, she thought for a moment that Arthur Collins might weep; then instead, some sort of awe flooded the puffy features.

'Such a wonderful picture,' he said. 'Beautiful as a Madonna, Lady Farrar, if you'll permit the observation.'

'You think it wonderful?'

'Of course. What else could it be?'

'It was the day I gave him up. The worst day of my life.'

'It's still wonderful,' he replied.

'When I came to the ironmongery and saw him, I thought my heart would stop, Mr Collins,' said Isobel. 'But when he turned away from me, I swear I almost wished it might not start again. Will you help bring Frank back to me, Mr Collins? You said in your letter that you might.'

'What happened in the shop was just a bump in the road, Lady Farrar,' said Arthur. 'But be prepared for that road to be a long one. And even once you reach the end of it, another road will stretch out before you. Getting to know Frank – to really know him – isn't easy.'

'And you have, Mr Collins?'

'Not really, though I've tried for long enough. I think that the only person who might succeed in that is you. That's why I want to help you if I can.'

The scratchy string quartet began to play a new melody. And Arthur Collins, softly, as if he hardly intended to, started to sing. For a moment, Isobel's instinct was to smile, but then she didn't. Out of this ageing man with the thinning hair came a voice of transcendent beauty. And it was singing not at her, but for her.

'*Pack up all my care and woe. Here I go, singing low. Bye bye blackbird.*'

And a measure of the comfort which, unwillingly, he had taken from her earlier, he now returned. In the comfort of a second chance. In the hope of redemption. In the possibility of possibility.

'We will find a way, Lady Farrar,' he said. 'We will plot and plan. Plot and plan. Remember, dear lady, this really is such a wonderful thing.'

On parting, he shepherded her to the street doors, walking half a pace ahead to clear a passage through the throng, just as he would have done in his own little kingdom. He waved down a taxi to take her to Waterloo, grasped her hand and raised it to his lips. It was a gesture she disliked as a rule, an unctuous trespassing on her privacy. But this time she found herself affected by it. Arthur Collins, she knew now, was her friend.

'Oh, look,' he said suddenly, his eye caught by one of the festive windows, sparkling in the growing dusk of the winter afternoon.

In the midst of an Aladdin's cave of desirable Christmas presents stood a small table, draped in satin, edged in tinsel. Isobel's gaze followed Arthur's fingertip towards a display of Russian dolls, painted scarlet and gold, spread out one by one from largest to smallest.

'There you are,' he said. 'There's Frank. That's him exactly. That's your challenge, Lady Farrar.'

As her taxi crawled into the traffic, she watched him saunter off along Jermyn Street. He raised his hat to a beggar on a corner and put a coin into the outstretched hand. She could've sworn he was still singing. Pack up all my care and woe. And for the first time in the two weeks since her child had fled from the sight of her, the sadness that had smothered Isobel's spirit, loosened its grip a little and let her breathe again.

In the womb of the taxi, she took the photograph from her handbag. Familiar with every grain of light and shade upon it, it seemed to her that it looked slightly different. She stared at it curiously until the change became clear. How wonderful it was, Arthur Collins had said. And in one sentence, he had transformed a lifelong testament to loss and yearning into one of infinite joy.

14

When, at the turn of the year, her usual time had come and gone, Isobel had not at first felt alarmed. It had happened before. After recent events, small wonder that her body was out of kilter. But the next date came and went too. Then she was sick in the basin three mornings in a row. When the truth could no longer be denied, she had slumped down onto the lavatory seat and wept for an hour.

'Alice, Alice, what shall I do?'

In those darkest months of Isobel's life, Alice was still the only one to whom she could turn. Alice had hurried to the little flat in Pimlico, served up a swig of brandy from a flask, then suggested a nice walk along the river towards Chelsea. It was a fine, crisp day. A bit of fresh air would do her good, help her to think calmly.

But Isobel had found it impossible to think calmly, even to think at all. Emotion engulfed her. Just one emotion. The visceral need to be rid of the presence she now knew was seeded in her belly. A burning certainty that she could never love that presence. Never ever.

Arm in arm, the women walked slowly along the Embankment in the weak sun of late winter. Alice remarked only on a yellow rash of crocuses in somebody's window box or how prettily the light danced on the river. Isobel said nothing at all. She watched a flock of hopeful gulls wheeling around a coal barge chugging slowly downstream. Most Londoners quite forgot how close their city was to the open sea. No doubt those gulls would cling to the barge until the river widened and the confining land melted away. Then they would soar off into the sky. How wonderful it would be to beg a ride on their wings and go with them. Far above every trouble and care. The past left behind, the future not yet discernible. The present moment everything.

They crossed the bridge into Battersea Park and sat on a bench looking over to Wren's great hospital in Chelsea. Alice reached out and took Isobel's hand.

'Well now, my duck, there's a fast train and a slow train,' she said, 'and it's up to you which one you get aboard.'

'Oh, the fast one, Alice. The fast one, please.'

But that, said Alice, was the one that carried most risk. The one that bore you into a dark and dangerous tunnel from which you might never emerge. Isobel was young and, despite recent ordeals, was healthy, but those dangers remained.

'Her name is Granny Robson,' said Alice. 'Lives above a bookie's in Frith Street. A sweet, cuddly old thing, wrapped in shawls. Listens to all your woes and feeds you chicken broth if you've got a cough. But the other stuff she pours down your throat is a lot less pleasant. Sometimes it works, I must admit, but sometimes it doesn't. Dear Granny Robson has dispatched far more of our girls than the madman in Whitechapel ever did. Including my little sister. So I'd think long and hard before you go to Frith Street.'

Isobel retrieved her hand from Alice's and went over to the river wall. Suddenly, the nausea rushed over her again, but she managed to push it away. For a time, she stared silently down into the water. She tried to picture the thing now growing inside her, but failed utterly. No shape, no face – however unformed it would still be – came to her. But then other faces did. The faces of those who had loved her and prayed that her life should be a happy and a noble one. Her father, her mother, her grandfather, the music teacher who had first told her she was gifted, the nuns at the convent, the old blind priest who had taught her the catechism. And, last of all, looming larger than any of those others, the face she had loved the most. And she knew with utter certainty that, wherever he now existed, he would want her to live.

'And the slow train?' Isobel said, turning back to Alice on the bench.

'You let things unfold as they should. A tedious business, of course, but by the time the buttercups are out on this grass, it'll all be over.'

'And then?'

'And then I will speak to my gentleman admirer,' replied Alice. 'Mr Godsal. You've heard me speak of him. The one who wants to marry me and save me from a life of sin. Mr Godsal is well connected. He will deal with everything. He will find a place for it.'

'What sort of place? An orphanage?'

'A home where a child is wanted,' replied Alice. 'You need never know where or who. You need never see it again. It's best that way. That's what Mr Godsal says. He's helped out quite a few of the girls.'

Some stray cat had appeared from the bushes and was rubbing against Alice's ankles. She lifted it onto her lap and stroked its matted coat until the purring came. But her gaze lay elsewhere, in some other space and time.

'Including me.'

'You? You never said.'

'Twins.'

'Oh, Alice.'

Alice shook herself as if she was suddenly cold, making the cat leap from her lap. A street seller had pushed his barrow into the park and begun to call out his wares.

'How about two cups of negus?' Alice said. 'That'll warm us up. I think we deserve it, don't you?'

She joined the queue at the barrow, returning with the spicy wine and a few sweetmeats to tempt the cat to return.

'I call them my ghost children. Isn't that nice?' said Alice. 'Little ghost children. Maybe that's not the right word, because ghosts are usually dead, aren't they? And perhaps mine now are, who can tell? I hope that somewhere they live and breathe and are happy, yet I'll never know if that's true or not. And so, they haunt me. Day and night. Summer and winter. And till my last breath, they always will.'

Alice reached across the bench and took Isobel's hand.

'Funny really. I thought I never wanted children. Noisy, smelly little blighters. I wanted pretty clothes and bright lights and fun. I just wanted food in my belly, not a bloody kid. But when the thing happened, all that changed. I changed. Of course, I pretended that I hadn't, but I had. And then Billy Godsal took them away, one by one. And they became my little ghosts.'

Now it was Alice who rose and went to look out over the river. And then, to her amazement, Isobel saw her friend's shoulders begin to shake. Alice never cried. Alice, so strong and capable. Alice who always had an answer for everything, a way out, a clever stratagem. Alice who had survived the streets of the city and the evils to be found there, but who still laughed as she walked proudly along them, her sharp nose in the air. But now, here was Alice with tiny rivulets coursing down her powdered cheeks.

'The same will be true for you, my duck,' she said, turning again to Isobel. 'You need to understand that. Mr Godsal will take care of things. But don't imagine it will ever be over. It will never be over. You will be haunted too.'

And the cat returned to her and took the sweetmeats from Alice's outstretched hand.

15

On the last Sunday before Christmas, Frank Brodie sat on top of the Number 9 bus from Hammersmith to the West End. Beneath his coat, he wore his winter suit and a fresh white shirt and tie. The coat was a little threadbare at the collar and cuffs, but he would take it off when they got there and carry it folded up so nobody would notice. He knew that was daft, because nobody would notice him let alone his coat, but nevertheless. Arthur had offered to buy him a new coat for Christmas, but he'd politely said no. Arthur was good to him in so many ways already. Enough was enough.

'Not far to go now,' said Arthur, as the bus crawled towards Hyde Park Corner. 'Thanks again for coming. Good of you.'

'That's all right,' replied Frank.

But it wasn't really. After a week of funereal cloud, the day was clear and crisp, the sky a limpid blue, the bare branches laced with hoar frost. He'd much rather have been out on the bike. Just a short ride, though, as it really was perishing cold. Over Hammersmith Bridge and around Barnes Common maybe. But Arthur had asked him to come to a carol concert in aid of the war widows. It'd be nice, Arthur said. Get them both in the mood for Christmas.

Since the appearance in the ironmongery of the white-veiled lady, the matter had not been mentioned between them again. As Frank always did, after losing his temper, he fretted terribly that he had wounded Arthur – a thought he found unbearable. As Arthur always did, he acted as if it had never happened. Normally, the dust would be allowed to settle until the air was clear again, but this time that had not quite been the case. The matter still hung in the air of 74 Pitt Street. Unspoken but ever present.

Frank had retreated into himself even more than usual and Arthur, for once, made no attempt to cheer him out of it. There had been no tapping on Frank's bedroom door to say that a fresh brew was ready in the kitchen or that the funny programme they both liked was starting on the wireless. Though Arthur went on serving the supper as usual, he had otherwise not sought Frank's company. And Frank knew how much Arthur loved company, anyone's company. His eternal need for an audience. It was one reason why he was a good floorwalker; there was a different 'house' every single day. Even his usual singing at home, a habit which sometimes brought complaints from the neighbours, had stopped now, and Frank, so impervious to the impact of his own silences, became deeply discomfited by the silence of Arthur. For he knew that Arthur, for the first time, was despairing of him. In Frank's life, only Arthur Collins had ever cared enough to despair. And so, on this winter Sunday, he sat on top of the Number 9 bus.

At the gateway of the church, he took off his coat even faster than planned. He'd expected a congregation of fairly ordinary folk, the pews occupied by the wives of long-lost soldiers, garbed in black like ranks of ravens, clutching the hands of their fatherless chicks. But it was not like that at all. Those going in were far grander, richly dressed in all colours of the rainbow, alighting from chauffeur-driven motorcars, their children well-trained little mice in the uniforms of posh schools. In the porch, a small woman with a strong jaw and shingled hair bustled around taking tickets and directing people to their seats. For a moment, she stared hard at Frank as if she knew him and, when he glanced back, her eyes followed him still. She could sense, he thought at once, that he did not belong here.

Their seats were in the middle of a wide pew, and they had to squeeze past a dozen others to reach their places. Above the altar hung a vast banner in white and gold. Below the name of *The Ladies' League for The Relief of War Widows* were embroidered the names of the great conflicts from Ypres to The Somme and of all the horrors in between. Frank Brodie had only seen one of these, but one had been enough. The sights, the sounds and the smells remained in his eyes, his ears, his nostrils. He knew they would never leave him, nor did he want them to. In the desolation of those trenches, he had found, deep within himself, reserves of strength. At first, this had surprised him, because he had never thought of himself as strong. Only slowly had the truth of it dawned upon him. That he didn't much care whether or not he came through this thing. And that if this was the end of his road, then so be it.

While others wrote endless letters to wives or sweethearts, to parents or to children, Frank had only had Arthur to write to. While others dreamed of all those faces, Frank had no such loving gallery. And when, blasted awake from the comfort of dreams by the nightmare of reality, others prayed silently for protection and deliverance, Frank slept soundly and prayed to nobody. He had given all that up long ago. For as far back as he could remember, it had gotten him nowhere. A load of old rubbish, he told himself.

Yet that bleak indifference to his own mortality had brought him a strange sort of peace. It had seemed also to provide some kind of armour. No whizz-bangs landed near him; no Hun bullet skimmed his ear. No limb was blown off, no eye blinded. Just perhaps a little deafness from the shelling, which he admitted to nobody, not even himself. The beauty of Frank Brodie remained magically untouched as if, despite appearances, God had loved him after all.

Yet there was a chink in the armour. The fact that Frank cared so little about himself never meant he didn't care for others. In those foul runnels of mud and duckboards and sandbags, nobody did more than Frank Brodie to look after his fellow man. He listened to stories of heartache and yearning, to confessions of fear and of the fear of that fear. He got to know the names of far-distant people he would never meet. He looked at their well-worn images, taken shyly from inside pockets. He even learned how to touch without hesitation, how to carry, how to bury. More than once, his was the last face that a stricken man would see. And in doing all this, he learned, more than he ever had before, of how other people led their lives. The worst of it. The best of it.

Now, as he sat in the church and looked at the pretty embroidery of the banner above the altar, so many names came back to him. Ten years on, Christmas was still the hardest. The same carols which these rich folk in their furs would sing today had been sung in the trenches by men with mud-streaked faces. That first Christmas of the war, he'd been one of those who'd left their dug-outs, walked into no-man's land and played football with the enemy. Christ, what a fuss that had caused. The high and mighty had gone bananas. For just one day, they'd stopped trying to kill each other, but the next morning it had all begun again. His mate Cyril had scored a goal that Christmas day but, within twenty-four hours, the same leg that had kicked the ball was blasted from his body and lay torn and twisted yards from its owner. Frank had tried to comfort him as he'd thrashed in his agony and screamed for his mother. Frank had happened to know that Cyril's mother was long since dead, but that hadn't mattered. Until his last breath left him, it had been her name Cyril had called again and again. That night in his dug-out, Frank had asked himself if he would have done the same. But to a faceless, nameless woman? A mere idea as opposed to an actual being. How absurd it would have been, but might he have done it all the same? It had been the only moment in those four years that he had turned his head away to weep.

Now, in St James's Piccadilly, the small woman who'd stared at him in the porch walked onto a dais. The audience applauded as if they knew her well; there was even a 'bravo'.

'Oh God, here she is,' sighed an unseen man in the pew behind Frank and Arthur. 'Why do we have to come to this damn concert every bloody year?'

'Because you're Miss Maud Farrar's solicitor, darling,' replied an unseen wife. 'As you also are to half of this congregation. These are the people who pay for Tristram to go to Eton. Do try and look as if you're enjoying yourself.'

Frank heard the name. No, maybe he'd not heard correctly. Yet why had the small woman stared so hard? A slight unease came into him.

The small woman thanked everyone for coming to support this excellent cause. She reminded them that, for so many, the war was still not over. The man behind Frank yawned. She announced that the carols marked with an asterisk in the programme were those for which the congregation should stand and sing along with the choir. The first of these was now. 'Hark! The Herald Angels Sing'.

It was only when they all sat down again that it happened. When a very tall man in front of Frank shuffled along his pew to make way for a latecomer of diminutive stature. Only now could the figure of the pianist be clearly seen. Seen by both Frank and Arthur in the same moment. To the former, a surprise. To the latter, not at all.

Frank half rose in his seat. Arthur gripped his elbow and pulled him down again.

'If you run this time, Frank Brodie, I swear to God I'll never speak to you again.'

'You knew about this, didn't you?'

'I certainly did.'

'You tricked me?'

'Hole in one,' said Arthur.

Frank knew he was trapped. There was nowhere he could run, no door he could slam. Never in a hundred years could he have squeezed past all the bodies between him and the aisle. It just wasn't in him. He felt the familiar surge of the raging rise up and Arthur felt it too, coming off him like steam.

'Calm down. Breathe slowly. Grow up,' said Arthur.

It was the last of these injunctions that stung. For Frank knew well enough that he had not grown up. Even those things he had seen in the war had not brought that about. In the blood-soaked fields of Flanders, his responses had been essentially those of a child: incomprehension, helplessness, indiscriminate compassion in the face of suffering. And now, at the age of thirty-eight, he remained that child because, in a paradox, he was still waiting for the nourishing childhood that would enable him to progress into being an adult. At the age of thirty-eight, he remained inchoate. And the woman whom he held responsible now sat at a piano thirty feet away from him.

When the first of the letters had arrived in Pitt Street, he'd guessed at once from whom it came. It had been a full day before he opened it and, when he did, the printed heading at the top of the page had taken his breath away. *Lady Farrar. Halcyon Hill.* She wrote from Halcyon. On that last Sunday, a month or so back, when the long-deserted house had suddenly been awake and he'd been scared away by a barking dog, it had been her return that the cleaners and polishers and beaters of rugs had been preparing for. Now she lived again in the place where he had so often imagined her.

My dear Frank, all I want is for you to hear the story. Yours very sincerely, Isobel Farrar.

It was the possessive adjective which had caught at his throat. She called him *her* dear. Did that tiny word acknowledge that he belonged to her, that they were somehow joined? And did the use of *yours* not mean that, in some way, she was offering herself to him in return? He'd sat on his bed reading the sentence again and again.

But the feeling which began to seed in him was a fragile thing. Like his hebe out there in the yard, the one which, no matter how hard he nurtured it, failed to grow. Inside Frank Brodie, there was still a cold, dark place, which shied away from even a glimmer of light. Not trusting in the light, not able to believe that it might linger. And it was this dark place which overwhelmed him now. By what right did this woman address him as hers? Once upon a time, she had rid herself of him. For thirty-eight years, she had offered him nothing of herself. He'd not even known her name. Christ, she probably used the same words in a note for the milkman; not that a woman of her station would ever need to do such a thing. And so, the letter in the rich creamy envelope had been torn in half and put in the dustbin. As had the one which shortly followed it, without its ever being read. Only Arthur Collins, holding it into the steam of the copper kettle, had heard her second pleading and answered her, while Frank had shut himself away in the dark place, in the cold chamber of the heart, curled up into a ball.

Now in the church, the singing of the choir drifted up past the gilded columns and the stained-glass depictions of God in His heaven and up into Wren's barrel-vaulted roof. They sang the words evangelically, as if without a shadow of a doubt, as if they had not even noticed the banner on which the names of infamous battles were embroidered, each one a testament to the fact that their God was not always merciful. A famous actress ascended the pulpit and performed a bible reading with the same passion she had recently given to her Saint Joan. Then, departing from her script, she asked the congregation to remember in their Yuletide prayers, not just the widows of the war but the brave wives of those miners who had gone on strike this very summer and who now faced deprivation. There are many kinds of war, said the famous actress, who was known to be a socialist. Unfortunately, her audience contained many of those who had eagerly volunteered to drive buses, trains and lorries to ensure this deprivation came about. What a lark it had been.

'Outrageous,' muttered the man in the row behind. 'And in a church too.'

After the last notes of 'Ding Dong Merrily on High', a short silence fell. And then, from the side of the dais, the pianist began to play. Until this moment, Frank had averted his eyes from her, keeping them lowered on the hymn book in his lap. But now, trapped in his pew, he forced himself to lift his gaze and, for the first time, look properly at the woman who had walked quietly into the ironmongery and caused havoc in his soul.

Isobel sat straight-backed at the keyboard, her profile to the congregation, the casque of silver hair illuminated by the quivering light of a candelabra. Among the brightly dressed women in the church, only she had worn simple, reverential black, as if only she really remembered why they were all there on this Sunday afternoon. It seemed to Frank that, like him, she did not quite belong here, that she breathed in a place apart from the eager choir, the famous actress and the extravagant Christmas tree. He had no idea of the piece she played. Arthur had tried to share his own love of the classics, but the magic Arthur spoke of had never quite touched Frank. Not for the likes of him, he'd said. But whatever this was now, he was lifted by its beauty. And, in truth, by the beauty of the player too.

That such a creature had carried him and given him life, he found impossible to believe. For all these years he had simply wanted to know the name of that person, but realised now that such narrow information was meaningless. He should want to know *who* she truly was. And in the notes she played, he felt she revealed that a little, even if he could never have articulated how or why it was. He watched her face as she gazed down at the keys or, for a moment, did the opposite and tilted her head up towards the roof of the church. He wondered how a person who could create such beauty could also commit the act of giving away the child of her body. And for the first time, Frank understood that there might not be a simple answer, an answer that a simple man like himself would be able to understand. In the letter, she had only asked that he should hear her story. Why was it that, in the war, he had so often listened to the stories of people he scarcely knew, but now flinched back from hearing what this woman wanted to tell him? That made no sense. What story could ever be more important for him to hear? For it would not just be Isobel Farrar's story, but his own too.

Suddenly, as he watched her play, Frank felt his breathing slow down and the tension in his body give way a little. Yet still, from that dark place inside himself, the doubts awoke and began to whisper. Perhaps the reverent black gown and the beautiful music were just window dressing. Maybe she belonged to this entitled tribe as firmly as the silly man in the row behind. A posh woman who'd once disposed of something unwanted with no more thought than she would abandon a hat no longer in fashion, but who now, in the autumn of her years, feared the judgement of some god or other. And if that were true, how could the gulf between them ever be crossed? Would it not just bring more grief to them both?

And yet. And yet now the spectral woman who, on his first visit to Halcyon he had imagined walking in its gardens, at last had a face. That mirror face of his own. Back then, of course, he'd pictured her as young and now she was almost old, but that didn't matter. Now, he could see her clearly out on the terrace or under the old oak tree, strolling past the pond down towards the coppice. On a hot day, a parasol above the silvery hair, she would shield her eyes against the sun and look out across the cornfields towards the distant ridge of the downs. He tried now to picture himself being there with her but, for some reason, that scene refused to come to him. Perhaps one day it might. Frank wondered if he wanted it to, but didn't know the answer.

When Isobel finished playing, the congregation applauded. Arthur nudged him in the ribs.

'Clap, you sod,' he said. 'Go on, it won't cost you anything.'

But when Frank tried to lift his hands, they were trembling and would not leave his knees.

'There, there, Frank,' said Arthur, noticing.

The small woman took to the dais again, announcing that the afternoon had raised one hundred and eighty-seven pounds, three shillings and ninepence for the war widows. The congregation applauded again, this time for itself. A vicar materialised and blessed them all. They stood for the final carol and then it was over. In Frank and Arthur's pew, the people between them and the aisle began to disperse. They were no longer trapped, but still the two of them sat where they were. And still Frank's hands trembled.

From among the shuffling crowd, Frank saw Isobel move in their direction. Her passage was slowed by compliments on her performance; there was time for Frank to run, but he did not.

'Thank you for coming,' she said. 'I'm so very happy that you did.'

Frank gave a little nod, but did not reply.

'Hoping that you might be here, I brought a little Christmas present for you,' she said. When she passed him a small, slim package, he saw that her hands were trembling too.

'It's just a book of poems written about the war,' she said. 'I believe that you served in France and I hoped these lines might have some meaning for you.'

Again, Frank could only incline his head. Arthur had melted away. It was just the two of them now, standing in the aisle of St James's Piccadilly, as the congregation chattered, embraced their friends and buttoned up their coats against the cold awaiting them outside. For a long moment, the woman and the young man stood silent in the vortex of the bustle around them. Each of them understanding that the weight of the words which needed to be spoken was as yet unsupportable.

'I wonder if you might give me something in return,' she said. 'Would you let me wish you a happy Christmas? I last held your hand very long ago and I should so like to hold it again.'

Just as she'd first done at the counter in the ironmongery, Isobel reached out her arm. Frank hesitated for a second too long, so that her face fell and her arm began to withdraw. But then he took it and, as he did so, was aware that his own shaking had quite gone and that his grip was firm. How soft her skin was. His own palms were calloused from the work he did and he hoped she didn't notice.

'Thanks,' he said. 'Happy Christmas to you too.'

Isobel smiled at him now. He had never received such a smile. Not once, not ever. And in that smile, Frank saw everything he had always wanted to see and it gave him voice.

'You're shivering,' he said. 'You'll catch cold in that thin dress. Go and put your coat on.'

'I will,' she said. 'Thank you, Frank. I will.'

And with that Frank Brodie turned away up the aisle. He hadn't run after all. In fact, he walked quite slowly and at the head of the nave he turned to look back at her. Still standing where he'd left her, Isobel raised her hand in a tiny wave.

Her coat was of thick astrakhan with a fat fur collar. A gift from Octavius the Christmas before he died. Until today, she'd always pictured Octavius standing behind her, holding it open for her arms. But, from now on, it would be Frank Brodie. And even when that coat had long gone out of fashion and the moths had done their worst, it would still keep her warm each winter. The symbol of her first inkling that her lost child might, somewhere in his secret soul, still care for her.

16

Just as Isobel Farrar had, for half a lifetime, refused to admit the existence on the map of Pelham Crescent, so Frank Brodie had tried to do with certain parts of the West End of London.

He'd wanted to please Arthur by going to the church concert, but Arthur hadn't mentioned which church. Fifteen years ago or more, Frank had known every corner of the churchyard of St James's Piccadilly. Especially by night. He'd known the position of every lamppost when light was required, every pitch-black nook when it wasn't. Nor was it the only churchyard with which he'd once been closely acquainted. St Anne's Soho. St Paul's Covent Garden. St Martin in the Fields.

It was always the cold he remembered most. Strange, he thought, when that was the least of the dangers. One of the other boys had confessed it was those very dangers that kept *him* warm, made his heart beat faster and pump the blood around what he called, with a wink, his extremities. But nothing had ever seemed to ease the chill in Frank Brodie's young bones. The bones that showed through the skin in those times when work was hard to find. Often, he'd try to shelter from the wind or the rain in some shop doorway, unless a courting couple or an ill-tempered tramp had got there first. But a shadowy doorway wasn't the best place to stand when, like the items in the window, you were on display.

Frank Brodie had never been one of those able to operate at an elevated level. He would never be invited for champagne in the gilt-mirrored spaces of the Café Royal or Monico's. He would never be taken for oysters at Kettner's then invited upstairs to a private room. Though his beauty would always attract passing eyes, if the eyes came closer and looked harder, many would retreat again. His clothes were not smart enough to be taken into such places. His hair looked like he cut it himself, which was indeed the truth. He certainly couldn't be passed off as a nephew down from Cambridge or a young friend of the family seeking kindly advice on launching a career in the City. But it was more than that. In his manner, in his posture, in the vibrations he transmitted into the crisp night air, he exuded no good cheer, no spark of flamboyance or *joie de vivre*, no sense that time spent in his company would be anything more enjoyable than the briefest mechanical transaction.

As he loitered under the notorious arches of the Circus, Frank Brodie could only be seen for exactly what he was. Thus it was that those who did business with him were confined to his own class or only slightly above it: the shop assistants, the bus drivers, the lowest ranks of soldiers and sailors, the waiters from the restaurants and the big new hotels. And there were rarely rich pickings to be had from such shallow pockets. Instead of the gilt-mirrored rooms, Frank would ply his trade in the churchyards, the parks, the railway termini and of course the Circus.

Naturally, his looks were remarked upon, not least among those in the same line of work. Yet they invited not just admiration but professional jealousy, so that where he might have found a degree of camaraderie, he found only isolation. But that was not unfamiliar to Frank Brodie; it was no less than his experience of life had led him to expect. What he'd never had, he didn't miss. Once or twice, some kinder soul had tried to befriend him and draw him gently into the gaudy warmth of their circle. One had given him advice on his clothes and his hair, suggesting just the lightest touch of rouge on his cheeks because he looked too thin. Another had passed him the card of a man who, for a small percentage, might be able to groom Frank for a more prosperous clientele. How old was Frank? Twenty-two? Better hurry up, dearie. Time is passing. Make the most of what you've got, while you've got it. Nothing sadder than an old tart down on her luck.

But Frank had not been drawn into the circle. While, just a few yards away, the rest of them had shrieked and giggled and dispensed graphic invitations to passers-by, he had stood alone under the arches, looking out across the lurid vortex of the Circus as, night and day, life whirled ceaselessly around it. In time, he'd become so used to his loneliness that he'd only really noticed it the one time it had been relieved.

'Want a cigarette?' the voice had said from the pavement.

At first, he didn't realise the remark was directed at him. He was used to hearing grains of other people's conversations blowing over him like sand in a wind.

'Yes please. Ta,' he said.

He'd not had a smoke for days because money was tight. And this girl was offering a proper fag from a packet, not just a roll-up.

'I've seen you here before,' she said. 'I walk past most nights.'

Her name was Dora. She worked in the Langham Hotel up at Oxford Circus, she said. Chambermaid. The mess some people left in their rooms. Posh people too. Dreadful, honest to God.

After that, she'd stopped quite often. Then one night she'd suggested a drink in the pub round the corner. And he'd accepted and he'd lost his heart a little. They'd gone to the pub a few more times, as often as he could afford it, whenever he'd just had a punter. Dora was a chatterbox, which suited him well as he didn't need to say much in return. If she knew, as surely she must, what he was doing under the arches, she never referred to it. She lodged with an aunt in Clerkenwell and when the aunt went into hospital for a few days, he found himself invited there. She'd shown him her bedroom and when the thing happened, it had taken him quite by surprise, before he'd had time to think about it. And it was fine, except perhaps that he was confused afterwards. Sands had shifted beneath his feet.

But then Dora had been rushed into the same hospital as her aunt. One of the other chambermaids had tracked him down, but by the time he reached the ward, the curtains had been drawn around the bed. A burst appendix. She must have had pains for quite a while, the nurse said. Such a shame. Such a pretty girl. The nurse had held her hand as she'd passed away. Dora had mentioned his name, the nurse said.

'You look bloody freezing,' said a new voice from the pavement. 'How long have you been standing there?'

'A while,' he replied. 'It's fine.'

'It's a while too long on a night like this. And you're not exactly dressed for the North Pole, are you, sonny boy?'

Frank tried for a smile, but his teeth were chattering. Now he looked properly at the man. Middle-aged, of course. Not appealing. The usual sort. But Frank, who had learned by bitter experience, by knocks and bruises, to sense the possibility of danger, saw no danger here. As the crowds coming from the theatres jostled past towards the Underground station, the man stood looking at him, though not precisely in the usual way. That usual way was present, but there was something else too. The man looked hesitant, as if debating with himself.

'Tell you what, I'll buy you a drink. A brandy to warm you. What d'you say?'

Frank's heart sank a little. As a rule, he liked to keep conversation to a minimum. Not just because it took up time, but because he was no good at it. He was always polite, of course; he prided himself on that. He just didn't know what to say. Sitting at a bar or at a café table, face to face with a stranger who would sometimes ask him questions he didn't wish to answer. Strangely, it had never been the case with Dora, though that of course had been quite different.

But tonight, the cold was so sharp it burned his nostrils. It would be good to get inside, and he'd had no other offers since he'd reached the arches three hours before. He let the man lead him across the Circus to the Criterion Bar, to the gilt mirrors and the chandeliers, to the mixed aromas of Turkish cigarettes, cologne and brilliantine. As they reached the entrance, Frank could see the mass inside, squashed together like bowler-hatted grubs. A commissionaire held open the tall glass doors. Frank felt his glance sweep over him and stopped dead.

'No, I'd rather not, thanks,' he said to his new companion.

'Why not? What's the matter?'

'It's just...'

The man looked hard at him and Frank knew that he understood.

'All right, what about Lyon's Corner House over there? No brandy, but a nice hot pot of tea and a crumpet or two. Suit you better?'

Just as Frank had imagined, they sat face to face at a table with the tea and the crumpets. As he had not imagined, the man, having asked his name, asked nothing more. He told Frank to drink up and eat up, while he himself looked through the evening paper. He'd been working late he said and hadn't managed to read it yet. When the tea ran dry, the man ordered another pot. Was there anything else Frank would like? After half an hour, the man folded the paper and smiled.

'Well, nice to meet you, Frank, but I must be getting home. The last tube goes soon. Early start tomorrow.'

Out on the pavement, the man shook Frank's hand and slipped two shillings into his palm.

'That'll make sure you get some breakfast tomorrow,' he said.

Frank didn't understand. Under the bright lights of Lyons Corner House, the man appeared to have changed his mind. So was it true, then? Twenty-two? *Better hurry up, dearie. Your time is passing.*

'But you've been kind already. I couldn't take...'

'Nonsense. Take it to please me.'

The man shook Frank's hand, wrapped his scarf tighter against the wind blowing rubbish across the pavement and was gone, swallowed up by the crowd disappearing into the Underground.

And that, Frank thought, was that. But it wasn't. A week or so later, the man appeared again. Again, tea and crumpets were taken in Lyons Corner House. Again, the evening paper was read and comments made about Lloyd George being a right bastard and that the new king seemed a bit of a stuffed shirt compared to his dear old dad, bless him. This time, questions had been asked but only one or two and harmless enough. How had Frank been since last time and had he managed to escape the flu? Very nasty the flu could be, especially if, like himself, you were knocking on a bit.

On the third occasion, one of the young men who followed Frank's trade had occupied a nearby table and winked when Frank and the man went past.

'So, you've got a gentleman admirer, then?' the same young man said the next night. 'That's nice. Not a beauty, but they never are, are they?'

'An acquaintance,' replied Frank. 'That's all.'

'Oh yes? And I'm Queen Alexandra. Well, get what you can from it, dearie. Get what you can. That's my advice.'

On the fourth encounter, an invitation was offered. Would Frank care to visit his house for tea on the coming Sunday?

There was a first-class bakery nearby, the man said, and he'd get in something special. What did Frank like best? A nice slice of Madeira? Or Victoria sponge? And maybe a bit of fudge too, though fudge could be hell on sensitive teeth like what he had. Anyway, Frank only had to say. It'd be his choice entirely.

And so it was, on a wet dank Sunday in December in the year 1910, that Frank Brodie had first caught the Number 9 bus to Hammersmith Broadway and walked the rest of the way to a small house in a nondescript street. On that afternoon, fate had looked down on Frank Brodie and decided that, after twenty-two years of shoddy treatment, it was time that it smiled upon him.

17

'He has been *here*? To Halcyon Hill?'

'Back in the summer. A scorcher of a day, that first time he came. On a bike. He stopped at the farm and asked for directions to the Farrar house.'

'You're sure it was him, Letty?'

'Oh yes. Handsome devil, isn't he? I told him the place was shut up and no Farrar lived there anymore, but it didn't seem to put him off.'

'And he came back again, you say?'

'Three, maybe four times after that. More, for all I know. Always on a Sunday.'

The encounter between Isobel Farrar and Frank Brodie in the nave of St James's Piccadilly had been seen by many, but observed by only two. The first of these had been Letty Blount, high in the gallery, her ticket a Christmas gift from her mistress. The following afternoon, bringing the tea to the covered court, she had thought it quite acceptable to mention the matter.

'His bike got a puncture once just outside the farmhouse. I took him inside and made him tea. Nice man. Shy, though. Never said much.'

'Did he not speak of himself?'

'Not a lot. Said he lived in the city. Worked in some shop. Loved getting out into the countryside. The last time was just before you came back. I was up here getting the place shipshape. He was down in the garden among the trees. My dog started barking and scared him off. I saw him running away.'

'How sad that he should have run away,' said Isobel.

'I suppose he saw himself as a trespasser,' replied Letty.

'A trespasser?' said Isobel, as if she had never heard the word before and was examining it for meaning. 'A trespasser. I see. Yes.'

'Though not really, of course, since you're acquainted with the gentleman.'

'Yes,' replied Isobel. 'I'm acquainted with the gentleman.'

When Letty had cleared away the tea things, Isobel went again to the cloakroom off the lobby. Here hung the astrakhan coat she had worn the day before. The coat Frank had told her to put on. Several times today already, she had gone into the cloakroom to look at that coat.

She put it on now and went out through into the wintry garden. Frank here! At Halcyon. But how? Alice Godsal must have told him of it. But why had he come? What had he hoped to find? In a deserted house, in an abandoned garden?

Isobel went from corner to corner, to the places where Letty said the man on the bicycle had been. Like the coat, these familiar spots were suddenly changed in her eyes, his presence now impressed upon them, his breath still hanging in the air. Absurdly, this thought made her look around for his footprints, in case the coming of the cold weather might have preserved them. Then, at the very edge of the coppice, under the skeleton of a larch, she saw a tobacco tin. Had he dropped it when he'd fled from the barking dog? Of course, it might belong to somebody else, some real trespasser, but surely it might just be his. She picked it up, wiped off the worst of the dirt and put in it her pocket. Somehow, she resolved, Frank must return to Halcyon Hill. She wanted to see his footprints everywhere: in the earth, on the grass, on the doormat, on the tiled floors of the covered court. And he must return not through the cornfield, but through the front gates. Not as a trespasser, not even as a guest, but as someone with the right to be here. For surely there was nobody with a greater right than her own child.

She went back into the house, into the kitchen, and sat down at the old oaken table that always smelled vaguely of onions and leeks. Letty turned, surprised at the sight of her mistress in the kitchen. As a rule, Lady Farrar wasn't the sort to stick her nose in. Was there something Lady Farrar wanted?

'Letty, dear, I think there's a question you're not asking me and which you might like to,' said Isobel.

'Me, Lady Farrar? Not at all.'

'Yesterday, in the church, you saw his face. And you saw mine beside it.'

'Yes, of course.'

'You're not a stupid girl, Letty. So, ask me the question, because I want to tell you the answer.'

Letty still stood by the oven, her cheeks red from its heat, the tea towel in her hand. Never at a loss for words, the young woman seemed to struggle to find them now. But then she asked it.

And so, gripping the edge of the old table into which her second child had once carved his name, Isobel told the farm girl she scarcely knew about the first. She told because she yearned to tell. Yet it was the simplest facts, nothing more. The gentlest possible limning of the tale, the worst pain surgically removed from the telling, anaesthetised by the most circumspect of adjectives, nouns and verbs. No need to upset the girl or burden her, however broad her shoulders. As Isobel spoke, Letty sat down beside her and when, once or twice,

Isobel needed to pause in the telling, she reached out with her hand, blotched and reddened by work, for the hand which was slim and pale as that of a ghost.

When Isobel was done, the women sat in silence as the smells of a pie leaked from the oven. Chicken and mushroom.

'That first time he came here,' said Letty slowly, 'I saw him on his way back past the farm. I was washing the dishes at the kitchen window. I could see that he was crying. Crying like you'd not believe, Lady Farrar. Crying so hard.'

Isobel drew in her breath.

'It's rare to see a grown man cry so it affects you, doesn't it?' said Letty. 'I wondered why, of course. Now I wonder if, though I'd warned him you weren't here, when he saw the locked-up house, it was too much for him. Maybe he cried because he felt he'd lost you all over again.'

'But now I'm not sure he wants to know me, Letty,' replied Isobel. 'He was tricked into going to the concert yesterday. He seems confused.'

'Well, of course he is. The poor man doesn't know if he loves you or hates you. But somebody else does. God does. God knows how much your child loves you.'

'Oh, my dear...' sighed Isobel, once the good Catholic, but whose belief in a benevolent God had been tried too many times.

'After all these years. God has brought your child back to you. He has given you a second chance. Not everyone gets second chances. I did, so I know what I'm talking about.'

The kitchen was suddenly filled with the smell of an over-baked pie. Letty dashed to the oven, grabbed for the baking tray and burned her fingers. Isobel rushed to pull the girl's hand under the cold tap, so that their faces were only inches apart. Once the pain had eased a little, Letty's other hand pointed to the scar that ran down the side of her eye.

'I should have died in the war, Lady Farrar,' she said. 'In the disaster at Silvertown. Over seventy souls killed in a moment. Hundreds injured. A munitions factory blowing up. It was like seeing hell. Do you remember it?'

'Who could forget?' replied Isobel.

'But I'd just ended my shift and was walking away, so I escaped with only this. So I try to live better than I did before. To do right and not hurt anybody. My second chance, Lady Farrar, and God has given you one too. Fight for your boy's love. It's already there, somewhere inside him. It must be or he'd never have tried to find you in the first place, never have wanted to come to Halcyon Hill. You must find a way to get it back.'

That night, a while after she'd already got into bed, Isobel rose again and went downstairs in her nightdress and dressing-gown. The robe was of flimsy stuff and the stoves that fed the pipes and warmed the house had been banked down until morning. The house was cold as she went once more to the cloakroom off the lobby. She took the astrakhan coat off its hanger, wrapped herself inside it and returned to her bedroom. She draped the coat over the chair beside her bed, so that it would be the last thing she saw before switching off the lamp and the first thing she would see when she awoke to the new morning.

'Go and put a coat on,' Frank had ordered. 'You're shivering.'

18

On Christmas morning, the second person who had observed that fragile meeting in St James's Piccadilly arrived at Halcyon Hill bearing gifts in the boot of an elderly Morris Cowley.

Miss Maud Farrar, she of the strong jaw, drove a car as she did everything else, with determination, confidence and a certain absence of finesse. The last of these characteristics testified by the woeful state of its bodywork. She'd driven ambulances in France for the Women's Auxiliary until they'd stopped her and sent her into the troop kitchens, a role for which she was even more unsuited, but which she had embraced with equal fervour.

Many people, those who didn't bother to look properly, were amused by little Maud Farrar. The ambassador's sister, the wealthy old maid who did good works and ran a bookshop in Chelsea, vigorously championing her 'waifs and strays' – those unsung geniuses of the garrets whom she had taken under her wing and whose works she promoted to the publishers of London, a group who were, in her view, idiots the lot of them. But people only laughed at Maud because she was not quite like them. A woman, well past seventy, who dyed and shingled her greying hair and wore the latest fashions, even though they didn't suit her. Who made a lot of noise in a world where ladies worthy of the name were still not supposed to do such things. Long before those troublesome females had marched to win the vote, long before the 'flappers' flapped, Maud had thrust out that jaw and shaped her immediate world to fit her notion of what it should be, never bowing to what it was. Little Maud who, beneath the silly hair and the Bond Street clothes, possessed a bottomless well of goodness.

As it was Christmas Day, Isobel had tried to insist that Letty should be down at the farm with her father, though the girl had seemed less than excited by that prospect. No, no, she'd replied, she'd prepare something nice and simple for Lady Farrar and Miss Maud, serve it up and then go home. Just this once, the dirty dishes could be left until tomorrow.

But Maud Farrar wasn't having that. Dirty dishes were meant to be washed on the day they became dirty. She'd learned that in the war, she said. To do otherwise was an act of barbarism. And so, when Letty had gone, Maud rolled up her sleeves at the sink and handed Isobel a tea towel. As they worked, they reminded each other of other Christmases in this house, when Octavius with his snow-white whiskers looked like Santa Claus in a Savile Row suit. Of Gladstone the dog knocking over the Christmas tree. Of Johnnie, hardly more than a toddler, wide eyed at his first tricycle which, festooned with scarlet ribbon, had been hidden all week behind a bale of straw in the stables. And of that last Christmas when Octavius had presided over the table, gently smiling and singing silly songs, giving no clue that he knew he would never do so again.

But in among these recollections, as the plates and saucepans rose steaming from the water, Isobel saw that Maud was not quite her usual self. At luncheon, her chatter had been thick and fast as usual, but with a current of agitation flowing underneath the torrent. And then it came. Maud dried her hands, sat down at the kitchen table and asked the same question which Letty Blount had asked.

In the fervour of her hope of seeing Frank Brodie at the concert, Isobel had quite forgotten that others would see him too and that Maud, taking tickets at the door, her nose into everything, would be one of them. Now Maud didn't even wait for Isobel's answer before volunteering some answers of her own. A young cousin perhaps? What a resemblance. Quite remarkable. She didn't recall Isobel ever mentioning that she possessed a cousin. Not in all these years. But surely that must be it. A cousin, a man too, in whom the mysteries of familial genetics had produced a facsimile.

Once more, Isobel sat at the kitchen table and said the simple words. But if Isobel had, in answering the question, underrated the effect that answer might have on Maud, she was sharply corrected now. If she had expected another caring hand to reach out for hers, she was mistaken. Miss Maud Farrar almost sprang out of the kitchen chair and leapt backwards against the sink, her hand flying to her mouth. When at last she uncovered it to speak, it was not in her usual way. She spoke slowly, almost in a whisper.

'There was a child?'

'Yes.'

'Whose?'

'Whose do you think?' asked Isobel, perplexed by the question.

'Not...?'

'Of course not! Not possible.'

'Then some other... before you married Octavius?'

'There was no other. Not in all those long years.'

'So who...?'

'Heavens, Maud, think. The child was made in wedlock.'

'Then he is the son of...?'

'Yes.'

'The result of the...?'

'Yes.'

Maud sat down at the table again and now at last the hand reached out towards Isobel's.

'Did Edwin Reed know?'

'No. Never.'

'Why not?'

Isobel paused, unable to answer. In the silence, she heard the old clock on the wall tick as it had always done. Octavius used to joke that the bloody clock was too noisy, reminding him all too loudly of his mortality. It should be covered with a cloth, he said, like the cage of a budgerigar. Isobel thought of his joke now as she looked his sister's last question square in the face. These days, mortality was much more often in her mind. More often now, she saw Octavius, his face twisted with pain, being dragged helplessly away from the light. She saw Alice Godsal on her chaise, halfway to being an apparition. And, in her nightmare, Hugh Pasco, eyes wide with surprise, the trickle of blood at the corner of his mouth. Life was short. Honesty mattered more now. Tell the truth and shame the devil, the local priest had taught her in childhood. So now she would.

'I didn't feel he deserved to know. I suppose I wanted revenge.'

'And for that you gave up a child?'

'In part. Shameful, isn't it?' replied Isobel. 'To deprive him of the heir he wanted so much. A son to mould in his own entitled image.'

'But he was your child, Isobel. How could you?'

The small, beringed hand that had clasped Isobel's was withdrawn again.

'How could I have kept him, Maud? I had hardly any money, almost no friends and my heart was broken after Hugh... My God, I could scarcely look after myself, let alone a baby.'

And then Miss Maud Farrar began to weep, something Isobel had never seen before. Her surprise was compounded by the way the little woman wept. Not the melodramatic tears that might have been in character, but an almost inaudible whimper, like that of a wounded animal.

'I always wanted a child,' she said. 'All my life. Did you know that? More than anything.'

'Yes, I knew that, Maud dear.'

'For me, it wasn't to happen, no matter how much I yearned for it. And you? You were given this great gift and you... you just threw it away.'

'It wasn't like that, Maud. Please believe me – it really wasn't like that.'

A silence fell on the kitchen table. From the day of her marriage to Octavius, his spinster sister had bustled into Isobel's existence, embracing her with a whole heart, never seeming for a moment jealous of any diminution of attention from the bachelor brother she had worshipped. As Octavius himself had done, Miss Maud had brought light into Isobel's life. A loving aunt to Johnnie. Someone to chivvy Isobel out of those melancholies which sometimes descended upon her. A friend and confidante who knew everything there was to know. Except this one thing which had been held back from her, as it had also been from Octavius. But no longer. And Isobel, to her infinite distress, saw that it had changed things. That a slight but tangible separation now existed between them. And both of them recognised and mourned it.

Isobel rose from the kitchen table, filled the kettle and put it on the stove.

'Has he asked about his father?' said Maud after a while, drying her eyes with the tea towel.

'He has asked nothing. I have told nothing. So far, we have exchanged no more than a few polite sentences in the nave of a church.'

'He will want to know at some point.'

'I dare say. I will cross that bridge in good time. All that matters now is that we have found each other.'

'But that boy could be rich,' said Maud. 'The legitimate son of a wealthy man.'

'All of that can wait for now.'

'But of course it can't wait,' said Maud. 'Now is the very moment for that boy to claim his birthright.'

'Why such a rush, dear?'

Maud, still clutching the tea towel to her like a child with a rag doll, glanced up at Isobel as the teapot and cups, the sugar and the milk jug were laid out on the table.

'Is it possible you don't know?'

Isobel shrugged her shoulders and poured out the tea.

'Edwin,' replied Maud.

Isobel still flinched at the very name, as she had done since the night she had fled from Pelham Crescent. She could just about cope with using the personal pronoun. Him. So vague, so dismissive. But the name itself had never lost its power to unsettle her.

'Two or three months ago,' said Maud. 'Some sort of haemorrhage, I believe. I assumed you'd heard, so I didn't mention it before in case it upset you.'

Isobel put the teapot carefully down on the table. She stared at Maud, waiting for the words. Praying for them, dreading them.

'He's dead, Isobel. Edwin Reed is dead.'

*

On the late evening of that Christmas Day, Isobel Farrar sat at her dressing table, alone again at Halcyon Hill. The precious photograph, now framed, stood on the table by her bed. She had unpinned her hair and let it tumble to her shoulders and, if she half closed her eyes and let the mirror play tricks, she could still almost see the young woman in the picture. One day soon, she would place it among the precious others on top of the grand piano in the covered court. For now, for just a little longer, she would keep it close.

As she looked at the photograph, lit by the soft glow of a lamp, it seemed incredible to her that she had ever been half-mad with the compulsion to eviscerate that child from her body and cast him away. Now she would give almost anything to hold him against her again and tell him that she loved him. But such had been the fetid legacy of the man who, she had learned today, was no longer alive.

She stared again at her mirrored face, but now with her eyes wide open. Would anything have changed in it after the news of today? Some faint shining in her eyes that had not been there before she'd heard it? Some dissolution, however slight, of the mask she had worn for so many years? If that were so, she would feel no guilt for it. No remorse that the passing of another human being had brought about that happy transformation. For her anger against her first husband still burned within her. Her contented years with Octavius and the birth of Johnnie had banked it down to a smoulder, but the flame had never completely snuffed out.

Octavius himself, believing that he knew everything there was to know, also knew when it flared up inside her. Usually for no reason at all. Some tiny association, some fragment of old music or the smatter of rain on a winter windowpane. Aware that she would never allow him in entirely, Octavius would say nothing, just take her hand for a moment or gently stroke her shoulder, tell some feeble joke he'd heard at the golf club or suggest some little treat. Tickets for a concert perhaps. A weekend in Deauville. Even just a nice glass of wine before the hour considered respectable.

Isobel was aware of the old saying about anger. That it was a poison which did more damage to the vessel which contained it, than to anything over which it was poured. Yet however true the truism, how hard it was to adhere to that wise philosophy. In her own case, quite impossible.

But in the mirror, Isobel saw no miraculous transformation. No beam of celestial light shone down upon her, a purified soul. Still, she looked into the eyes of a woman who had long lost the facility for forgiveness. Above all else, that was what Edwin Reed had taken from her. She knew it all too well and that was what she grieved for on this Christmas night in the house on the hill.

And it came to her that perhaps it was that same corrosion which had eaten into the soul of the child in the photograph. Cradled on the warmth of her breast, he had looked to her for everything but ended up with nothing. The child who had been cruelly treated, who had few friends, who had no wife, no children of his own. The sad boy.

She got into bed and traced her fingertip across the tiny framed face on the bedside table. Better late than never, could her love, restored to him, assuage that sadness? Could his in turn do the same for her? She switched off the lamp. Out in the old oak tree, the usual owl hooted beneath a wan Yuletide moon.

Edwin Reed is dead. My God. And, as Maud had added for gruesome effect as she got back into the Morris Cowley, covered in his own blood.

19

'There you go,' Arthur had said. 'Valentino still lives.'

The evening before, in the scullery, Arthur had draped an old towel round Frank's shoulders and trimmed his hair, as was the custom every month or so. Frank didn't much like this ritual; such great care was taken that he found it a bit embarrassing, but he knew Arthur liked to do it. In the morning, Arthur brushed and pressed Frank's suit, ironed his shirt and chose his tie. The hair was smoothed with a drop of brilliantine, the cheeks splashed with Arthur's cologne.

Frank hadn't known what to take as a present and was cross that he didn't. But if you leave school at fourteen, how *could* you know? The nuances of etiquette, second nature to your betters, are as incomprehensible as some foreign tongue. In midwinter, flowers were expensive and no doubt she had plenty anyway. He might get a staff discount on a tiny bottle of perfume, but even so it'd be an arm and a leg. Arthur had offered to pay, of course, but Frank didn't want that. Yet he was a bit skint at present. He'd gone over a pothole on the bike and twisted both the wheels. Getting it fixed had nearly cleaned him out. Then Arthur suggested a Christmas cake from the bakery up the road. Their stuff was first-rate and anyway it didn't really matter since it was the thought that counted. And so, it was carrying a cardboard box from a Hammersmith bakery that

Frank Brodie set out for Halcyon Hill on the first day of the virginal year.

The familiar creamy envelope had arrived two days after Christmas. Might Frank be able to accept an invitation to luncheon on New Year's Day? The trains would be less frequent but, if that wouldn't inconvenience him too much, it would be a great pleasure to see him. If Frank didn't go, Arthur had said, he'd bloody swing for him. As Frank had sat at the dining table writing his acceptance, Arthur stood over him, checking the spelling and grammar. Then, in pouring rain, Arthur had walked to the nearest letterbox and posted it himself.

At the front door of 74 Pitt Street, Arthur had shaken his hand and wished him well, as if they were polite strangers or Frank was going on an expedition to Antarctica and might never return, like poor Captain Oates. Often when Frank left the house, it was Arthur's habit to come to the door and wave him off and Frank's habit to turn at the gate and wave back. But when Frank did so now, the door had already closed behind him.

*

From the little station, Frank Brodie pedalled along the lanes towards the house on the hill. The air was harsh on his face, the clouds massed above the naked treetops threatening snow. Between the frozen branches, he caught glimpses of the land rolling away out towards the distant downs, the landscape stripped of the summer lushness it had possessed when he had first laid eyes on it and it had entered his soul. Yet even in the sharp claws of January, the first wild snowdrops were pushing their way up along the edges of the lane.

When he reached the drive leading off the road, then saw the sign with the name of the house, he stopped. It felt different approaching this way, not across the waving field of corn and up through the coppice with the sun beating down on his neck. After that first Sunday back in high summer, he'd told himself he would never go back, but he had. He'd not returned immediately; it had been a good month between his first and second visits. On those other Sundays, he'd gone to the great parks at Hampton Court and Bushy or along the dappled towpath between Richmond Bridge and Teddington Lock, but with much less pleasure than before. He had seen Halcyon now and that was where he wanted to be.

He'd thought of it on the way to work and as he carried out the daily tasks that numbed his brain and deadened his senses. He thought of it as he and Arthur sat by the fire in the evenings. Mostly, though, he pictured it as he lay in bed, kept awake by the trains on the nearby line or by the Italian couple through the wall. It was then that he carried himself back to the silent garden on the hill, disturbed by no more than the buzz of the insects and the whisper of a breeze brushing across the blades of unmown grass. As he lay there, the images projected themselves onto the dark ceiling of his little room. The first glimpse from the lane of the distant house. The nice farm girl with the scar on her face who'd invited him in for tea. The pond, the old oak tree, the terrace in the sunshine, the green of the roof tiles against the cobalt blue sky. All of it.

But now, on this midwinter day, there would be no lark song, no dragonflies, no sun beating down on his neck. In comparison with the path through the corn, the gravel drive seemed alien in its formality and the nervousness which he had held at bay on the journey seized him now. The compulsion to run came over him as usual, but he heard Arthur Collins in his ear, promising to swing for him if he did any such thing.

Yet when, from around the bend in the drive, the house itself appeared, Frank's heart began to pound in his head and, despite the cold, sweat leaked into the fresh white shirt that Arthur had ironed. For the house had changed since he had last seen it. The chimney pots were no longer crowned with abandoned birds' nests and spirals of silvery smoke escaped into the sky. In the porch, flagstones the colour of buttermilk had been rescued from under the drifts of rotting leaves. The fractured drainpipe, once hanging off the wall, had been reattached. The windows shone and their curtains were no longer drawn against him. The rusty padlock no longer disfigured the front door. Frank rang the bell and, from his inside pocket, took out the letter of invitation in case it was required for admission.

The door was opened by a face he knew, though not the one he expected. The young woman from the farm stood there. The one with the scarred face. Surprised, he took a step or two back from the porch, but she was smiling and acting as if she'd never laid eyes on him before.

'Come away in, Mr Brodie. I hope the journey wasn't too difficult.'

Riding on the warmth of that smile, Frank crossed over the threshold. He flushed a little as she helped him out of his coat. Damn it, she'd surely notice the collar and cuffs. He'd not reckoned on somebody doing that. Nor could he remember anyone ever doing it before. How strange to be the one served and not serving. As the young woman led him through the lobby, he straightened his tie and ran his palms over his new-trimmed hair.

And there she was. In a big room with a gallery running around it and a glass roof and the windows looking out over the countryside. Even on this grey day, the room was filled with so much light, he almost felt he was outside again. She was standing beside a piano, just as she'd been in the church. Now, in his mind's eye, she was somehow inseparable from a piano and from the music she had made that day. She was holding on to the side of the instrument and he saw her draw herself up and come towards him across the big room. She stopped a yard away.

'Happy New Year, Frank,' she said. 'I'm so very pleased you've come.'

He didn't know what to do. Did he just reply in kind? Did he stretch out his hand? Was she expecting a kiss or an embrace – both of which he wouldn't have a clue how to carry off? He saw that she was uncertain too, so he reached out his arm, remembering a second too late that it might smell of brilliantine.

'Same to you, Mrs... Lady...' His voice trailed away. 'I don't know what to call you.'

'Why don't you just call me Isobel?' she replied. 'We can be Isobel and Frank. Would that suit you?'

He nodded. She led him over to the chairs by the window. Instinctively, he went right up to the glass and stared out. In his imagination, he had already come here in winter and it was exactly as he had pictured it. Pared back to the bone, its skeleton showing, but almost as beautiful in the sense it gave him of what would come again. Of the resurrection and the light.

'Rather desolate at this time of year,' she said.

'Oh no,' he replied. 'It's not desolate. Not at all.'

The young woman came and asked if they'd like a sherry before luncheon. When he paused, the woman asked if he'd prefer a beer. She thought there might be one in the larder. No, he said, a sherry would be fine. When it came, he sipped it cautiously, as if he suspected some menace in the glass. He'd only had sherry once before and thought it revolting. But he was not going to ask for the beer.

In the chairs by the window, they spoke at first of small things. Of his getting there on a day when the trains were fewer. Of the splendid cake he had brought. Of the chance of snow. Of the concert in the church which had raised so much for the war widows. That was good news, he said, as he knew a war widow himself. The wife of a mate who'd not made it back. Out near Acton. Three kids. Not much to live on. He went to see her now and again. Isobel said that, if he gave her his friend's name and address, the woman might be helped by the fund. He said that would be really good. Thank you. Thanks a lot.

'I hope you liked the book I gave you?' Isobel asked. 'Though I worried that you might find it too sad.'

'Yes, sad all right. But I was glad to read it,' he replied. 'I didn't know people had written poems about all that.'

'Do you like poetry?'

'I don't know anything about it, really, though at school they made us learn bloody great chunks of it. Sorry. Pardon me. I can still do "The Charge of the Light Brigade". Cannon to right of them, cannon to left of them. All that stuff.'

For the first time, Frank Brodie smiled at the woman who had given birth to him. More than a smile indeed, a grin. He saw the effect of it, saw the light come into the dark eyes. Still, he found it hard to believe that she was flesh and blood, no longer imaginary. Somebody who brushed her teeth in the mornings, took a bath, got headaches, broke wind, yawned when she was sleepy. A corporeal creature like everyone else, not just a confection of shadow and light and the faint whiff of perfume. And of his own yearnings.

Isobel took their empty glasses and crossed to the decanter of sherry on top of the piano. With her back still turned to him, she spoke.

'I'm so very grateful that you came through the war, Frank. So relieved. I often thought of you in those years and prayed that you would be safe. I couldn't bear to think that…'

Frank nodded, even though she wasn't looking at him.

'Thanks a lot,' he replied. 'Very kind.'

'Kind?' she said, spinning round to face him, almost as if the remark had angered her. 'Kind? If so, it was the smallest of kindnesses, Frank, among the many owed to you.'

In turning so quickly, she had split some sherry on top of the piano. Don't worry, he said, he had a clean hanky. He dabbed at the little puddle, then polished, then dabbed some more. His glance absorbed the framed photographs arranged there. Stern-faced men and women, costumed and coiffed by another century, posing beside potted palms or painted backdrops of an Alpine lake. Others, more recent, when the techniques of photography at last allowed the capture of a smile. Isobel sitting on the terrace beyond this very window. Isobel with her arm through that of an older man, his gaze fixed lovingly upon her. Isobel and a boy in a school uniform. A wedding photograph of a young man and a toothy girl – a young man who faintly resembled himself. Then, of course, he understood. There had been another child. A child after him. One who had not been sent away. And all the time, he was aware of Isobel by his side, looking at him looking. He smelled the perfume and felt the warmth of her body near him.

'Do you play any instrument, Frank?' she asked.

'Me? Oh no. Well, just the penny whistle,' he replied. 'But I liked what you played in the church.'

'You like Debussy?'

'I didn't know what it was, just that I liked it.'

'I could play it again for you now,' she replied. 'If you would care for that?'

As Isobel played, Frank's gaze went to and fro between the woman at the piano and the landscape rolling out beyond the great window. In the years to come, long after she was dead and despite everything that was still to happen between them, it was a moment he would always carry with him. Never having believed it might ever come to pass, it would always bear a sense of unreality and, because of that, hold an unassailable magic.

*

'It's shepherd's pie,' said Letty Blount, 'and one of my best, even if I say so myself. I hope you're peckish, Mr Brodie.'

He was relieved it was shepherd's pie. He could cope with that. He'd worried it'd be something posh, something foreign even, and that he'd struggle to eat it or not be sure which knife and fork to use. With cutlery, you work from the outside in, Arthur had drilled into him. But shepherd's pie he could cope with. And the apple crumble and cream for dessert. And the box of chocolates that appeared after it. She could eat anything, Isobel told him, and never seemed to put on a pound. He was just the same, he replied, wasn't that a strange thing? She smiled and said it was maybe not strange at all. And when he tucked his napkin into his collar, he noticed that she lifted hers from her lap and did the same.

In the dining room off the covered court, they continued to speak, in fits and starts, of more small things. She talked a little of Canada, of Niagara Falls and the great lakes of that continent. No, she'd never seen any Red Indians. She asked about the shop and how long he had been there. Sixteen years, apart from the war? Goodness me. Did he find ironmongery interesting? No? She was sad to hear that. Then, between the apple crumble and the box of chocolates, he took a sip of water and cleared his throat.

'When you came into the ironmongery...'

'It's all right,' she replied.

'It was a bit of a shock, you see. Your friend, old Mrs Godsal, said she thought you might possibly be...'

'I know. I know. I understand,' said Isobel.

'Anyway, I'm sorry.'

'It's all right.'

They took coffee back in the chairs by the window and ate more chocolates.

'I know it's rather cold, but might you like to see around the garden?' she asked.

'I would, please,' he replied, feeling the blush rise up from his too tight collar.

Isobel half rose from her chair and then stopped.

'Goodness, it must sound as if I'm treating you like a guest, any guest, to whom the gardens should be shown. You're not that, of course. You do know it, I hope.'

He didn't know how to answer, just nodded in his usual way.

'There are things I must say to you, Frank,' Isobel said. 'A story to tell you.'

'No,' he said.

'I beg your pardon?'

'No,' he repeated. 'I don't want to hear it. Not now.'

'You don't want to hear it?' she replied. 'But Frank, dear, I thought that would be the most important thing to you. I thought that was why you might come.'

'I thought so too,' he replied. 'But maybe it isn't after all.'

'And what is?'

Frank Brodie stood up now. He went behind his chair and gripped the back of it, struggling to bring out the words he needed. His voice, quiet at the best of times, had almost shrunk to a whisper.

'Being here,' he said. 'I think it's just being here.'

And for a moment, he saw Isobel Farrar tightly close her eyes.

Out on the terrace, they watched the banks of snow-cloud edging towards them from the west. Then Isobel went through the charade of showing Frank Brodie the ground he already knew like the back of his hand. She showed him the old oak tree, the pond, the sagging pergola. She showed him the kitchen gardens and the broken glass in the growing frames. She told him the tale of the place, what had been done, when and by whom. There had once been a fernery over there which she herself had swept away and made into a rose garden. Did Frank think that had been a mistake? And over *there*, the yew hedges had grown so tall that the view to the little river had almost been lost. Yet the yew hedge was a thing of great beauty. What did Frank think of that? Cut it back or leave it be? A dilemma. So many decisions.

It seemed, she said, that the old lord who'd owned the house for a few years had not cared for gardens. Such a pity. The architect who had built the house would hate to see it like this. A genius far ahead of his time. Long dead now.

He asked if she'd mind if he smoked. Did she want one? No, she'd stopped smoking years ago now. Bad for the complexion, she smiled. But when he lit up, she asked for a puff or two and when she coughed and her eyes watered and he patted her on the back, they both laughed without tension, each of them noticing the fact and pleased that they had done so.

'Frank, I've been thinking. I understand you're very interested in growing things. You have a garden at home, I believe.'

'Just a yard with a few pots,' replied Frank. 'Not a proper garden. Not like yours.'

'I was wondering if you might consider helping me bring this garden back to what it once was?' she asked.

'Me? But I've got no experience of anything like this.'

'Maybe, but I feel you have the only qualification that matters. A love of the thing.'

He looked out over the garden. The idea thrilled him at once, though it frightened him too. What if he messed it up, somehow offended nature with his coarse, untutored ways? Suppose it rebelled against him and refused to do his bidding? Slapped him down and told him to know his place? He couldn't bear the thought of that. But then again, what if that were not the case? What if Isobel was right? That the simple love of the thing would somehow show him the way. Never once had Frank Brodie thought to leave any mark on this world, but supposing he might leave even a faint one on this tiny patch of it? That would do him well enough. More than enough. It would be more than he'd ever hoped for.

'Might you at least think about it?' she asked. 'It would give me great pleasure to have you here and I hope you might find that too.'

'Yes,' he replied. 'I'll l think about it.'

For a moment now, Frank Brodie felt more alive than he had ever done before. But then, just as the banks of snow-cloud began to roll over the garden, that moment was over. It happened quite without warning. She said it casually, as she turned up her fur collar against the cold and moved back towards the house.

'Of course, I'd be happy to pay you.'

'Beg pardon?'

'I'd be happy to pay you,' she said again. 'For your time. Whatever you think would be fair.'

'Pay me?' he asked.

'Yes.'

Frank Brodie turned away from the garden and from the woman in the astrakhan coat. He climbed back up the sloping lawn, went around the side of the house, past the stables and out along the gravel drive towards the gates. He heard her voice calling his name, but he did not look back.

20

On the morning it was to happen, she woke with the dawn cooing of the pigeons on the roof above her head. They seemed to be bustling around even earlier than usual. Perhaps they knew what today would bring. Perhaps they hadn't slept well either.

In Alice's room under the eaves, all was otherwise silent. Not a sound from him all night. In the first days after the birth, this had alarmed her. My God, had the child died in his sleep? But when she'd gone to him, all had been well. The breath in the little body rising and falling without distress, the eyes tight shut, only the occasional twitch of a tiny finger. She wondered if babies dreamed, but surely not. Of what could they dream, when nothing had so far happened to them?

But maybe that was wrong. Were the very first slivers of memory already embedded in that infinitesimal brain? The breaking of the sac. The fight to get out. The very first time he had taken a breath on his own. Or felt the light touch his face. As soon as she'd been strong enough to get out of bed, she'd carried him over to the window and shown him the world. The jagged rooftops, the chimneys and the steeples. One of the pigeons had landed on the windowsill and peered in at him, cocking its head from side to side. But the tiny eyes, though open, were as yet unfocused and he had closed them quickly against the July sun.

An armchair with a curved back had been turned into a cot, the only concession that had been made to economy. Long before the birth, Alice had gone out and bought all the swaddling clothes, the nappies, the safety pins and the dummy-tits. Alice had knitted too; dwarfish jumpers, bootees and woolly hats. Isobel, swollen out of all elegance, her back aching, her bladder turbulent and exhausted by the unexpected ferocity of a hot summer, had leaned yet again on Alice, just as she'd done on that foggy night on the Embankment. Once more, Alice's strong arm had gone around her shoulder and Alice's words of encouragement whispered in her ear. It would all be fine. Just fine. Like falling off a log, Alice said. No worse than a really difficult shit. Isobel had laughed then. Such a crudity had never before passed her lips, but now she repeated it to herself all the time, sometimes even aloud. No worse than a difficult shit.

But that had not turned out to be the case. A few days before her due date, Isobel had left the flat in Pimlico and returned to the sanctuary under the eaves, so that Alice could take care of her while still attending to her own profession. The doctor, well-known to Alice, had called once or twice to examine Alice's friend, whose name he had neither been given nor had asked for. But when the waters had broken, all over the hearthrug, they had not been able to find him.

It had taken nearly twelve hours. The pain indescribable. She had bitten into the pillow until it had torn open, the feathers spilling out and sticking to the sweat on her cheeks. In midsummer, the little room was stifling. Through the open window, she could hear the noise of the traffic far below, the neighing of the carriage horses, the shouts of the newspaper boys. How odd that the world was going on as normal and that it didn't seem to care. The doctor, found at last, came and went and came again but only Alice really cared and Isobel clung to her hand to stop herself falling into the abyss.

She'd begun to wonder what the presence in her belly wanted of her. Instead of struggling to be born, was it struggling instead to stay in the darkness and the warmth? Did it not *want* to be born? Did it have some sort of premonition of what was to happen to it after it left the darkness? Was it punishing her now for that, causing her as much suffering as it could before defiantly breaking free of her? In the short lulls between the waves of the pain, she told herself all that was nonsense. But when the waves crashed over her anew, those questions pulsated in her head.

When the ordeal was finally done, the two women and the baby had cried together in the hot little room, among the blood-stained sheets and smell of sweat and other pungent odours. When the doctor appeared for the last time, he'd complimented Alice and joked that she'd missed her vocation. Midwifery, he laughed, might not pay as well, but at least it was an occupation unaffected by the passing of the years. Then he accepted a glass of port.

In all of Isobel's long life, there would only be two occasions when her emotions had changed so utterly in the blinking of an eye. The first had been in somebody's grand drawing room in South Audley Street when, from a former position of polite indifference, she realised that she had fallen in love with Hugh Pasco. The second was the moment she first held her baby in her arms. For all these months, she had wanted nothing more than to rid herself of the ultimate evidence of Edwin Reed's possession. Her visceral revulsion had never lessened on the endless journey of carrying it inside her. Feeling each kick of the creature as a new blow from the husband she had come to loathe. Watching Alice knit the garments, Isobel had wanted to tear the needles from her friend's grasp, seize the end of the wool and unravel every stitch until there was only empty air. But when, cleaned of bloody debris and wrapped in a flannel, Alice had first handed her the child, all of that was forgotten. Gone in a moment. As if the warm breeze coming in through the window, had dissolved it, made it harmless and carried it off across the rooftops and the steeples.

'He has your eyes,' Alice said, and it was true. But though Isobel searched and searched the tiny face, there was no other sign of his genesis. That might come, of course, and probably would, but as yet the face was unblemished by the circumstances of his making. She prayed that it would remain so, that the child would never know. At the first sight of him, when she knew in an instant that she loved him more than life, it was this which became her reason for sending him away from her. At that first sight, her selfish motives, those which had consumed her for all these months, were suddenly as nothing. The desire for the cleansing of her body, the fever for revenge against a man desperate for an heir to mould in his corrupted image, no longer signified. Not even the fact, stark and merciless, that she was a woman alone, who could only just afford to keep herself and who would now need to work for her living, teaching other people's children to play 'Für Elise'.

All of these melted away when she first felt his breath against her cheek and the warmth of his skin against her own. All that mattered now was that she should be unselfish. And that meant releasing him from the tangled wreckage of her own life, letting him fly free towards the chance of something better. Let him survive. Let her survive too, in whatever way she might, even if never to be quite whole again.

Now, a week later, this was the day he was to be taken from the little room under the eaves. She would never know to where; she would never ask. Billy Godsal had fixed everything and only he would know. She and Alice had talked it through a hundred times. A clean break. Painful at the time, Alice said, but best in the long run. Best for the kiddie, best for her.

Isobel lay in the summer dawn, listening to the pigeons on the roof. From the bed, she reached out her hand to the child in the chair which was his cot. With her little finger, she brushed his own and felt it gripped in return. He opened his eyes and she told him yet again that she loved him. He closed his eyes again and so did she. She never knew how long she had slept but, when she awoke, he was gone.

She let out a cry and stumbled from the bed, calling out his name. Alice came running in and took Isobel in her arms. The kindest way, Alice said. No big scenes of parting. No melodrama. The kindest way.

The next day, Isobel had returned to the flat in Pimlico. The window of her sitting room had an oblique view of the river and she sat there long into the evening until the sun dipped behind the treetops of Battersea Park.

The feeling, by now familiar, was creeping across her as she had known it would. The feeling that would come to her so many times in her life. For Isobel Leigh, that girl who had been born to love and be loved in return, there was nothing more awful than the loss of it. And this was to be the worst of them all. Worse than that of her father and mother. Worse even than that of Hugh Pasco and, waiting far in the future, of Octavius Farrar. This time, the love she had lost had been unconditional. It had not relied upon her being a good little girl who had perfect manners and faithfully practised her catechism. Nor, later, that she had been beautiful, desirable, the cynosure of every eye. The love that had been spirited away from the room under the eaves had cared nothing for any of that, caring only that she existed. A love not of approval, but of need. The evacuation of her womb, that event so fervently wished for, had left an emptiness that, even in its eventual occupation by another child, would never be completely filled.

Soon after, the post brought a package to Pimlico. From Alice. In a gilded frame, the photograph of a mother and a child, each clinging to the other, as if against the world. Knowing that the world was going to defeat them, but defiant nonetheless.

21

On the morning of New Year's Day, when Arthur Collins had closed the door on Frank Brodie, he had gone straight to the silver tray that stood on the mahogany trolley in the parlour window. It was a bit too early, but he and Frank had both taken the day off work and who was to know? He could always take a little nap later.

Sipping his gin, just a weak one, he settled into his armchair beside the wireless. He reached out for the knob in case there was something worth listening to, then changed his mind. For once, silence was what he wanted. That was unlike him for, if anyone loved noise, it was Arthur Collins. Noise meant life to him. The music on the wireless or from the gramophone. The constant hum of the customers in the shop. The cars, the buses, the underground railway, even that yelping poodle across the street which drove everyone else crazy. Then there were the noises of the memory, mostly from his days on the halls. Still, he could hear the vulgar comics joking about ladies' undergarments, the blowsy chatter of the chorus girls backstage, the pit musicians tuning up. Above all, he could still hear the music of his own voice and the applause that it brought.

My lords, ladies and gentlemen. We are proud to present, for your delight, Mr Arthur Collins, the Camden Caruso.

Arthur was not a man greatly given to reflection. That way, he believed, only led to gloom and doom. Just look at Hamlet. No matter what ailed you, the best medicine was to put on your top hat and tails, apply a little greasepaint, go out onto the boards and sing. So it was out of character that, on the first day of the virginal year, he felt the need to embrace silence.

When, on that day in 1910, Frank Brodie had moved in with his meagre possessions, it had taken Arthur a good while to adjust to this new lodger who didn't talk much. His predecessors had been a colourful crew, young men working in the theatre or in the hotels and shops of the West End. Of each of them, Arthur had nourished secret hopes, none of which had ever been rewarded, though he'd always accepted that cheerfully and borne no resentment. By the time Frank Brodie had arrived to occupy the small bedroom that overlooked the yard, those hopes had faded to no more than the final flare of a dying candle. So it was to his great surprise that the boy he had found beneath the arches was the one to at last fulfil them.

The unaccustomed silence that Frank had brought with him had, in time, become acceptable to Arthur because of the unspoken dependence which suffused it. Nobody had needed Arthur for a long time; not since the passing of his mother, whom he'd nursed devotedly to the very lip of the grave before helping her ease gently into it. Since then, the gift for loving that was the essence of Arthur Collins, the gift he shared with Isobel Farrar, had been unwanted, until the day a piece of flotsam from Piccadilly Circus had arrived to take tea on a Sunday afternoon. And soon the realisation of Frank's dependence had seeded the same emotion in Arthur. And it was a fine thing that began to grow in the little house in Pitt Street. A thing never spoken of between them and all the stronger for that.

As he sat now with his early gin, Arthur remembered the first time he'd cut Frank's hair, just as he'd done last night. In the shop, he'd mentioned a young lad to his drinking pal Wilf Jones, who ran the ironmongery. There was a junior position going, wasn't there? This lad he knew, the nephew of a friend, had been stuck in casual, labouring work until now. A bit on the quiet side, but intelligent and polite. Arthur swore he'd be perfect. Do me a favour, Wilf?

So, the night before Frank went to see Wilf Jones, Arthur had got the scissors and tidied Frank's hair. He'd lent him a shirt and one of his own jackets, even though it was much too big. He'd spoken words of encouragement and faith. And when Frank had got the job, he'd pushed the boat out and bought two rump steaks from the fattest cows that had ever grazed on English grass. In an envelope in the drawer of his bedside table, Arthur still kept the lock of hair he'd rescued from the sweepings off the scullery floor.

And today, he thought now, it'd been the same performance all over again. Sending Frank out through the front door, all spick and span, towards a different future. With heart and soul, it was what Arthur wanted for him, but this time he was afraid. Lady Farrar was quite a different matter to Wilf Jones.

Despite being a man who usually liked noise, or perhaps because of it, Arthur was strangely sensitive to the nuances of silence. The silence of Frank sitting opposite him by the evening fire was quite different to that when Frank was out of the house all day on one of his bicycle trips. That silence in turn was as nothing to the one which now hung like a pall in the parlour of Pitt Street carrying, as it did, the prospect of fundamental loss. Of the end of everything.

This worst of all silences was not new to Arthur Collins. He had gone through it before when, in the dog days of summer, somebody shot an Austrian toff whom nobody had ever heard of, and the world had lost its mind. When Frank, egged on by the older men in the ironmongery, had gone and joined up. What a joke that was. Frank who, despite his temper, was really the least bellicose of men, who saved ladybirds from falling into the water butt in the yard. Frank with a gun and a bayonet? Don't make me laugh.

For four long years, as the piles of corpses grew into mountains on the ravaged fields, Arthur had endured that worst of silences and his absolute certainty that Frank would never return. Only the occasional letter, short and bland, brought a few days of merciful relief before the anxiety gripped him once again. Until then, Arthur Collins had been an abstemious man, careful of his figure and his tendency to gain weight, but he'd soon made the discovery that a gin or two took the edge off the anxiety and that three or four would deliver the dozy oblivion that his sleepless nights no longer allowed him. In that oblivion, he could no longer hear the silence.

He'd been gently dozing in this self-same armchair when he'd heard the front door open and the footsteps in the hall. And then the face had peeked round the door of the parlour. Older, thinner, but otherwise unscathed. I'm back, he'd said, as if he'd just been out on the bike. And more rump steaks were bought from the butcher and cakes from the bakery. And, in the privacy of his room, Arthur had wept. And the worst of silences had lifted from the little house in Pitt Street.

Now, on the first day of 1927, Arthur wondered what was happening at this place called Halcyon Hill. He'd never imagined that, one day, Frank Brodie would go in search of his past. That past had been the very thing Frank had always shied away from, the very thing that Arthur Collins had had so much trouble worming out of him. Well, well, he'd thought, life was full of surprises.

But in the event, what a blessing it was; what a relief too. It was two years now since Arthur had finally gone to the doctor about his pain and been told to cut down on the drink. Think of it like a boxing match between your liver and your habits, Mr Collins. It's gone ten rounds and, if you're not careful, it'll soon be on the ropes. But he hadn't been careful. Life was for living and having a good time. For a while, the pain had eased away but had returned as bad as before. Of course, he'd not said a word to Frank. Frank would only worry.

Once again, Arthur tried to picture the beautiful house beyond the city. If, in some way, he was to lose Frank to that house, he would have to grin and bear it. Indeed, rejoice in it. For sixteen years, he had looked after Frank Brodie and would gladly do so until his last breath. But now he knew that moment was no longer far off in the comforting mists of an unknowable future. That was why he had steamed open the creamy envelopes. Gone to meet a strange lady for tea at Fortnum's. Ironed the shirt, brushed down the suit and brilliantined the hair. Frank's visit to the country must go well. It really must. The baton would need to be passed. There had to be somebody else who would care when Arthur Collins no longer could.

22

At the end of the first week of January, with the snow still crusted onto the ground, Isobel Farrar made a pilgrimage. Two in one day, in fact, indissolubly woven together. One into the past, the other into what she still hoped might be the future.

When she got out of the taxi at the monumental arch of the necropolis, everything looked exactly as it always had. She smiled at the absurdity of that thought. If any place was unchanging, it must surely be a graveyard, unless of course one counted the process of decay.

It was five years since she had last visited the grave of her parents but, when she reached the place, she couldn't find it at first and was flustered until she discerned the stone, lopsided now, half consumed by the tentacles of rotting bindweed and broken brambles. It was only a small stone, but money had been tight at the time. If she could, she'd have built them a temple for, if any child had adored her parents, it had been young Isobel Leigh. She tugged back the foliage, ruining her gloves, then took a handkerchief to wipe away the encrusted filth until their names saw the light again.

Millicent Leigh. Died 1875. Aged 38 years.
'A rose was ne'er so sweet.'

Francis Leigh. Her loving husband. Died 1881. Aged 51 years.
'Must here the burden fall from off my back?'

She had always walked under the arch of the necropolis with a faint sense of disbelief. This was not right, not how it was meant to be. Theirs had been an idyllic family. The respected concert pianist and teacher at the Royal Academy and his beautiful wife, the gifted cellist who had once been his pupil. She had been twelve when her mother died; not quite eighteen when her father followed. And though the shadows always hang heavy in a graveyard, there was an especially bleak one above the grave of Millicent Leigh. A suspicion. Faint as an echo on the wind. A gossiping maidservant. Questions asked, but answers accepted. Just a tragic accident. So very sad, everyone said.

Six years later, her father had died on the stage of the Albert Hall and with him had died the greater part of a young girl's still developing sense of herself. But Francis Leigh had had a secret, a secret quite separate from the one his young daughter had already discovered. He had left gambling debts of spectacular dimensions. When her childhood home was sold to repay these, there was precious little left to support his only child. From then on, she had withdrawn into what little remained of an only half-formed self. The genesis of what, after a while, people would begin to think of as her mystery. That mystery which, throughout her life to come, would alienate some and intoxicate others. Now, as Isobel bowed her head beside the grubby tombstone, she asked the question she had asked in this place so many times before. Oh Papa, why did you have to die? Everything went so wrong after that.

Yet as well as sadness, these annual visits had brought comfort too, especially during the desolation of her first marriage. Here, for a short while, in the silence of the sepulchres, Mrs Edwin

Reed had become Isobel Leigh again. A girl with her life before her, of whom fine things had been expected.

'It is always harder for a woman,' her father had once told her. 'But I promise you, my dearest, there is still so much you may do in this world, if you wish it. Let nothing stop you flying.'

But when the moment came when Isobel might have flown free, her nerve failed because Francis Leigh was no longer there to encourage her. Short of money, she'd found herself alone in a world in which she was viewed as a very different kind of commodity. And so, presented with a dubious but insistent proposal, she had retreated into what that world expected of her. A wife. Dressed in satins and furs. Wings clipped. Gilded cage. To fly free, now quite impossible. An object now possessed.

Yet the creature she had appeared to become was just an apparition. The truth was that Isobel Leigh could never be entirely possessed, even by those who assumed that they did so. Especially not by them. And from that simple fact, all trouble came.

*

First pilgrimage made, she embarked on the second. In the taxi, the package sat beside her on the seat like a companion. The object cossetted inside the layers of thick brown paper had not existed a week ago, but she gripped it tightly against the jolts of the journey, seeing it already as an almost holy thing.

The notion had come as she woke on the morning after New Year's Day. She had slept but little, that sleep disrupted by the storms of her dreaming. In these dreams, she might have expected to see Frank Brodie in the garden, looking at her with the hurt etched on his face, then turning away without a word. Yet Isobel had dreamed not of his presence but of his absence. The chair by the big window in which he'd sat. The seat at the dining table where he'd eaten the shepherd's pie. The spot where he'd wiped the spilled sherry off the piano. All of these places where he had breathed and which were now bereft of him. If he never came again, was Frank Brodie destined to become just another of the ghosts who haunted this house? Alive and dead at the same time. The thought of that was quite unbearable.

But as Isobel had lain in the struggling light of a January dawn, her gaze had rested on the photograph beside the bed. Suddenly, she had known what she would do. It was worth a try, she decided. Anything better than sitting at the window, numbed by desolation, staring out at the spot where Frank Brodie had turned on his heel and walked away from Halcyon Hill.

Obsessively, for the next three days, she sat at Octavius's desk in the old studio, stopping only for the light meals and cups of coffee which Letty Blount pressed upon her. The family albums, musty from the years of storage, were piled high beside her. She stripped the contents from one of the least memorable, then raided the others to create a new collection. Its contents were not numerous, no more than a dozen or so images, once sepia and now yellowing, but they chronicled the early life of the girl who had been Isobel Leigh.

In the way of those times, the poses were wooden and unsmiling, but that couldn't be helped. Her mother and father when young. Her mother in a vast crinoline, pretending to play a cello. Her father on a piano stool, holding the music of some concerto. The two of them on the occasion of their engagement. On the day of their wedding at the church on Kew Green. There was Isobel herself in a bassinet, swaddled in Venetian lace. A view of the solid house in Kew Road. Isobel in the garden, pushing a doll's pram twice her size. Isobel on the same piano stool, her hair falling down her back; her father standing over her, older and moustachioed now: teacher, mentor and deity.

Her mother in the conservatory, with a little dog in her arms. Isobel and her father, dressed in black, standing on either side of a milk-white tombstone.

A rose was ne'er so sweet.

Under each picture, she wrote a caption. If Frank didn't yet want to hear her story as it related to himself, he might care to hear those parts of it which didn't. To see glimpses of the girl she had been before it all went wrong.

It wasn't far by taxi from the necropolis of the middle and upper classes to Pitt Street, Hammersmith. A mile or two at most and yet another city. She had often tried to picture where he lived and, to her surprise, had imagined it perfectly. It was no slum, no alley of Dickensian misery, but it was cramped and workaday. A street in which to muddle through. Somewhere in which to be born, live, die and always know your place. A street without vistas.

She told the driver to stop a short distance from the house. Would he kindly deliver her package to the doorway, putting it carefully where it could not get wet. He was to ring the doorbell and return to the cab without waiting for an answer and drive off at once. All this was done and from the shadows of the taxi, Isobel caught a glimpse of the door of Number 74 being opened. Looking back through the rear window, she saw Frank in his shirtsleeves peer up and down the street, then be swallowed up again by the humble walls he called home.

The last photograph in the album was the one she had carefully extracted from the frame she had only recently bought for it. It was given a page all to itself and she had written a message beside it. It asked him to excuse her for her crassness last Sunday. She had been nervous. She had wanted so much to please him and she had made a stupid mistake. Silly old woman. Would he please give her another chance?

The people in the photographs belong to you as well as to me, she had written. *They are your family, and I would like you to know them and accept them as yours. The last picture is my greatest treasure, but I send it to you now in the fervent hope that you will return it to me soon at Halcyon Hill.*

She had signed it *your loving mother*. An act that had required some courage. What would he think of that? Might it somehow break through the barrier? Would he just laugh? Or would he think it the grossest possible impertinence?

When she got back to Halcyon, she took the now empty picture frame from her bedroom, carried it downstairs and placed it on top of the piano among the precious others. She put it at the very front, in pride of place, where it would surely be noticed by anyone who might come to call. And if such a person remarked on the oddity of an empty frame, her answer would be ready.

'It's awaiting a new photograph of my son Francis. You must come again soon and meet him.'

23

In the wreckage of his visit, both Isobel Farrar and her son Frank had reached for something to cling to. That night, in the pretty bedroom at Halcyon Hill and in the plain one in Hammersmith, both had lain sleepless, searching for answers, desperate to find them. And Providence had been kind to both. In the first days of January, as Isobel strove to create the album of photographs which she would deliver to Pitt Street, Frank Brodie would labour also.

The first thing he did was to write a note to Wilf Jones in the ironmongery for Arthur to deliver. Frank was still owed a few days' holiday carried over from last year. Could he please take them at once? A family matter. Wilf would moan and groan at the short notice, but he was all bark and no bite. The second thing was to go to the printer's shop at Hammersmith Broadway and buy as many large sheets of paper as he could afford. The sort on which architects and draughtsmen worked. From the newsagent, he bought pencils, a ruler and a box of children's crayons in bright colours. Then he went home, gathered up the tomes on gardening from his bookcase and settled at the table in the little dining room.

The volumes piled high on the chequered tablecloth had been unlikely companions for Frank Brodie. In the house of his childhood, there had been few books. The woman supposed to be his mother had believed that all you needed to know was contained in just one book. The Good Book. Bound in black, its countless pages edged in gold leaf, the monstrous slab of a thing was produced every Sunday evening and she would read it aloud in the sitting room. She would tolerate the butcher half asleep in his chair, but any loss of attention from the boy would bring a shouted rebuke or a cuff on the ear. Every week, she set him to learn several verses and, if he failed in this, another cuff would rattle his teeth. And so, Frank Brodie had come to see books, school books, any books, as punitive objects and had spent most of his life avoiding them.

But that had changed when he discovered that people had written books about the subject that had slowly begun to obsess him. In the barrenness of his childhood, the green spaces of the city had sustained him. The parks, the heaths, the commons, even the churchyards. A municipal flower basket hanging from a lamppost, a hopeful window box on a north-facing wall, a lonely yucca in the dentist's waiting room; all of these and more had possessed the power to cheer him.

Yet it went deeper than that. Between the child and God's good earth, a communion was nurtured, more meaningful than that which he'd so far found with any other human being. The smell of the rich, dark soil, the sight of it caked on his hands and under his nails, the very feel of it running through his fingers. All this he loved. The fragile strength of the first snowdrop pushing its way towards the light could, in the same moment, almost make him weep and yet fill his heart with hope.

As Frank had grown, the butcher and his wife had cared less and less about the boy they had once taken in; where he might be or what he was doing. There was no season in which he would not go up onto Hampstead Heath or down to Primrose Hill, to Highgate Woods or Alexandra Park. There was no joy greater than to stand on the brow of the Heath, throw back his head and gaze up into the unfathomable depths of a blue sky. The sound of larksong, the barking of pampered dogs and the chatter of the ducks on the ponds would, even just for a while, overcome the harsher noises of his childhood. The whine of the butcher's wife as she spouted the gospels. The slamming of the door to the cold chamber. The voice in his head which asked him, again and again, who he really was.

This, then, was the communion which sustained Frank Brodie through the years above the butcher's shop. His reason to get up in the morning and face the day. On one of these mornings, he'd passed a second-hand bookshop in Kentish Town and seen a gardening book in the window. And inside, he'd found even more. It hadn't crossed his mind before that such books existed. The bookseller, a kindly woman, had let him have the first one for a sixpence. As time passed and this strange quiet boy had come back again and again, she'd always knocked something off the advertised price. It was the light in his eyes, she told her husband later; the passion, even, as he brought the books up to the cash desk as if he'd struck gold. Which of course he had.

Inside the covers of his growing library, he both lost and found himself. Here was the companionship that his strangeness denied him among his school fellows. It was the end of Frank Brodie's loneliness. Soon, he could almost recite chunks of those fat books in a way he'd never been able to with the verses of Genesis or Exodus. He tutored himself in the mechanics that created all those miracles beneath the soil. He got to know the stories of plants, trees and flowers. He read of their different characters, their strengths and frailties, their moods and idiosyncrasies. He learned about their enemies, the pests and the parasites, but also that mankind itself could be their greatest friend. And that was what young Frank determined to be. How wonderful that it might be up to him whether a living thing in a terracotta pot would be happy and contented or turn its face from the sun, wither and die. He learned both of the sad penalties of neglect and of the unimaginable bounties of love. And somehow, quite instinctively, he understood all that.

Now those same volumes, battered by usage and the passage of time, were spread out on the dining-room table in Pitt Street,

Hammersmith and for three or four days, stopping only for food and sleep, Frank worked. The first few sheets of paper ended up on the floor, crumpled into balls, tight little fists of frustration. But gradually, over the days and nights, he relaxed a little, letting go from his mind the importance of his task and so the thing that he sought for came to him. The pencils and crayons began to fly across the paper. The terrifying blankness of the paper disappeared beneath straight confident lines, fanciful circles, oblongs and rectangles. These were filled in with rainbows of green and blue, yellow and red. Neat captions, underscored, were written beside the circles and the rectangles, sometimes with the names in Latin that he'd purloined from the books. He wanted to impress her. To make her feel he knew what he was doing, even when he didn't really. Yet that was not exactly true. He did know. The vision coming to life on the sheets of paper came from somewhere deep inside him. A flowering of the spirit long suppressed and now released. He was surprised by the power of it, swept away by the joyousness of creation. He had never expected such a thing to happen to him, but now it had. And that would change everything.

Arthur Collins, glancing down as he went to and from the kitchen, asked no questions and was given no answers. Without the request being made, the wireless in the parlour was kept low of an evening.

When, well past midnight on the third day, the task was done, Frank leaned back in his chair and rubbed his tired eyes. That blessed stillness which he always sought but found so rarely, swept over him now. Yet there was exhilaration blended with it too. That same mix of emotions when, coming round the bend of the lane on his bicycle, he had first glimpsed Halcyon Hill.

The next morning, he sat down again at the table and, with Arthur at his elbow, wrote to Isobel Farrar. He had a small gift in return for the book of poems she had given him at Christmas, he said. Might he call on her to deliver it, whenever was convenient? If so, she must not go to any trouble. A cup of tea would be more than enough, but only if that was convenient too.

24

How hard he found it to kill. She saw that at once and it pleased her. He would crouch down and take the ailing thing gently in his hands. Perhaps shake his head and sigh. He might even talk to it.

'Well, what a sorry state *you've* got into. What are we to do?'

Then he'd take a few steps back, as if he couldn't bear for it to hear the diagnosis.

'It's a crying shame, but this probably has to go,' he'd say to her. 'What do you think?'

'It's what *you* think, Frank,' she'd reply. 'I leave it entirely to you.'

She'd watch as his brow would crease, the power of life and death weighing heavily upon him.

As they walked around the gardens, a cardboard tube was tucked under his arm. From inside the tube, he'd now and then pull out the roll of paper to consult it or to make a point. Like some parchment proclamation, the paper would curl up at the edges, so he would need to hold one side and Isobel the other. Excitement filled her at the prospect of what might be to come. She had resolved not to flinch from any of the changes Frank might suggest. It was sad, of course, when the condemned was something she held in affection. A bush from which Octavius had once cut her a single rose. A magnolia that little Johnnie used to hide behind when it was time for his bed. But all that was in the past. Frank was the future of the garden now. She understood that.

On the first Sunday when he had shyly returned to Halcyon Hill and unrolled the paper across the dining table, she had been astonished. In pencil and pen and coloured crayons, he had shown her a dreamscape. No corner had escaped his attention. Whatever had been good about the garden he had made better, whatever had been inferior was to be replaced and made glorious. As it must once have been with Hugh Pasco, there was no vista with which Frank was not familiar and hadn't taken into account. That view to the little river, to the twisted chimney-tops of Blount's Farm, to the far-off crinkle of the downs. Except for midwinter when, he explained to her, every garden has the God-given right to rest, in every season there would be something of interest. Some colour, however muted, to hold the eye and catch the breath. He had eradicated flowerbeds in one place and moved them magically to some other where he felt their inhabitants might be happier. The steps from the terrace down onto the lawn could be lined with small camellias in pots, like soldiers on parade, uniformed in pink and red and white. A new bench by the oak tree looking down towards the little river. Maybe even a tiny summerhouse, if that were not too expensive, so she could still enjoy the view in cooler weather.

He had thought too of those creatures for whom this land was home. Their presence cherished, their tenancy respected, their disturbance minimised so they wouldn't flee. In Frank's plan, not a single dragonfly would wish to desert the big pond, no lark or swallow abandon its nest or a fox its hide.

He spoke of Miss Jekyll who had designed such wonderful gardens all over Europe. Miss Jekyll had once been a painter, he told Isobel, and had wanted her gardens to be like paintings too. In her books, he'd read how plants, shrubs and flowers should be about more than just some pretty colour, but about the texture of their leaves and blossoms and the way they might move in the wind. A garden should be a depiction of man and nature working together with the tools of soil and sunlight to create something fine, something almost worthy of a frame, from which the beholder could take a step back and sigh at the beauty of it.

All across Frank's roll of paper, in tiny writing, were the Latin words Isobel didn't know and which he had to translate and call by their common names.

'Goodness, Frank, you're very clever,' she said once.

She caught his look of utter surprise, as though he thought her deranged. She wondered, and doubted it, if anyone had ever said such a thing to him. She had wanted to take him in her arms just then, the impulse so powerful that she'd excused herself and gone into the house until it passed.

He took great care to warn her not to expect too much too soon. It was already January, too late now to do much new planting for the coming summer. Maybe just a splurge of daffodils in the border below the terrace. All that could really be done was the clearing away, the tidying-up, the digging of the new beds and the hope of a decent display from that which had been rescued. It might even look a bit worse before it began to look better but, he promised her, everything would be happening under the ground. That miracle, as he put it. So, she must be patient. This year, the foundations would be laid and they could only wait to see what would grow for them. She would wait, she answered. She was happy to wait.

'But you mustn't exhaust yourself,' Isobel said. 'You work all week in London, then you'll be here on Sundays. Why don't we try to find you some local help? Just with the heavy stuff. There's a nice young man called Jed Simmons. A friend of Letty's.'

At once, she saw the look on his face at the notion of an intruder. She saw too, as she often did in a certain light, the first tiny markings of age on his features and could imagine how he would look when they were more deeply scored. It was hard for her to accept that her child was no longer a child, nor a boy, nor even a young man. The years of his zenith were nearly past and how little had come to him during them. The man who loved the sunlight because it made life grow, had spent the best of them in the windowless gloom of the ironmongery and the trenches of Flanders. Always submerged, so rarely in the light. This, Isobel vowed to herself, would change.

'Just for a few weeks, to help you out,' she said again.

'If that's what you think is best,' he replied. 'It's your garden, after all.'

'No, not now,' Isobel replied. 'Now it's yours too.'

She paused for a moment, unsure of saying more in case she should stumble as she had before.

'Anyway, I think it's been yours for quite a long time, hasn't it? Months before I ever returned to Halcyon.'

Frank blushed and lowered his eyes.

'You knew about that?'

'Letty recognised you in the church. The handsome man on the bicycle, she called you. Why didn't you tell me?'

Frank took out his cigarette and lit one. He passed it to her and she took a few puffs. She no longer coughed like the first time and, though she didn't care for it much, she liked this small ritual that had been established between them, this silly little connection.

'Then just tell me why you came,' she said.

'Old Mrs Godsal told me you'd lived here. I was just nosey. That's all.'

'But you came again. Quite often, I think.'

'Once or twice. I liked it here.'

'Is that all?'

Frank stubbed out the cigarette, picked up the stub and put it in his pocket. He walked a few paces away and, when he spoke, his back was turned to her.

'She said you'd gone to Canada and might well be dead by now. She had no idea, so neither did I. It'd taken me years to pluck up the guts to try to find you and find out why you'd given me up. That matters you see, knowing why I'd been given up, what I'd done wrong without knowing it. And now it seemed I'd never know. But I could still come to a place where you'd been. And if I came here, I could breathe the same air. Bloody silly, I suppose.'

'Oh, my dear.'

Isobel took a step towards him, but his back was still turned and her step faltered. Under the gardening jerkin he always wore, she could see the muscles of his shoulders working and knew she must wait.

'I used to sit on a dirty old canvas chair under the oak tree and picture you here, though I hadn't the foggiest idea what you looked like. I'd picture you on the terrace, by the pond or down towards the coppice. All around the place. That's how I came to love this garden, every corner of it. Not just because it was so beautiful, but because you'd once walked in it.'

Isobel took another pace forward until she could have reached out and touched him, but still she held back.

'Then let me tell you why I gave you up,' she said.

'No, please,' he said. 'Not yet. We're here in the garden now. You and me. That's what matters most to me now. In the past few months I've dreamed of that, and now it's happened. So no sad stories. At least not yet. Do you understand? Tell me you understand.'

The wave of words from this quiet man washed over her, knocking her off balance. So many sentences, uninterrupted by nervous pauses or silences, had never come out of him before. She rejoiced in it. Some dam had broken or, at least, fissured.

'I will try,' she replied. 'But when you're ready, you must tell me and then we will speak of it. Because speak of it we must.'

His hand went back into his pocket for the cigarettes. Only when he had lit one did he finally turn round to face her.

'Give me one of my own this time,' she said.

They stood together smoking, gazing down towards the little river.

'I meant what I said about the garden being yours too now,' said Isobel. 'And when it is beautiful again, it won't be because I live in it, but because you do too.'

He looked at her now. And for the first time, the look was unguarded, no longer nervous of what harm the dropping of the guard might bring. And the two pairs of dark eyes, each the mirror of the other, forged again the fathomless connection not made since, in the tiny room under the eaves, he had first looked into her face as she held him in her arms. How she longed to embrace her child again now, but she knew that it must be Frank who came to her. And so she would wait. She would wait forever.

Then suddenly, into that moment, an intruder did come. Letty called down from the terrace. Lord Marchwood had arrived. He apologised for appearing without warning, she said, but was driving past and wanted to pay his respects.

'Will you not come up and meet him?' she replied. 'He's a nice lord, as lords go. I should like to introduce you.'

'I'm best left out here I think.'

'I should like to introduce you as my son,' she said.

A second figure appeared on the terrace beside Letty. Short, portly, grey-whiskered. He raised his hat and waved it, calling out Isobel's name.

'Sorry, old girl. Thought I'd drop in for a minute. Is it a frightful bore?'

Isobel smiled and waved back. She stretched out her hand to Frank.

'Come,' she said. 'Take your place beside me.'

She saw both pleasure and fear flit across his features, jostling for precedence. But she kept her hand outstretched and, after an endless pause, he took it.

25

On the third Sunday after Frank started work on the garden, another intruder came to Halcyon Hill. By now, Isobel had learned to recognise the screeching of tyres on gravel, the slamming of the car door. Miss Maud Farrar had come again.

Since, on Christmas Day, Isobel had confessed the existence of her child, Maud had telephoned several times, asking more questions, wanting more details. Where did Frank live, what work did he do? Who was the man with whom Frank had come to the church? Where were the people who had once taken him in? Why was there no wife or children? Such a good-looking boy after all. Isobel had answered the questions she could and ignored the ones she couldn't.

When Letty had called Frank in for his lunch, he had stopped at the entrance to the dining room, cap in hand, surprised by the presence of the small woman who'd looked at him oddly in the church. She was sitting in the chair he normally occupied. He backed away slightly, like a nervous pup, still shy of faces he didn't know and trust.

'Oh, Maud dear, you're sitting in Frank's place,' said Isobel.

'Frank has a place now?' asked Maud. 'How very nice.'

She stood and advanced on Frank, still in the doorway.

'Isobel is my sister-in-law,' she explained. 'I'm not at all sure what that makes you and me. Friends at least, I hope.'

Frank gave one of his tight little smiles, still something of a rarity, but which lit up Isobel's heart. Over the luncheon, he said little. Maud fired the questions to which she still wanted answers, but this had the reverse effect, making him retreat into the safety of monosyllables, his gaze fixed on his bowl of chicken soup.

After a while, Maud gave up and talked of trivialities. Her bookshop always did badly in the winter, she moaned. It's an antiquarian shop, she told Frank. Her bread and butter was the educated American tourist seeking leather-bound editions of English literature. The Henry James brigade, Maud called them. Had Frank read any Henry James? No? Well, an acquired taste. Anyway, if they didn't arrive in the spring, Maud sighed, she'd be going without shoes by the autumn.

'And how is Lord Marchwood up the lane?' she asked Isobel. 'Such a *roué*. One of the Prince of Wales's set back in the eighties. A very naughty boy indeed. And you young people today are even worse, Frank.'

'But I'm not young,' said Frank. 'Not sure I ever was.'

Isobel caught his eye, but he looked away.

'Nonsense,' said Maud. 'We were all young once. Full of hopes and dreams. Weren't we, Isobel?'

Now it was Maud's eye that Isobel caught and Isobel's eye that now turned away.

'I'm not sure I was ever young either,' replied Isobel. 'At least not for very long.'

'Oh, what a pair of dreary creatures you both are,' said Maud. 'Now do listen to this rather risqué new joke about Lloyd George.'

And so Maud chattered on. The shouts of Jed Simmons and another helper drifted in from the garden. From the kitchen came the faint sound of singing. Letty liked to listen to the Sunday service and join in the hymns. As she brought in the pudding, she was still humming 'Nearer, My God, to Thee'. Isobel noticed how, when Letty put Frank's dish in front of him, the young woman quickly patted his back. Over the Sundays, Isobel had noticed the warmth growing between them. *Letty understands him*, she thought. *She senses how he feels, this boy from the pinched city street. Being in this elegant room with two women of a different class, one of whom he doesn't know at all and other he is struggling to know. Letty knows Frank in a way that I still do not.*

When Maud had finished, she pushed her plate away, leaned back in her chair and placed two tiny palms flat on the table. Isobel recognised the mannerism and felt her stomach tighten. Octavius's sister was about to pontificate.

'Frank, my lad, what has Isobel told you of your father?' she asked.

'Maud, please,' replied Isobel. 'Frank has said that, for the time being, he doesn't want to know the details of... of how things were.'

'He knows nothing of Edwin?' asked Maud. 'Nothing at all?'

'He has asked not to, for now.'

'But that is insane,' said Maud. 'Quite insane. Considering what it could mean for him.'

Frank was looking down at the remains of his apple crumble. Maud stood up from the table. She paced the room, going over to the window and back again. Isobel watched, knowing it was only a matter of moments. And sure enough, Maud spun round, gripped the back of her chair and fixed Frank in her gaze.

'Frank, your father was a man called Edwin Reed. A man from a tribe of people who, in those days, ruled the world. The so-called heroes of the Empire. Men who pretended to be giving when they were taking instead. They weren't all wicked, but most of them were corrupted by wealth and position. Of this tribe, your father Edwin was one of the worst. A trader in rubber and ivory. A man whose family wealth was built on the hard work and enslavement of other human beings. Dear Isobel here, because she was poor enough herself, made the mistake of marrying him and paid a terrible price for it.'

Frank did not raise his eyes from the table. Punctiliously, as he always did, he rolled up his napkin and pushed it back into its silver ring.

'What you need to know, Frank, and without delay, is that Edwin Reed has just died. A couple of months ago. He knew nothing of your birth, but you are his legal son. You have a claim on his estate. Don't you understand me, Frank? You could be a rich man.'

Frank's eyes stayed cast down, but Miss Maud went on undaunted.

'Edwin Reed's relatives, who are yours too I suppose, would probably contest your claim in the courts. Isobel would no doubt have to give evidence.'

'Would they believe her?' asked Frank, his voice scarcely audible.

'Possibly not,' said Isobel. 'You see, Frank dear, the unhappiness of my first marriage led me to... to become involved with somebody else. It wasn't a secret for long. The thing was widely known in the society I inhabited. There was great scandal and ultimately a divorce. So it would lead them to presume...'

'And all that would be dredged up again?'

'The Reed clan would fight it,' replied Maud. 'I'm sure of that. They're all cut from Edwin's cloth.'

Isobel gave a little shiver.

'Are you cold?' Frank asked. 'Shall I get your shawl?'

'No, dear, I think somebody just walked across my own grave.'

She tried to laugh, but it caught in her throat and lodged there. Frank came round the table and stood behind her chair. He put his hands on her shoulders and gently rubbed them. Apart from their usual formal handshakes, her child had never before touched her. Isobel raised her own hands and took hold of his. She felt the warmth of him bleed into her and hers into him. Thirty-eight years after she had first felt it in the tiny room under the eaves.

'No thanks,' he said to Maud. 'I don't want it.'

'Think hard,' said Maud, her little body arched like a cat, spitting the words at him. 'Think hard right this minute. You might never need to work again. No more ironmongering. No more shabby overcoats. The life of a gentleman for the rest of your days.'

'I don't need to think. I don't want it. I don't need to be a gentleman.'

'But he was your father. You are his son. It is your right.'

'But he was a bad man. You said that, Miss Farrar. He made Isobel so miserable she eventually had to run away.'

'That's right. If Edwin has, by some remote chance, reached the Pearly Gates, he probably had to write St Peter a cheque to get in.'

'Then I don't want him as a father. I don't want to make a claim on him. I want nothing that belonged to him. I don't even want his name.'

'Are you sure?' asked Maud, her voice raised, almost shouting. 'Really sure? Just think of the money.'

Frank and Isobel, their hands still clasped together, were both trembling now, in the face of The Fury with the shingled hair.

'But I've already had one rotten father,' Frank shouted back across the table. 'I don't want another, even if he's dead. I renounce him. I won't be the son of any man who was cruel to others. Cruel to my mother.'

Just as he had never touched her closely before, neither had Frank yet called Isobel by that word. The word spoken in anger was the word that finally spoke of love. Each aware of it, they looked at each other, the shyness between them not quite gone, but now undermined. Frank lifted Isobel's hand to his lips and her heart danced.

Letty came into the dining room. Jed Simmons was at the back door, she said, asking for Mr Brodie. Some urgent decision needed making in the garden. Could Mr Brodie please come?

When the door had closed behind him, Miss Maud Farrar sank back down in her chair, all passion spent. She closed her eyes for a moment, then opened them with a look of triumph on her face.

'A job well done, I think,' Maud said. 'And it needed doing, Isobel. You hadn't done it, so I did. He had to be given that information and offered the chance to act on it, if he wished. And he didn't.'

'Oh, but Maud, I was so afraid that he might. That even in death, Edwin would reach out to claim him.'

'Well, whatever his bloodline may be, your son doesn't have the soul of the Reeds and their ilk. Not a trace of their cancer. And isn't that a wondrous thing?'

The two women took coffee by the great window in the covered court. They watched Frank and Jed Simmons down by the old oak tree, two heads bent over the rolled-up paper from the cardboard tube. Frank offered Jed a cigarette and they smoked together as they stalked the gardens, Frank pointing this way and that. When they went their separate ways, Jed Simmons lifted his cap to Frank. Isobel saw it and was pleased.

'You know what he's doing, don't you?' said Maud suddenly. 'It's not just bulbs and shrubs he's planting. He's planting himself.'

'I ask for nothing more,' said Isobel.

*

'Did you know the man?' he asked later in the darkness of Maud

Farrar's car as it headed back into the city.

She'd give him a lift, she'd said. Hammersmith was on her way. No point in travelling on a bumpy train when he could experience the amazing suspension of the Morris Cowley. The other day, she'd given a ride to a friend who wore a truss and he'd not had so much as a twinge.

Frank had changed out of the gardening clothes he now kept in a cupboard in the stables and back into the suit he always wore to arrive at, and depart from, Halcyon Hill. His face and hands had been scrubbed in Letty's scullery and his hair combed through.

'What man?' asked Maud, as she took the roundabout by the gates of Richmond Park.

'The man who became her...' he said, his voice almost lost under the screech of the brakes.

'The lover?' she asked. 'His name was Hugh Pasco. An architect. The man who designed and built Halcyon.'

'Did you know him?'

'Only slightly. I was still quite young when my brother commissioned the house.'

'What was he like?'

'Oh, very handsome, very charming. Everyone liked Hugh, especially the ladies. I can still picture him, dashing around the half-built house, climbing up and down ladders, pencils and rulers sticking out of his pockets.'

'What happened to him?'

'He died. Unexpectedly. The day before Isobel finally fled from Edwin Reed's house in Pelham Crescent. Such a waste. All that genius.'

'Did you know her then?'

'Oh no. Not till a dozen years later. After her divorce from Edwin, she lived all alone in Pimlico for years and often came to my little bookshop off Sloane Square. One day, my brother Octavius was there too. Confirmed bachelor, we all thought, and so did he. Fell hopelessly in love on the spot and married her. And so, by the strangest twist of fate, she came to live in the house created by her lost lover. Divinely romantic, isn't it? We are the playthings of the gods, don't you think?'

For a while, there was silence in the car as it headed north towards Hammersmith.

'You must understand that Halcyon, both house and garden, was the vision of Hugh Pasco. Nobody else,' said Maud. 'The Farrars may own it on paper but, in truth, it will always belong to Hugh. That's why young architects still come to see it. It is his memorial. And I think, like him, it will never grow old.'

'From the first time I saw it, I wondered about the man who'd imagined such a place,' said Frank.

'Then do your work for Hugh,' said Maud. 'Not just for Isobel or for yourself. Do it for Hugh and some of his genius might reach down and touch you.'

The little woman reached across and squeezed his hand in hers. The car zig-zagged across Hammersmith Bridge to a chorus of frantic horns.

26

'Eurydice has risen from the underworld,' he called as she got out
of the hansom on the brow of the Heath. 'Is it safe for me to turn
and look at you now?'

And though she would smile, she was only too aware of the truth
in the jest. These afternoons, once a week if they were lucky, were
now indeed the pulse of life for which Isobel yearned above all else.

As a rendezvous, Hampstead had been his notion. He had
recently completed a small commission there, a summerhouse for
a bourgeois garden, nothing more, but it had paid his bills for
a month or two. He had been seduced by this village on its city
hilltop, he said. In the curving, cobbled lanes, along the alleyways
of precipitous steps, behind the doors of bow-fronted cottages, all
kinds of interesting people lived. Artists, writers, sculptors, even
struggling young architects and women who might teach piano
for a living. Our sort, he'd told her. Maybe, when the time came,
might they not find somewhere up here? Had Isobel not noticed
that, as soon as the horses pulled the cab up the slope from Swiss
Cottage, the clouds would fragment and the sun begin to push its
way through? And by the time the hansom gained the hilltop, the
sky was the rich deep hue of a bluebird's wings? And because she
loved him, she let herself begin to believe it.

In Flask Walk, they discovered a small Italian restaurant where,
after a few visits, they were given the same corner table, beneath

an indifferent watercolour of Lake Como. Had Isobel ever been to Lake Como? No? Then he would take her one day. The little town in the picture was called Bellagio, admiring itself in the mirror of the lake, with fir-clad hills clambering up to where the frosted Alpine peaks began, encircling the skyline and keeping it safe from the outside world. There was nowhere on this earth lovelier than Bellagio, he said. If he had a choice of where to die, it would be there, lying in her arms, looking out over the water. And then he'd blushed and laughed at himself, saying she must think him a soppy fool and ordering another half carafe of wine.

Afterwards, warmed by the wine and the haze of unreality, they walked onto the edges of the Heath. For a time, they would mingle with the dog-walkers, the kite-fliers and the children sailing boats on the ponds. And other lovers too, of course. He liked to play a whispered game, guessing which couples were respectable and which, like themselves, were sinners – even if, like themselves, it was largely in thought rather than deed.

'*They're* hitched,' he'd say. 'But *they're* not.'

'Hush,' she'd reply. 'They might hear. Anyway, how do you know?'

'It's to do with the stoop of the shoulders.' He laughed and then he stopped when he saw her face. Jokes about the yoke of marriage held no humour for the wife of Edwin Reed.

Just then, two young men strolled past them, their heads bowed close together.

'And they *definitely* are,' he said.

'Hugh, really,' she replied. 'You shouldn't say such things.'

'Don't be so stuffy,' he said, a whipcrack of snappishness in his voice she hadn't heard before.

'But aren't you...?'

'What? Disgusted?' he replied. 'Nothing that is human disgusts me as long as it is loving.'

After a while, a private nook was discovered, among a tangle of trees and wild white hydrangeas beside the little viaduct that spanned one of the less visited ponds. Two long-dead stumps did service as stools and he took to bringing a piece of sheeting in a rucksack, so that her dress would not get dirty. Here, they sometimes spoke of everything; at other times few words were used at all, as they kissed or simply held each other, looking out over the flat blue-green water.

And yet, despite the setting, there was little romance in any of it. No poetic language, declarations of eternal devotion or daisies picked and threaded in her hair. Why say or do such things when they were quite superfluous? How much nicer to take what had happened almost for granted, as the natural unfolding of what simply *had* to happen. The two palms meeting in the formality of a drawing room in South Audley Street. The look between them. The look that, in a moment, had shown him everything there was to know of the girl born Isobel Leigh, now Mrs Edwin Reed, wife of a prosperous man of business. That quality called her mystery had been quite invisible to Hugh Pasco. She had sensed that in a single moment and the relief had been indescribable. Like a swimmer trapped underwater by some impediment, she was suddenly free of what chained her and broke through the surface to take the most precious breath of her existence.

Though not especially tall, he was broad and sturdily built with the cheekbones of a Botticelli prince. What in those days was called his 'presentation', though it just passed muster, hardly measured up to that of the effete young men around him. Hugh Pasco's moustache was quite unknown to the barbers of Jermyn Street, the suit not quite well-pressed, the cravat carelessly tied, the collar not as starched as custom dictated. This collar was grazed by dark chestnut hair, tousled and a worn a little too long. And at least one of his fingernails was always dirty.

But in that moment, both Isobel Reed and Hugh Pasco knew that, from now on, their lifelines would somehow run in parallel. She had always thought such things only happened in silly novels. What the French, in their florid way, called a *coup de foudre*. But now it had happened and it wasn't silly anymore. Yet there was no thunderbolt to shake the high windows in South Audley Street. The chandeliers did not so much as quiver, nor the tassels tremble on the pelmets of swagged silk.

But the soft brown eyes of Hugh Pasco looked at her in a way no other man's had done before. What made it so striking was not what the look expressed, but what it did not. By now, she had reached her early twenties, the misty border between girlhood and womanhood firmly crossed. Married womanhood too, that strangest and most frightening of all foreign lands. She was now accomplished in the interpretation of the ways men regarded her. Not that this was difficult, since the spectrum was narrow. Desire, mostly, of course; either blatant or discreet. Sometimes, an appreciation of her playing the piano. Even now and then, she noticed, a sweaty whiff of fear. But whichever it might be, it would always be underlaid by the other thing too. The monster which lurked behind the smiling eyes and perfect manners. The urge for possession and the sense of a right to it.

But in the face of Hugh Pasco, Isobel had seen none of those responses. What she saw, in that first long look of his, was simply the greeting of someone who, by some unfathomable alchemy, already knew her as well as one human being might ever know another.

One Hampstead afternoon, when the sun was almost too hot, they found shade in the little chapel on the rim of the Heath, where the Low Church people went to pray. Its walls were the creamy white of a wedding cake, its lines simple and clear, without ostentation. Everything that Hugh Pasco strove for in his own work. As he wandered up and down the aisle, the wonder on his face, she saw that she had lost him for a while. She sat down in a pew, her new shoes pinching her toes, and waited until he remembered her again.

'Keats lived in this street – did you know that?' he said. 'He must have come here, I imagine. Even just to peek, as we're doing now.'

He sat down in the pew across the aisle from her and looked around him again.

'Oh, Isobel, there is so little time,' he said, turning to look at her. 'So ridiculously little. And the awful thing is that we don't know how much. Is that not the cruellest cut of all?'

He stood up and reached for her hand. Together, they walked down the aisle until they reached the tiny altar, scarcely more than a table draped with a simple cloth. A coarse crucifix of bold, bare wood. Two crumbling candles. They stood there together for a few minutes. No word was spoken, no vow was made. Nothing exchanged, not even a kiss. And yet the deed was done.

When they returned up the aisle and went out again into the afternoon, their eyes were blinded by the summer light.

'Not long now,' he said. 'Not long now, I promise.'

And when it was time for Eurydice to descend once more into her darkness, the roles of the myth were reversed. Now it was she who would never look back. It took all her willpower, but she knew only too well what she would see and that it would cleave her heart. The figure at the cab rank, the hat being waved above the tousled head demonstrating, even in the mundanity of that gesture, the exhilaration of his love for her. Too bleak to see the waving trilby shrink into one pointillist dot among the hundreds of others on the streets. Far preferable to shut her eyes and do the very opposite. To picture his face so close to hers that it blotted out the entire world, to smell the scent of him still clinging to her, to feel on her body the ghostly pressures of where his hands had lingered.

As predicted, when the hansom reached the bottom of the hill, the clouds rolled in. Then down and down, the black horse pulled Eurydice's carriage, down into the bowels of the city, down towards her immuration in the house in Pelham Crescent and the life which held no light for her. But again and again, she clung to the lifeline he'd thrown to her as they'd stood before the altar of the little chapel.

'Not long now, I promise.'

27

Alice Godsal refused to die. It wasn't in her nature. Expected to pass before the turn of the year, she was still breathing as the first of the daffodils appeared outside her window in Goldhurst Terrace, West Hampstead.

The doctor was amazed. The tumour should have seen her off long since, but her heart was strong. Perhaps it was all that exercise in younger days, opined the doctor, a man given to coarse remarks, quite aware of Alice's earlier life. She'd told him of it once when he had called to inspect her gout and been tempted into staying for tea and a shortbread finger.

But though the strength of the body clung on, that of the mind had deserted her. Wandering now between present and past, between sense and nonsense. From day to day, there was no knowing exactly where the mind of old Alice might be. Those few who came to see her could only hope to hold onto her coat tails and try to follow her into the labyrinth. Often, they would fall by the wayside, abandon the effort, telling the little maid they'd return on a 'better' day. Sometimes, though, she would pull them with her into dark places, mumble dark things that were not fit for respectable people to hear. They would make their excuses and hurry off, secretly hoping she might pass away soon so they need never come back.

Isobel Farrar was, of course, one of those who came to the ugly house Billy Godsal had built. Every other day, she telephoned for news and, at least once a week, made the long journey to Goldhurst Terrace. Before and after Christmas and New Year, when her thoughts had been obsessed with Frank Brodie, a corner had still been reserved for the shrivelled creature lying on the chaise longue by the window. Anyway, Frank and Alice were hopelessly entangled. The woman who had rolled up her sleeves and brought him into the world then soundlessly removed him from the tiny room under the eaves. The woman too who had been the channel in his restoration.

Isobel had not informed Alice of that day in the ironmongery when Frank had fled from the face behind the white veil. It was only after the meeting in the church, once a frail seed of hope had taken root, that she dared to tell Alice that she had found her boy. And Alice had wept and wept until the little maid had hurried into the room and managed to soothe her, as only the girl seemed able to do.

After that, on those days when Alice was even faintly connected to the world, Isobel told her something more of the man on the bicycle. Sometimes, Alice cried again, asking if she'd done the wrong thing by Isobel and the child. Had she given her friend the wrong advice? Billy Godsal had said he'd take care of everything. Alice and her friend needn't worry, he'd promised. Easy as pie. A good, respectable couple, the man and his wife. But where the hell was Billy today? He'd be sorry to have missed Isobel's visit, Alice said.

'Have you found out why the boy is sad?' Alice asked more than once. 'I remember how sad he was when he came.'

'Only a little,' said Isobel. 'I hope he will tell me more in his own good time.'

'Oh, I hope so,' said Alice, grasping Isobel's wrist in her cold hand. 'And then you can put it right. You can put back happiness into him.'

As the weeks went by, the fierce closeness between them, diminished by the recent years of separation, was revived. The little maid would be set free for a few hours and Isobel would attend to Alice's wants. She spoon-fed the broth, the soft-boiled egg and the buttered toast that made up the old woman's diet now. But the thing that seemed to nourish Alice most, was simply being held. And so Isobel would pull a stool right up to the chaise and draw Alice gently into her arms. Every time she did this, the surroundings of the plush drawing room seemed to evaporate and the tiny room under the eaves would materialise in its place. She could almost hear the pigeons on the roof and the shouts from the street far below. As Alice's arms had held Isobel together in her bleakest moments, now Isobel returned the favour.

On a good day, Isobel would talk of trivial things, of merry times spent together over the years. The luncheons in Soho, the birthday teas at Brown's Hotel. When they'd gone ice-skating on the Serpentine and landed on their *derrières,* showing off their bloomers. When they'd stood in a crowd for hours to watch the old Queen's coffin pass by and cried together when it did. On a bad day, when sense had fled, she would simply stroke Alice's head and let the gibberish tumble out. Sometimes, Isobel would flinch and try not to hear. Besides, who knew the effects of the opiates which the doctor was injecting with increasing frequency? Who knew what was truth and what was fantasy? Were the inhabitants of Alice's mind real or not? Had Alice really slept with one of the old Queen's sons (though she wouldn't reveal which one as discretion, she said, was the watchword of her trade)? She spoke of her mother, a seamstress like herself; her father, a soldier killed at Balaclava. She spoke of many others too, as they paraded across the ruins of her mind. Isobel only half listened, trying not to follow her into the labyrinth, as long as the old woman in her arms seemed happy to lose herself there.

'Maurice is a doctor now, you know,' she said more than once. 'And Mary has married well, thank God.'

'That's nice,' said Isobel.

'He was such a devil when he was young,' said Alice another day. 'Who, dear?'

'Maurice. Such a scamp. I often had to give him a good smack. He's a doctor now, you know. Harley Street no less. Who'd have thought it?'

'That's nice,' said Isobel again.

'And Mary married to the son of an alderman,' said Alice, dropping her voice to a whisper. 'He took on a handful with her, I can tell you.'

Isobel had been on the train going home when the penny dropped. The ghost children. The twins to whom Alice's body had given birth and her imagination had then given life, long after she had bid them a physical farewell. Half a century on, they were still with her. And when she departed this earth, they would be kneeling here beside the chaise, cradling her in their arms and sending her on her journey on a wave of love.

*

'You moved those *pieris japonica*,' said Frank, clutching his cap, looking for something to say. 'I said they'd be better there, didn't I? They'll do well this spring. You wait and see.'

On one of her good days, Alice had clutched Isobel's arm and asked her to bring Frank Brodie back to Goldhurst Terrace. She longed to see them together, she said. It would do her old heart good. And so, one Sunday, instead of in the garden at Halcyon Hill, Isobel and Frank arranged to meet outside West Hampstead station.

She watched him come up the busy escalator, hemmed in by all those other lives. She wondered if he might kiss her again.

It had only happened that once, when he had faced down Miss Maud over the dining table and, in that tumultuous moment, had become Isobel's knight in shining armour and called her Mother. She longed for him to do both these things again, but he never had, reverting to calling her Isobel and shaking her hand. One step forward, one step back. At the entrance to the Underground, that was what happened again. Oh well, she thought, maybe soon.

As they walked towards the ugly house, Isobel thought that something should be said about Alice. That she had been Isobel's friend from long ago was all Frank knew. He knew nothing of the circumstances of their meeting, nothing of the little room under the eaves. Still, after all these weeks, whenever Isobel drifted carelessly towards the circumstances of his birth, she would see Frank back away from her. Still, he did not want to know. This inexplicable conceit. If only she could understand of what he was afraid. And then, one Sunday, when she had dozed off in her chair by the window, she had woken to find that he'd come in from the garden and was sitting opposite, silently watching her. And it came to her then that perhaps he didn't want to know because he feared making a judgement of her, that he feared he might hate her. And the thought had given her strange comfort. That he did not want to hate but, if possible, to love. Yet the story must eventually be told. It had to be. Truth was merciless. It had to be faced. When would Frank be ready?

At the gate of the house, Isobel stopped him.

'There is something you have the right to know about Alice.'

At once, she saw the shutters come down over the dark eyes. He took a step back from the gate, as if he suspected some harm was about to come to him.

'It was Alice who brought you into this world,' said Isobel. 'When the doctor didn't come. It was Alice.'

'All right,' he replied, with one of his nods.

But today was not a good day in the fading of Alice Godsal. Today, her connection with the world came and went like a faulty telephone line. The doctor had been early and given her another injection but, the little maid said, each one seemed less effective than the last. Yet at first, it seemed that the sight of Isobel and the man on the bicycle did indeed do the old heart good. She seized one hand of each and clasped the two together. This was lovely, she said, just lovely. Tears came, which Isobel had to wipe away because Alice could no longer lift her arms. Then she mumbled about nappies and knitting bootees and of pigeons on a roof. She stroked Frank's cheek and told him how handsome he was. Heavens, if only she'd been forty years younger. She'd not even have asked him to pay.

But by the time tea arrived, Alice had wandered off into the labyrinth. Maurice was a doctor now. Harley Street no less. Maurice was handsome, just like Frank. Was Frank a doctor too? And Mary had married the son of an alderman. Was Frank an alderman? Isobel watched him as he played with the cat, seeing him begin to understand what was happening. The shyness fell away from his face and compassion took its place. No, he said, he worked in shop. He sold hammers and screws and wheelbarrows and things that carpenters and builders needed to make furniture and build houses. Hadn't Alice's husband himself been a builder? Maybe Frank had served him once. Well, you never knew, did you?

But the mention of Billy Godsal was a mistake. Alice seized Frank's hand again.

'Oh, I'm sorry! So very sorry, my duck. Billy swore the people would be all right,' said Alice, the tears starting again. 'They wanted a son, Billy said. They'd lost one and needed another. I never thought they wouldn't be kind. I never thought *that*.'

Frank pulled back from her a little and stared silently out onto the spring garden. Isobel poured more tea, raising the cup to Alice's lips, but the eyes had closed. For a while, there was silence in the room, apart from the purring of the cat. Then Alice sat bolt upright, her eyes blazing open.

'Damn you, Billy Godsal! Damn you to hell! You took this sad boy. You took my boy and my girl. Damn you, Billy Godsal. I hope you've rotted at the bottom of the sea!'

Alice cried out again and again. The little maid came running and comforted her mistress, until at last she fell back onto the cushions.

'Maurice is a doctor,' the old woman muttered. 'And Mary has married well.'

*

The funeral was a sparse affair. Some ancient women with dyed hair and too much powder. A few distant relatives of Billy Godsal, trying not to look hopeful. A solicitor. The doctor, who kept peeking at his watch. The little maid. Isobel and Frank. 'Yes, of course I'll come,' he'd said. 'Of course I will.' And when Alice had been lowered into the ground, Isobel, in distress, had needed his arm, and he had not withheld it.

As they walked towards the gates, she thanked him again for coming. Suddenly, he stopped on the path.

'Was Alice... you know?' he asked quietly, though nobody else was close enough to hear him. 'Was Alice once...?'

'A woman of the streets? Indeed she was. Those cold, unmerciful streets.'

And Isobel saw a strange look come into the eyes of her son.

'Bless her, then,' he said.

28

The silver-plated tray of bottles and glasses sparkled in the strengthening sun of a late March morning. Arthur Collins had polished them until he could see his carefully shaved reflection. The purpose of the tray, that of impressing people with the sophistication of 74 Pitt Street, had never been more important than today. On this particular Sunday, Frank Brodie was not going to the country. Lady Farrar was coming to luncheon.

Though Arthur felt nervous, the invitation had been his idea. *Every week now*, he'd said to Frank, *Lady Farrar offers you her hospitality. It would be gentlemanly to return it at least once.* And Arthur was keen that the mistress of Halcyon Hill should see Frank as such, even if only in embryo. If Frank was to take his place in her world, and it was vital to Arthur that he should, that perception mattered. So, it was lucky that there was in Frank an innate strain of gentlemanliness already, though God only knew where it had come from. In the shop, Wilf Jones had said, customers had sometimes spoken favourably of the quiet young man behind the counter in the ironmongery, of his courtesy and his willingness to help. And Arthur had taken pride in that.

He had been up since six. Not only had the bottles and glasses been polished, but so too had his mother's harmonium, the wireless and every other wooden surface. He'd rubbed Brasso on the door knocker, though not too much lest Lady Farrar stain her gloves. Arthur was quite certain she would be wearing gloves. There wasn't much he could do about the faded chintz of the armchairs, but cushions were judiciously placed to conceal the worst of the wear. His main concern was that Lady Farrar might wish to use the bathroom and see the scabs of rust on the cistern and around the bath. Hopefully she would be a woman with a capacious bladder, though, in his experience, this was less likely among the gentry than with working folk.

Frank had been of little use. The man who would tut at the sight of dust on the leaf of a plant seemed oblivious to it on a piece of furniture. The evening before, Arthur had got out the iron and pressed Frank's suit as well as his own.

'But she's used to seeing me in my gardening clothes, Arthur.'

'Well, you're not a gardener tomorrow. You're the host and you're going to bloody look like one. And behave like one too, please. Don't leave everything to me.'

Arthur had splashed out on the luncheon. A good leg of lamb with all the trimmings. Peach Melba for afters. When he was young, he'd worshipped Nellie Melba, even more than he'd come to worship Marie Lloyd. He'd save up for a seat in the gallery at Covent Garden and she'd always made him cry. He'd chosen the pudding because it would allow him to tell Isobel of this – something to talk about that might interest a woman of her breeding.

When he saw her getting out of the taxi, his heart gave a little lurch. Not just at her beauty and her fine clothes, but at the way she moved, the way she smiled and spoke to the cabbie as she paid the fare. And when, for a moment, she stood and looked up and down Pitt Street, it was not with distaste or even conde-scension, but with an open curiosity. In the shop, he was quite used to wealthy women, but so often they were vulgar creatures, over-dressed, over-powdered and painted, mummified in the self-importance given to them by a husband's money. But Isobel Farrar was not of that tribe. She was, in Arthur Collin's eyes, quite simply a goddess. Or, as he put it to Frank, class.

That Frank's search for the woman who had borne him should have uncovered such a person still seemed to Arthur Collins some kind of miracle. Heavens, Frank might as easily have unearthed a washerwoman, a factory girl or even a tart. But no, he had found this exquisite creature now coming through their gate, who could give to Frank everything Arthur would have wanted to give him and so much more he had never dreamed of. On that afternoon when Arthur had first met her in Fortnum's, he'd got off the Number 9 bus in Hammersmith, and gone into The Church of The Holy Innocents, a place he'd not entered in years. In a quiet pew, he had got down on his knees and given thanks. Hallelujah, Arthur had said to God. Hallelujah.

'My goodness, what a beautiful object,' Isobel said, when she saw the harmonium. 'One rarely sees the like anymore. Quite lovely.'

'My mother's,' replied Arthur. 'She was a singer like myself, though far superior to me.'

'In the music hall?'

'Gracious no. In the chorus at Covent Garden. A wonderful voice. I'm sure she could have risen higher, but then she married and I was born and, well, you know...'

'I do know,' said Isobel. 'So much is lost to women in marriage, is it not?'

Arthur offered sherry. Sweet or perhaps dry? Dry was accepted. He had decided that he wouldn't touch a drop while she was here. He'd not had anything last night either, even though it was a Saturday. The bottle hidden in the wardrobe had stayed untouched too, though it'd been a close-run thing. Later, when she'd gone, he might have a nip.

In the parlour, Frank retreated into near silence, as he usually did when anyone came over the threshold. Was this what he was like at Halcyon Hill, Arthur wondered? Surely not. Surely by now, some rapport must have been built between them. If so, there was little evidence of it today, on Frank's side at least. But perhaps they were both shy in front of him, so he excused himself and went to the kitchen to see to the meal.

Frank asked Isobel if she would like to see his pots in the back yard. Arthur, at the stove, watched unseen through the little kitchen window. Frank went from pot to pot, squatting down, talking about each one; Isobel stood above him, asking questions, smiling sometimes. At one moment, with Frank's gaze fixed on his plants and thinking herself unobserved, Isobel glanced around the shabby yard and the grimy backs of the little houses. A shadow of regret passed across her face. Arthur saw it and was wounded. Well, he'd done his best by the boy, given him what he could, though knowing it wasn't enough. But, when Frank looked up at Isobel again, Arthur was compensated, the little wound forgotten. Because now he saw what he yearned to see. That which had been quite absent in the parlour. The sign of feeling between mother and child. The cord, once brutally cut, slowly growing again.

At the dining table, they spoke more of music. She talked of her father, the distinguished professor and concert pianist. He had longed for his daughter to be a prodigy, she said, and had been a hard taskmaster. She had practised eight hours a day, until her neck ached and her fingertips were raw. But she hadn't quite been a prodigy after all. Talented yes, but not first-rate. A career as a teacher the best she could hope for. Her father had told her that himself. Quite coldly, as she recalled. She still remembered the day. She'd cried for hours. She had been only sixteen.

As he had planned, Arthur spoke of Nellie Melba over the pudding, of Luisa Tetrazzini and Adelina Patti. Of Gigli and of course Enrico Caruso. He had heard Caruso at the Queen's Hall the night before the war broke out. Like Lady Farrar, Arthur said, he too had cried, knowing that what he'd always wanted would never be within his grasp. There had been no money to study as a serious singer. Such opportunities didn't happen to a boy like him.

'Then you and I must be content to be disappointments to ourselves, mustn't we, Mr Collins, and stumble on as best we can?'

'Too true,' Arthur replied. 'Opportunity is everything, isn't it, Lady Farrar? The lack of it such a waste.'

Arthur looked at Isobel and saw that she had taken his meaning. The unspoken understanding between them that had seeded at the elegant table in Fortnum's grew stronger at the humbler one in Pitt Street.

The Italian couple next door had started one of their arguments; they ignored the noise until something heavy thudded against the other side of the wall.

'I'm so sorry, Lady Farrar,' said Arthur. 'Foreigners, I'm afraid.'

'It's a scene from Puccini, don't you think?' She smiled. '*Gianni Schicchi*?'

'Exactly. Perhaps in a moment they will break into song.'

'Lady Farrar, I wonder...' Arthur paused. 'Would you play something for us? I don't play myself, so the instrument is never used. I have it tuned now and again, but otherwise it's sadly neglected.'

'The harmonium isn't my instrument, Mr Collins, but I'll try, if you will sing for me.'

And so they did. Isobel sifted through the sheet music until a simple aria was found which she could play and Arthur could sing. Standing by the harmonium, he puffed out his chest and held onto his lapels as he had always done on the stage. For the first few bars, the harmonium wheezed a little and so did Arthur, but then it cleared and with it went whatever awkwardness had hung in the house since Isobel crossed its threshold. In the exhalation of the music, the three of them found an ease which had not been there before. There was mutual applause, laughter, a search for an encore to perform.

'Arthur, do "Keep the Home Fires",' Frank said, from the corner. 'Go on. It's lovely, that.'

Arthur hesitated, but Isobel said she could do it without the music. It had been a favourite of her late husband Octavius. And so the old song was sung, no less potent with the passing of time. Arthur's voice gave way a little in one or two places, but it was not from a failure of talent. All three of them knew that. There was no applause this time, just a silence, but the new-found ease between them had deepened.

'It must have been hard for you,' said Isobel, when Frank excused himself from the room, 'during the war.'

'I never believed he'd make it back,' replied Arthur, his face still flushed from the singing. 'The odds against it were so high.'

'That's what I believed, too,' said Isobel. 'I thought of him with every ghastly newspaper headline.'

'Yet, Lady Farrar, you didn't even know if your child had grown to adulthood.'

'Oh, but I did,' she replied. 'Don't ask me how, but I did.'

Isobel still sat on the stool at the harmonium, but now she turned to face him.

'I'm so glad you asked me here today, Mr Collins,' she said. 'It's clear to me now that Frank has not been quite alone in the world all these years.'

'No, he's had old Arthur Collins chivvying him along,' he laughed. 'Nag, nag, nag.'

'But I think it's more than that, Mr Collins,' she replied. 'It seems to me that once Frank came to this house, he was no longer parentless. And I cannot tell you what comfort that gives me.'

Standing beside the harmonium, Arthur knew that Isobel Farrar spoke the truth, yet it was not the one he had hoped for. But that other truth, that which had begun when young Frank, the boy from the arches of Piccadilly, had first come to tea in Pitt Street, had faded with the years. Arthur only had to look in the mirror to understand why. Still, he was grateful to God that the first truth had been replaced by the second truth, since it was one which would never fade, even though the transition had hurt him at the time.

'It's you, Mr Collins, who has brought up my son,' continued Isobel. 'Those qualities I see in Frank – his kindness and gentleness, his courtesy, his nobility of spirit – come, I think, from you.'

Arthur was touched and didn't know what to say. He looked at the shining bottles on the silver-plated tray in the parlour window. He wondered if she'd take a small brandy, so that he could have one himself.

'But have you seen the rage too?' he asked. 'It appears from nowhere like thunder from a clear sky.'

'Once, yes. It distressed me.'

'That comes from what happened to him, Lady Farrar. The anger he holds inside about the injustices committed against him. I've tried to help the healing, but I think that only you truly can.'

'I know that, Mr Collins,' she said. 'Believe me, I do, and I'm trying, but there is some distance still to go. The wounds are deep, I think.'

'Deeper than you know, Lady Farrar. Possibly deeper than he will ever let you see.'

'I will take my chance, Mr Collins.'

'Would you also take a small brandy, Lady Farrar? Frank should have our coffee nearly ready by now.'

'With a little soda if you have it.'

Arthur went to the silver tray and poured out two measures. He looked for the soda but found none. There was some in the cold cupboard in the kitchen, he said. So sorry. He'd be back in a jiffy.

Frank was laying out the coffee things.

'It's gone quite well, don't you reckon?' Frank said quietly.

'I think so, yes.'

'All down to you, of course,' said Frank. 'Thanks, Arthur.'

Frank slid his arm round Arthur's waist and kissed him on the cheek. Arthur did the same in return. For a moment, Frank rested his head on Arthur's shoulder and they stood together looking out over the yard. It was only when the faint scent of perfume reached their nostrils that they turned in unison and saw Isobel standing in the doorway.

29

From an upstairs window, she had seen the police carriage stop outside their house and the constable come up the path with the big parcels under his arms. She had known at once it was her mother's clothing. The woollen cloak, the heavy dress and the petticoats which had dragged Millicent Leigh down to the bottom of the river, the poor little dog clutched in her arms.

That afternoon, another policeman, one who didn't wear a uniform, had gone into her father's study and spent a long time there. After his departure, the maid had been summoned to the study but for a much shorter time. She left the next morning and did not return. Isobel's father told her that the girl had gossiped about the family's private business and caused all sorts of bother. The last thing that was needed on top of their grief. Unforgiveable, he said. A viper in their bosom.

But the maid was not the only one to overhear the turbulence that rocked Professor Leigh's respectable house just days before his wife's tragic accident. When Isobel had come in from the convent school, the drawing room door was open by a sliver. It seemed her mother had come home early and now her parents were arguing. They never argued; they would have thought it vulgar. The familiar hat on the hatstand meant that Uncle Giles must be there too, as he often was, especially on those days when her mother was rehearsing for some concert and Isobel was imprisoned in her classroom. Not a real uncle, just her father's best friend from their Oxford days. He always brought her some little present, of sweetmeats or of ribbons for her hair. And he was so handsome that she was quite in love with him, though she'd have died if anyone had known of it. How awful that Uncle Giles should hear.

The rules of acceptable behaviour for a young lady, which her father handed down in tablets of stone, had not included listening outside doors. But now, she hid herself in the shadow of the great grandfather clock and did just that. That there was an earthquake happening in this sylvan avenue in Kew was not to be doubted. Right beneath her feet, beneath the foundations of everything she knew and understood. And she had to know why.

Yet what was being said, and the fury with which it was expressed, seemed quite out of kilter. Her parents seemed to be arguing about the summerhouse. At the furthest end of their large garden, tucked away behind a wall of hydrangeas. Isobel heard her mother shouting that the summerhouse be torn down, wiped off the face of the earth. Her mother would never enter it again. Her father was shouting back, though less loudly, an echo of conciliation in the voice. From Uncle Giles, there wasn't a sound.

Though her heart was pounding, Isobel grew bold and slipped out of her hiding-place towards the sliver of open door. Inside the drawing room, three figures sat, each well separated from the other. Her mother had slumped onto a sofa, her little dog by her feet, curious and discomfited, its tail between its legs. Her father sat on the piano stool, his head in his hands. Furthest away, by the open French windows, Uncle Giles smoked a cigarette with the faintest of smiles on his lips.

Her father and Uncle Giles were both dressed in their tennis clothes. Though early October, it was still mild enough to play on their court. Yet it was the convention that tennis dress should not be worn indoors; the summerhouse was to be used as a changing room. How odd, Isobel thought. Had something interrupted their game?

And then Millicent Leigh stood up, her back ramrod-straight again as it usually was. Quietly now, she told Uncle Giles to leave her house and never to return. He had simply smiled, tossed his cigarette into the fireplace and headed for the door. Isobel darted back into the shadow of the grandfather clock, but he had spotted her.

'Bye bye, poppet,' he said and blew her a kiss.

Inside the drawing room, the silence which had fallen did not last long. The words the professor's wife normally spoke – those that articulated intelligence, gentility and restraint – were quite gone. In their place, she spat words of condemnation and revulsion, which her daughter did not understand and over which restraint seemed to hold no sway. The voice of her father, by contrast, seemed weak and broken, weighed down with desperation and pleading.

Suddenly, the door was thrown wide, crashing against the lintel. Seeing Isobel shrunk back against the wall, Mrs Leigh stopped and stared, as if the child was some stranger. In her mother's eyes was wildness and fear.

'Millicent! Millicent!' came the voice from behind her.

Gathering up her skirts, the professor's wife ran across the hall and up the staircase, the little dog barking as it scampered in her wake. A door slammed somewhere above.

Now it was her father standing in the doorway of the drawing room. He seemed smaller than he had that morning when she'd left for school, half leaning against the doorframe as if intoxicated. Isobel took a few paces towards him.

'What is the matter, Papa? What is wrong with Mama? Is she ill? Have you lost all your money?'

Her father looked at her and did not reply. He went back into the room and closed the door. It was the first time he had ever turned away from her and, when he did so, a fragment of Isobel Leigh was lost and would never be regained.

For three days, the maid took a tray up to Mrs Leigh's room, though it was reported that precious little was eaten. Her mother was indisposed, her father said. Nothing serious; no doctor need be called. Just some fatigue caused by too many concerts. A few days rest and she'd be fine. No need for Isobel to worry, but best not to disturb her. But Isobel did worry and so she was glad when, on the fourth afternoon, she returned from school to be told that the mistress had risen and dressed that morning, though she still didn't leave her room. For two hours or more, she had played her cello. The same piece over and over again, the maid reported, as if she couldn't get it quite right. Then Mrs Leigh had come downstairs and said she would take the dog for a walk along the river. That'd do her the power of good, the maid thought. And Isobel had smiled and agreed.

It was to be two long days and three sleepless nights, before the doorbell rang in the respectable house in Kew. Isobel rushed to answer it herself. The expressions on the faces were enough. She walked backwards away from the door, every step a retreat into herself. To a place of greater safety.

30

On the first Sunday after Isobel's visit to Pitt Street, Frank Brodie went as usual to Halcyon Hill, but Lady Farrar was not at home. She'd left a note to say she had gone to an impromptu birthday celebration for Lord Marchwood at his house across the little river. So sorry. Letty would of course provide his luncheon and anything else he might need. She hoped, Isobel wrote, that he would have a productive day in the garden. On the Sunday after that, another note said that she had needed to go up to town unexpectedly. So sorry. She hoped, she wrote, that all was coming along well in the garden.

On that second Sunday, he told Letty not to bother laying the table in the dining room. He'd be happy to sit in the kitchen with a bit of bread and cheese. No, honestly, that'd do him fine.

'I hope she's all right,' he said to Letty as she poured out two bowls of soup to cheer up the bread and cheddar.

'As far as I can tell. She's not that easy to know. Just like you.'

'Why's she gone into London?'

'To see Miss Maud, I think.'

He was glad that Letty had made that comment. It gave him his excuse. He didn't find Isobel Farrar easy to know, but then he didn't find anyone easy to know. That was why he stuck with plants rather than people. He tended to cope a bit better with the simple, cheery, outgoing sort, since they'd usually come towards him rather than the other way around. The sort who wore their hearts on their sleeve like Letty Blount, not wreathed in shadows as Isobel did. As he did too. But then, how could she not be like that? A woman who'd once given away her child.

Whenever he came to Halcyon Hill, Frank felt most at ease in the kitchen. He felt easy too with Letty Blount. The dog she sometimes brought with her from the farm, which had once scared him away, had become his best friend. It sat now at his knee, hoping for a bit of cheddar.

'Can I ask you something?' said Frank. 'A bit cheeky, I suppose.'

'You can ask.'

'Does that hurt?' he said, pointing to the scar.

'A dull ache, when I'm tired. That's all.'

'Good,' he said. 'I'm glad.'

'I only got what I deserved,' said Letty.

'What?'

'Back then, all I wanted to do was kill,' she replied. 'Kill Germans. My fiancé had died at the Somme. It was all I could think about. I left the farm and went to work up at Silvertown so that I could help make the bullets and the bayonets that might kill the bastard who'd killed him. Then the whole bloody place blew up and I got this.'

'But why on earth did you deserve it?'

'Because God knew what I was doing and taught me a lesson. He didn't let me die, but He left me with a reminder of what I'd become every time I looked in the mirror. All eaten up, full of pity for what had happened to me, when millions of other women had suffered the same fate but had faced it with more Christian charity than I'd been able to muster.'

'I don't think anyone would blame you for how you felt,' replied Frank.

'It doesn't matter what other folk think,' she said. 'It's how you live with yourself. Once you've become somebody less than the person you'd hoped you were.'

Letty went to the sink and filled the kettle to make some tea.

'You reach a point, Frank, when no matter what huge pile of dung has been dumped on you, you have to climb out of it and walk on,' she said. 'If you can't manage that, you'll be buried in it for the rest of your days. Now, that German soldier? I wish him well.'

When the pot was filled, she brought it to the big oak table and left it to brew. From the larder came a plate of rock cakes, a pat of butter, a dish of jam. As Frank buttered one, he caught Letty gazing at him, her elbows on the table, her chin resting on her hands.

'Why are you staring?'

'I'm just wondering what your pile of dung is,' she said.

'No doubt she's told you something.'

'The bare bones, no more. That things didn't go well for you.'

Frank looked across at her, the low spring sun reaching through the window and melting into the thick wavy hair, tied back with a ribbon. Scar or not, she was still pretty; not in a porcelain way but pretty in her strength of character. He realised that he felt safe with this girl as he had with poor Dora all those years ago. He examined the feeling and asked himself why it should be there. Yet he was aware that there was something more to it than that, as there had been with Dora. Those sorts of feelings, the ones his fellows in the shop or back in the trenches had joked about, been coarse about and seemed to find so uncomplicated, had never been so with him. With Frank Brodie, the confusion of who he was led in more than one direction.

So he found himself telling Letty Blount about life above the butcher's shop and, for once, words came to Frank Brodie without struggle. The smell of the meat, the blood and the saw-dust, the racks of the cleavers and the hacksaws. He told her of the long windowless hallway leading to the sitting room where the butcher and his wife sat on those evenings when the man hadn't gone to the pub. He told her of the Sunday nights when he'd trembled as he tried to remember the passages of scripture the woman had set him to learn. And though, as he thought of it, the words stopped coming with ease and his throat tightened, he told her too of the cold chamber. Of the darkness, the pain, the shadowy shapes of the carcasses hanging from the hooks.

When he stopped speaking and lit a cigarette, Letty too was silent for a while.

'That's a lot of dung,' she said at last. 'Tough to climb out of.'

'I've tried,' he said. 'Honest.'

'Where are they now?' she asked.

'They sold the shop and retired to Scotland. I'd just turned sixteen. I'd have to fend for myself now, they said. They'd done their bit. She's dead now, but he's still half-alive the last I knew. I send a card at Christmas. God knows why.'

'And how *did* you fend for yourself? Where did you go?'

'I lived in lodging houses, in a hostel sometimes. You don't want to meet the fleas in a hostel, you really don't,' he said. 'They're a breed on their own. Indestructible.'

He laughed, but Letty Blount did not.

'I did odd jobs. Labouring and the like. I even worked in a butcher's once. I knew the trade after all. But I couldn't stick that. Couldn't stick that at all. Christ, no.'

Into his mind now came flashes of the other things he'd had to do. But he'd never tell her of that. He'd never tell anyone. Only Arthur knew. Only Arthur understood.

'But you've survived,' said Letty, feeding crumbs of rock cake to the dog. 'Just like I have. I survived Silvertown and I survived what happened inside of me. People look at me and think, poor Letty Blount. She was pretty once, but she'll never get a man now. On the shelf forever. But they know nothing. Nothing. I'm proud of my scar now, Frank. Honest to God I am. Because every day, I rise above it. The scar is my strength.'

He looked at her through the wisps of smoke, then put the smouldering cigarette into his saucer. He unbuttoned his shirt cuffs, rolled up his shirtsleeves and stretched out his arms across the rock cakes. The gouges where the hairy string had been tied around his wrists. He always marvelled at how livid they still were.

Letty reached across the table and took his hand in hers.

'Never hide them, Frank,' she said. 'Never be ashamed. Look at them without flinching. Because right underneath, your pulse still beats strong.'

The two of them sat for a moment as the clock ticked on the kitchen wall and the dog licked the last crumbs from its grubby paws. Only with reluctance did he let go of her hand.

'I'd best be getting back outside,' he said. 'Jed Simmons is coming at two.'

They rose from the table. She walked with him out of the back door and round to the terrace. The wash of daffodils he'd planted in the long bed below were in full bloom, their blossoms quivering in the languid breeze rolling up from the downs.

'A southerly wind,' he said. 'Can you smell spring in the air, Letty?'

Big, cheery Jed Simmons had emerged from the coppice and was waving up to them. Letty turned back towards the kitchen, but Frank grasped her arm.

'Do you really wish him well, Letty? That German?'

'Yes,' she replied, looking hard into his eyes. 'Can you do the same for the butcher and his wife?'

'I don't know,' he said. 'I don't think so.'

'Try it. Go on. Right now. Before Jed Simmons reaches us. Say it to me. Say it to the spring air. Or just say it to yourself.'

'What do I say?'

'Anything really. The exact words don't matter, as long as they are free of hatred and of anger. Try saying that you wish the Brodies well, dead or alive. That you let them go.'

Frank took a step back from her.

'I can't, Letty,' he said. 'I can't make myself feel it.'

'That's all right,' she said. 'Keep on trying and one day you will. I promise you that.'

A stronger gust of warm wind came up from the south and rippled across the long bed of daffodils. The crowd of startled yellow heads turned this way and that.

'It's hard,' he said. 'Too hard for me, maybe. I'm not made of strong stuff the way you are.'

'It's not that hard, really,' she said. 'If you decide to look it in the eye, the fear of it will get less. Stare it out. Every time it passes through your head, stare it out even longer until it blinks and looks away from you. Then you've won. Then it can't touch you ever again.'

31

From the farthest reaches of the rambling old apartment, Isobel heard the soft closing of a door. Having served luncheon without a word, the housekeeper had slipped back into the shadows. A strange creature. Tall, thin, Greek, dressed all in black. A refugee from some war or other. One of Miss Maud Farrar's 'waifs and strays'. But the woman was gone now and they would not be overheard.

Isobel had rarely entered Maud's private world. Through the years, it had been their habit to meet in a restaurant, at a concert or in the bookshop, where tea would be taken in the chaotic office at the back. Yet the little woman's domestic setting seemed no more organised. What cleaning or tidying the Greek housekeeper might do was scarcely apparent to the casual eye. In the big drawing room, books, periodicals and unopened letters spilled over little tables like milk frothing from a pan. Behind a hearth dusty with unswept ashes, a fire couldn't make up its mind between smouldering ineffectively or suddenly roaring up like Vesuvius, belching smoke across the coffee tray. Between the two tall windows, a cage of Chinese bamboo housed two canaries the colour of a sunset, its door left open for them to fly free and perch wherever inclined. Often on Maud's shoulder or even atop her shingled hair like some flamboyant decoration.

'I've never told anyone that before,' said Isobel, after she'd said what she had come to say. 'I'm sorry to burden you.'

'It's no burden to me, dear,' Maud replied, 'but it clearly is to you.'

Isobel had just finished perambulating the room, seeming to examine the pictures on the wall, some of which were by Octavius. It was a way of not looking Maud in the face. For nearly a quarter hour, as she circled the sofas and the little tables, she had been talking. Talking quickly, which was not like her at all.

She reminded Maud that her mother had drowned in the river near Richmond. Yes, said Maud, she remembered that fact. So dreadful for a poor little girl. But now, for the first time, Isobel had spoken of the terrible argument a few days before and the look on her mother's face as she had run from the room, the little dog behind her. She told of the glimpse of her father with his head in his hands. And two days later, of the ring on the bell. The policeman in the study. The bags of clothes, still damp, reeking of the pungent river. And, finally, out of sequence, she spoke of Uncle Giles as he had passed her in the hall that afternoon never to be seen again. That trace of a smile on his lips.

'You understand what it is that I'm suggesting?' asked Isobel, her back still turned, looking out of the tall window at children playing in the small park opposite.

'Of course, dear,' replied Maud. 'I've moved in artistic circles all my life. Now, do come and have some coffee.'

Maud poured the coffee, with her usual imprecision, into tiny Dresden cups. From the distant vaults of memory, Isobel recognised them as once belonging to one of the old Farrar aunts and was surprised that they had so far survived their new owner. Now Maud leaned back in her chair and contemplated her unexpected visitor. Isobel had telephoned only late the night before and asked if she might come up today. Most odd.

'It was somehow the start of everything going wrong, do you see?' Isobel said. 'The beginning of the road that led me to...'

'To marry Edwin Reed?'

Isobel closed her eyes against the power of the imagery. The wedding dress. The church. The certainty in her gut that she was walking down the aisle to calamity.

'Quite so.'

'But why are you telling me now?'

Unable to sit still, Isobel crossed again to the window and looked out at the children on the roundabouts and the dogs chasing their tails. Then she took a deep breath and spoke of being in a different house, one far less grand than that of Professor Leigh of Kew. The house in Hammersmith where, two Sundays ago, she had had a pleasant time, played the harmonium and where, standing in the doorway of a tiny kitchen, had seen what she had not been meant to see.

'For God's sake, Isobel, come and sit down,' Maud said, pouring out more coffee and offering a plate of fancies. 'Have one of these. Maria's an absolute wizard at the stove. I should be twenty stone by now, but luckily I burn it off.'

Isobel took one, scooped a corner of it onto a cake fork, then laid it aside. Maud sighed.

'I *quite* see that it's difficult for you,' she said. 'I quite understand that. The issue coming back into your life in this way.'

'What shall I do?' asked Isobel.

'Do, dear? What can you possibly *do*?' asked Maud.

Isobel stared at her, suddenly aware that she had come here today expecting a solution. Practical and down to earth, just as Alice Godsal had been, Maud usually had an answer for everything. Why should this be any different?

'You could walk away,' said Maud, answering her own question. 'Reject him for the second time in his life. Is that what you want?'

'Dear God, no.'

Isobel began to shake violently. She tried to put the Dresden cup down on the side table, but missed the place and it was to be Isobel who broke the first of old Aunt Clara's heirlooms.

Maud crossed the carpet and, ignoring the broken cup and the dregs on the rug, knelt down and took Isobel's hands in hers.

'Then you quietly accept it and go on as before. Never mention it unless he does, which I imagine he won't, bearing in mind the way the world is.'

'Oh, Maud, why did it have to be *this*? Anything but this.'

Maud dropped Isobel's hands and sat back on her haunches on the rug. Suddenly, the empathy had faded from her face. Now the Farrar jaw stuck out.

'I don't seem to recall that when you were offered love, you hesitated for a moment before grabbing it with both hands. You didn't give a damn about what the world thought. You, the respectable married woman, the rich man's wife with a house in Pelham Crescent. You hardly even tried to hide it, I believe. Octavius spoke of it to me once, just before he married you. *Le Scandale*, as he called it. Passion swept all before it. So, if you now regard your son as beyond the pale, then maybe it's in his blood.'

'Maud, Maud, oh, please don't.'

'What a damn hypocrite you are,' said Maud. 'The scarlet woman now climbing into a pulpit.'

Now it was Maud who stood up and paced around the room. Now it was Maud who kept her back turned, her shoulders heaving.

'If Frank had been my boy, I would have kept him. I would have found a way.'

'But Maud, you would have had money. I had almost none. I had no choice but to give him up. For the chance of a better life.'

'From what you've told me, you sent him into misery.'

'Do you imagine I don't think of that every night as I try to sleep?'

Maud spun round from the windows and gripped the back of a chair, made of bamboo like the canary cage.

'Then what right do you, of all people, have to make a judgement about where the child you abandoned finally turned for love?'

Isobel could make no answer. Maud's breath came hard and fast. Blood had appeared on her knuckles where her fingers had cut into the chair.

'I ask you again, Isobel, what right do you have to make a judgement?'

The canaries had flown down onto the side table beside Isobel, to investigate the half-eaten fancy. But their interest turned to her instead, their heads cocked to one side, waiting for her answer too. But none came.

Maud noticed the blood on her fingers and bound them with her handkerchief.

'You once made a dreadful mistake, Isobel, which has marked you forever. Don't make another one now,' said Maud, colder than Isobel had ever seen her. 'Because, if you do, and if Frank Brodie is half the man I think he is, he would simply turn and walk away from you. I would applaud him for it and he would always be welcome in my house.'

And a little memory came to Isobel now. Long buried, long forgotten in its insignificance. Yet now, she realised, not insignificant at all. On Hampstead Heath, walking with Hugh. The two young men coming towards them, their heads close together, as much lost in each other as she and Hugh had been in that same moment.

'Nothing that is human disgusts me as long as it is loving,' he had said. And as the canaries, their interest in her gone, took off to some far corner of the drawing room, a shame enveloped Isobel Farrar.

Maud crossed to the door and called out. From somewhere in the gloom of the long corridor, the housekeeper came. At the sight of the bloodied fingers, the woman began to fuss until she was shushed into silence. Then Maud took her by her other hand and steered her towards the middle of the room. The housekeeper looked frightened and tried to pull back but Maud, though much the smaller, was the stronger too. Their hands still joined, the pair stood before Isobel.

'In case you don't remember,' said Maud, 'this lady's name is Maria. She is the reason I live.'

32

At the same time as Isobel was taking luncheon with Miss Maud and as Frank sat with Letty at the kitchen table, Arthur Collins still lay in bed. The same bed, once occupied by his mother, in which he had been born and in which he expected, quite soon, to die. He'd always like the symmetry of that idea, the romance of it. He'd even wondered if it might make a sentimental ballad, but he'd never got around to writing it and now he never would. Besides, sentimental ballads were out of fashion, unless you were Al Jolson, a singer in whom Arthur found no musicality or grace. The Jazz Age, Arthur had long ago decided, was not for him. The parade, he knew, had passed him by and, after a long struggle, he had at last made peace with that.

It was a big bed, a monster in mahogany, too large really for the front bedroom of 74 Pitt Street. In childhood, it had seemed vast when he'd sneaked into it to snuggle up to his mother. Naturally, when he'd grown up and, in time, inherited the bed, it had somehow shrunk to a perfectly reasonable size. So it was odd that, once again, it appeared to have expanded into a chilly wasteland of sheet, blanket and quilt. Hefty as he still was, Arthur decided he must have diminished a little.

Perhaps it was the pain. It'd been worse again this past week. He'd been putting off going back to the doctor, but he'd really need to go in tomorrow. The booze, origin of the ailment, was no longer also its best treatment. Something more was needed now. Something that would help him conceal things from Frank. He didn't want Frank worried. He'd spent seventeen years trying to bring calm to Frank Brodie. He wasn't going to stop now.

As Arthur lay there, the midday light sneaking in through a crack in the curtains, the loneliness he felt in the big bed came over him again. He remembered lying here the night Frank had come back from the war, waiting for the soft knock on the door and for the warmth and pleasure which the knock would bring. Just like it'd been in those few years after Frank had first come to tea in Pitt Street and had then become the new lodger. How close Arthur had come to walking past the waif under the arches – the beautiful face pinched with cold and the desolation of the life he led. That reflection still made Arthur shudder. But he hadn't walked past and from the impulse to stop for a moment, such joy had come.

In those early years, it'd been a while until the very first knock had come to Arthur's bedroom door. He'd never been sure what had prompted it on that particular night, though the boy had been unusually silent at supper, even for him. The boy's eyes had been fixed on his plate, but Arthur had sensed they saw nothing of it. Frank had been somewhere else entirely. In those dark places beyond a curtain which was always drawn. But perhaps that night, those places had been even darker than usual. And so, the knock had come to Arthur's bedroom door. And pleasure was both given and taken. In his sleep, the boy had wept on Arthur's chest, then woken to an awareness of it. He'd made to turn away, but Arthur had held him fast and stroked his head until he slept again. And so, pleasure became entwined with comfort and, over time, the latter had gained dominance over the former.

But the knock hadn't come on the night he got back from the war. Frank must be exhausted, Arthur had decided. There were so many stories of the men returning, damaged and even shattered, like puppets lying crumpled amidst broken strings. He must be patient, he told himself, and he was. But on the second night, the knock still didn't come. Nor on the third, nor the fifth, nor the tenth. And Arthur knew then that it would never come again and that things would not be the same as they had once been.

It would not be true to say that Arthur hadn't minded the loss of that. But he had accepted it, grateful for the quick hugs by the kitchen sink, the peck on the cheek before they went to their separate rooms. More grateful still for the presence, however silent, of someone else by the parlour fire listening to the wireless, someone who boiled his morning eggs exactly as he liked them and who cared if he went out without his scarf on a cold day. He had never hoped to find such a thing and could never believe his luck. So many times he had searched for it, but the bars of the Alhambra or the Empire, the conveniences of the railway stations, the pathways of the parks at dusk had never yielded it. Distraction yes, but comfort never. How amazing, then, that it had finally come to him from the most notorious place of all – the lurid rack of temptation under the arches.

From outside in the street, Arthur heard the children playing as he'd once done on the very same spot. But now they kicked footballs where he'd only had marbles made of clay and a stick to propel a wooden hoop along the pavement. Nor had his mother ever allowed him to play outside on the Sabbath. Such things had changed now, of course. Everything had changed since the war. A new sloppiness he couldn't abide. Ways of thinking he couldn't understand. Old certainties gone. A nervousness in the air which had not been there in the days of his youth. Of the ground shifting under the feet, the ground beneath which lay twenty million dead.

From the big bed, beckoning to him from a more confident age, he could see the photograph of his heroine. It was she who'd told him in the wings one night that, with a voice like his, he could've made it to the stage of Covent Garden. She'd been a bit drunk, as she often was, but he'd seen that she meant it. He'd kissed her on an impulse, which he shouldn't have done since he was near the bottom of the bill that night, hardly fit to kiss the feet of Marie Lloyd, let alone her cheek. He'd had tears in his eyes then and that had brought them to hers. *We poor folk*, she'd whispered, *must just do the best we can. That's the way of it, love. Always has been, always will be. Come and have a gin in my dressing room after the show.*

But all the disappointments of his life, the ones that had led him into a world of too many gins, had been made bearable by the gift that had come to him from under the arches on that night when he'd felt at his most hopeless and seen that hopelessness reflected in the eyes of a young stranger. They had rescued each other, swum towards the raft of each other's affection and clung to it through thick and thin.

Arthur told himself he really must get up now. He'd take a bath, have a shave, make himself look as nice as he could. He didn't want Frank coming back to find him looking like something the cat dragged in. He didn't see that much of Frank these days. Sometimes, in the shimmering shop, he'd find an excuse to go down to the ironmongery, perhaps on the pretext of a word with his old mate Wilf Jones. If Frank was serving a customer, Arthur would only get a quick nod and half a smile. If he wasn't occupied, they'd ask each other how the day was going, then agree that, oh well, we'd better be getting on. But it was something.

Arthur swung his legs onto the floor but sat there until he could face the rest of the effort. He reminded himself sharply that this was what he'd wanted; even planned and schemed for. Frank at Halcyon Hill. Restored to the woman who had delivered him into this world and, however indirect the path, into Arthur's too. Arthur had had him now for seventeen years and now he must be handed back. It was that simple really. The last stanza of another sentimental ballad, the one about the mother and son, lost and found again. A real tear-jerker. And far superior to the one Al Jolson now croaked out on the same subject.

When she'd come to luncheon, Lady Farrar had invited Arthur to visit Halcyon Hill. He was always welcome, she'd said. He'd replied with the appropriate words, but knew he never would. It was a place he preferred to imagine rather than to see. Listening by the parlour fire to Frank's intoxicated descriptions, Arthur had mythologised it in his mind. A little Camelot perched on its low hill, the summer sun glancing off the roof. And Frank in that bloody garden he never stopped going on about. Yet Arthur never pictured Frank digging the soil or mowing the grass or cutting the hedge with his collar off and sweat patches in his armpits. Instead, he would be sitting in a wicker chair under a tree, in shirt and trousers of white linen, his beautiful mother beside him, a parasol in her lilac-gloved hand. There would be a wicker table with a jug of chilled lemonade and two thin crystal glasses. The mistress of the house and her son, looking out across the fields towards the downs.

That was all Arthur wished for. But he knew it had to remain in his imagination where he could control it. To see it in reality might be too much. The last stanza of that sentimental song. The tear-jerker. The tears being Arthur's own.

In 74 Pitt Street he had been born, and here he would stay. All he prayed for now was that Frank would not abandon him entirely. Not just yet anyway. He didn't want to die alone. He knew quite well his prayer was plain silly, that Frank would never do such a thing. Yet still the thought of it haunted him. The fear of the dark at the top of the stairs.

There was a dull thump against the outside wall of the house. Bloody kids and their footballs. They could have broken the window. He'd give them a piece of his mind. But as he stood up to do so, the pain grabbed him in the guts, the worst yet, and he fell back onto the big bed. For a few minutes he lay there winded, then rose carefully again and shuffled to the wardrobe where the secret gin bottle that wasn't a secret still hid behind the socks and cufflinks. Maybe a few nips would ease the worst.

Arthur Collins sat down at the little escritoire and stared at Marie Lloyd. Covent Garden, she'd said. A voice good enough, she'd said. He drank some gin. It had been poor old Marie's ruin in the end, and he accepted that it had been his too. What fools we are, he said aloud to the walls of the room. Yet he knew he'd not been a fool about Frank Brodie. He'd got it dead right there. Ten out of ten, Arthur. When the cold, pinched face under the arches had stared up at him, he had felt a great surging of the heart and had never, not for a single second, regretted it.

33

That damn rabbit hole. He'd meant to fill it in, but it had slipped his mind. He sat on the grass, cursing and rubbing his ankle. Already he felt it tightening. In a few hours, it'd be the size of a grapefruit.

After lunch in the kitchen with Letty, the things she'd said fluttered around his mind. He knew she'd spoken the truth, because Letty Blount never spoke anything else. He would look his life in the eye, instead of averting his gaze from it as he'd usually done. He'd stare it down until it blinked and looked away. At least he'd try. Your scars are your strength, she'd said.

With that vow made, his afternoon's work had gone well. There were small flushes of warmth in the air now, as March rushed into April as fast as it could get there. The plants that he'd spared in his great cull, just cutting them back, were already in bud or even, like the old camellias, already past their full glory. The scrubby patches of lawn that he'd re-seeded and roped off with twine now sported the first fuzz of fresh green against the dull brown of the earth. As he made his way round the gardens, he'd been aware of the smile on his face. In the winter sleep, the miracle had indeed taken place. Of course it had. Why should it not? Why had he, absurdly, doubted it? Or ever doubted that he, Frank Brodie from Pitt Street, could help it along its path? The fear that had come over him when Isobel had first suggested he should come to the garden, seemed daft now. Nature had not been offended by his untutored care. It had not rebelled, told him to know his place and refused to do his bidding. On that barren winter's day, Isobel had been right. His love of the thing had been enough.

But that was hubris. Pride before the rabbit hole. He was alone in the garden today as the rough help of Jed Simmons was needed less frequently. He'd liked Jed well enough but was far happier alone. The only intrusions he welcomed were those of Isobel coming out to see how he was getting on or when Letty brought fat mugs of tea. Then he'd have the chance to point out some little thing he'd achieved, or a new idea for improvement that had come to him in the night or at the counter of the ironmongery. The smallest compliment from either woman, the briefest smile of pleasure, would be squirrelled away inside his head against the tedium of the week to come until, the next Sunday, he could return.

Now, sitting on the damp spring ground, the pain worsening, he called out for Letty, but she didn't hear. But the dog came and crouched by his side, barking, until Letty bustled out. A curse escaped him, as she put her arm under him and got him to his feet. He blushed and apologised.

'Lordy, you'll have to do better than that to shock a farmer's daughter,' she said.

So, as they hobbled back towards the house, he cursed again, only better this time. Then, under the weight of him, she did too. They competed to find foul adjectives to describe the rabbit hole.

'This is shameful,' he gasped, between the pulses of pain running up into his calf. 'Talking to a lady like this. What am I thinking of?'

'What lady's that, then?' She laughed. 'I don't see one anywhere.'

'I do,' he replied.

And he caught her eye. And she stopped laughing as she saw that he meant it.

Letty decanted him into an armchair in the covered court. He'd not be going home tonight, she announced. Not a chance of it. She'd telephone for old Doctor Palmer first thing in the morning. Since Frank would never manage the stairs, she'd make up the divan in Sir Octavius's old studio. Easy as pie. Then she'd find something to strap up the ankle. Lady Farrar would surely be back soon.

All these things were done. Aspirin was given and a cup of warm milk. She'd be in the kitchen with the door open. He only had to shout. The dog came and flopped down on the rug beside the divan. After a while, the pain eased a little and the milk calmed him. Through the uncurtained window, he could see dusk creeping over the stables. The clock struck six. It had been repaired now, so that time no longer stood still at Halcyon Hill. Frank knew that he was part of that change and rejoiced in it.

But where was Isobel? For two Sundays now, she'd not been here when he came. It had niggled at him during the day as he sold the hammers and the nails. Both he and Arthur felt the visit to Pitt Street had gone well, though he remembered that she'd seemed a little distracted when she'd climbed into her taxi. Had he done something without meaning to? Said something wrong? He'd searched his memory but could think of nothing.

He'd looked forward to seeing her today of all days, because he had brought something for her. Something she had lent him, asking for its return when he wished to do that.

On the rug, Letty's dog began to snore and have dreams, the furry legs twitching and flailing. Was it running through the cornfield on a summer day? Chasing the rabbits? Especially the sod whose hole had brought Frank to this pretty pass. Then he himself drifted off into that same landscape, strolling down across the lawns, past the pond where the iridescent dragonflies floated above the water, looking out across the rippling sea of corn husks towards the horizon. All the warmth of summer sequestered in his soul.

*

Afterwards, he'd wonder if Letty Blount had put some whisky into the milk. He wasn't used to whisky so maybe, with the aspirin, it'd knocked him out. He certainly never remembered sleeping so heavily as he had then, as that late afternoon gave way to evening. It must, he decided, have been the depth of the silence, like diving gently down into a fathomless sea.

In his little room in Pitt Street, whatever the hour, there was never total quiet. The noise of the underground railway, the warring Italians through the wall, the last of the drunks from the pub, the tossing and turning of the sleepless city. But maybe it wasn't the aspirin or the putative whisky. Maybe he was just tired. Maybe, he thought, he'd been tired for years, perhaps for always. Though he cycled up hill and down dale and scampered up the ladders in the ironmongery, he'd often been aware of a weariness inside him. One that had nothing to do with muscles and ligaments. One that no amount of rest had ever quite relieved.

Yet however profound the rest that came to him now, faint noises still reached him from way up there above the surface. The muffled opening and closing of doors. Fragments of whispered conversation. The chime of the stables clock – light, hesitant, as if wary of disturbance. Once, a narrow shard of light came into the old studio and fell across his quilt. Then it closed again, leaving behind the nebulous scent of a perfume. But these moments of half awareness vanished quickly as the silence reclaimed him and he eagerly surrendered.

And then the scream.

Frank had heard the screams of animals caught in traps. He'd heard the screams of his shattered fellows in the trenches. But he'd not heard a scream like that which now, in a single second, ripped him from sleep, every sense awakened, every nerve alerted. It was a scream that seemed to contain more than simple fear; there was disbelief in it, anger too, fury even.

His ankle forgotten, Frank was on his feet and hobbling out of the studio and into the covered court. For a few seconds, he was blinded by the brightness of the lamps, then he saw Isobel on a sofa, her body rigid as a frightened cat. A man was half on top of her, gripping her forearms to deflect her clenched fists. Her hair had come loose from its pins, spilling down her neck. There was a tear in the bodice of her dress. Her necklace had been broken and pearls lay scattered on the rug like the stones of a hailstorm. But it was her eyes that Frank would remember most, the pupils holding such terror that their rich dark brown had blanched almost to nothingness.

'Leave her be!' Frank shouted.

The man turned and Frank looked into the face of Lord Marchwood, his features puffy and flushed, the few remaining strands of pepper-grey hair sticking to the sweat on his forehead. Frank lunged for the man's shoulder, pulling him onto his feet. Then he punched him in the jaw, not once but twice. A tooth flew out and landed among the pearls on the rug. Lord Marchwood crashed into the side of the piano, setting the strings jingling, then crumpled to the ground.

'I'm so sorry. So sorry,' Lord Marchwood stammered. 'I'd thought we were alone.'

'And that would make it all right?' Frank said, his fists still raised even as his opponent lay flattened.

'Isobel, dear,' said Marchwood, the blood trickling from his mouth onto his starched evening shirt, 'my humblest apologies. I fear I misread the signals.'

'Signals? But I gave you none,' she croaked. 'None at all beyond my friendship.'

It was then that Frank saw it. The buttons on the man's trousers half undone. All the rage that existed in Frank Brodie, the rage he himself so hated, came flooding into him now. Putting his weight on his good ankle, he lifted his other foot just above those open buttons. He knew he would hurt himself too if he brought his foot down, but it would be worth it.

'Give me one good reason why I shouldn't,' said Frank, spitting out the words. 'Which do you fancy? A kick or a stomp?'

'Oh, dear boy, please don't, dear boy. I do entreat you. No harm done, after all.'

'No harm? Christ, look at her.'

Isobel still sat on the sofa, her body still rigid, her eyes still wide.

'Don't, Frank. I entreat you, too,' she said. 'That solves nothing. Let him go.'

He hauled Lord Marchwood to his feet, took him by the collar and propelled him towards the lobby. He found the coat and hat, threw them onto the floor and watched the man scramble for them.

'Now get out of my mother's house,' he said, 'and never come back to it.'

Lord Marchwood dabbed his bloody mouth with a handkerchief. In the open doorway, he stopped for a moment and looked back at Frank.

'Guttersnipe,' he sneered, then was gone. The car roared away over the gravel towards the lane.

Frank hobbled back to Isobel. Now the rigidity had left her and a dreadful trembling had taken over. He sat beside her on the little sofa and wrapped her in his arms until the worst had subsided. But her body hadn't ended its responses. Tears came now, which all of Frank's gentle words could not staunch. For ten solid minutes, Isobel wept softly and did not speak.

'I thought he was going to...' she whispered at last, her head curled into his shoulder. 'That it was going to happen again.'

'What?'

'The thing that was done before,' she said so quietly he could hardly hear. 'The thing done to me. By the man who was your father.'

'I don't understand,' said Frank. He took her chin in his hand and turned her face up towards his own to make her look at him. But Isobel's eyes were closed. 'Make me understand.'

'When I was taken by him,' Isobel said. The closed eyes suddenly flew wide open and looked directly into those of her child, her eyes bearing the same disbelief he had heard in her scream. 'Against my will.'

'You mean...?' he asked, the actual word unnecessary.

'God abandoned me that night,' said Isobel. 'I thought He had done so again tonight.'

'I understand,' said Frank, stroking the tumbled hair as the gesture seemed to calm her.

'You don't,' she replied. 'You can't. No man can.'

Frank rose painfully from the sofa and hop-scotched to the piano stool. He swivelled it so that he was looking out of the big window. Though the rest of the garden was in darkness, a half-moon sent a weak beam right down onto the waters of the pond, creating the illusion that the house was a ship floating on a sea and thus might suddenly tilt beneath him and throw him off balance.

'That's not true,' he said, turning the stool round to face her again. 'This man can.'

Isobel looked back at him from the sofa. He could see that she was still disorientated, her mind not completely present in the room in which she sat. Suddenly, she slid down onto her knees and began to pick up the scattered pearls, then stopped and let the gathered handful fall back onto the rug.

'Frank,' she said, 'we must tell our stories now. Right now. It can wait no longer. I must tell you mine and you must tell me yours. There can be no sleep tonight until we do. Before the sun comes up tomorrow, we must both know what each needs to know about the other.'

Frank gave his sharp nod. He had decided the same thing less than a minute before.

Isobel helped him hobble back to the old studio. She would make a pot of tea, she said, and then they would talk.

Returned to the divan, he propped himself up against the pillows as best he could. He caught his reflection in a mirror, his hair untidy, his nails dirty, still in his collarless shirt and gardening trousers, one leg rolled up above the bandaged ankle. What a sight he looked, especially for a moment like this. But then, that hardly mattered. The elegant Lady Farrar was damaged too tonight, her hair untidy, her dress torn. And anyway, it was damage they must talk about, so such things didn't matter.

He lay still in the sanctuary of the old studio, waiting for her to return. He breathed as slowly as he could and tried to prepare himself, for what he would have to hear and for what he would have to say, wondering which would be the harder. The watch on his wrist said bang on ten and he realised that the stables clock hadn't chimed. It was still temperamental; he'd meant to rewind it this week. So now once more, time was standing still at Halcyon Hill. But tonight, Frank thought, that was perhaps as it should be.

34

Isobel put the tea-tray on a small table between the divan and Octavius's old rocking chair. In the depth of the spring night, she and her lost child faced each other across the teapot and the cups. The silence in the room so profound they could hear each other breathe. But silence which, for both of their lives, had been as addictive as laudanum, must now be ended.

Twin soliloquies.

*

She'd promised herself she would never return there. Not after the last time. The day a few months ago when she had, on misguided impulse, gone back to Pelham Crescent. After that, she'd vowed she would never go again, not even in her thoughts. That latter goal had, of course, been impossible. But now, tonight, she really must return. For Frank's sake, she must. Perhaps, she allowed herself to hope, going there this time with his hand in hers might break its malignant spell. So now, she turned her head and looked Pelham Crescent in the eye.

It had never occurred to her, she told Frank now, that she could ever marry for any reason other than love. Don't all young girls dream of that? Yet, in the event, she had not. A fact of which she had always been ashamed. Not that love was entirely absent from the equation. It was only fair to remember that. The man she'd married, the wealthy man, had indeed felt love for her. But she had been unable to return his love, she said, because she soon recognised that his love had been a curdled thing. Soured by the standards of the society in which he lived and in which he and most men of his clan believed. Soured by many corruptions of the soul but, above all, by the ferocity of the need for possession. It was not long before she realised that, like the wine in the cellar, the fine art on the walls, the certificates of stocks and shares locked away in his study, Edwin Reed saw her as entirely his possession. Her beauty, her charm, her accomplishments were secondary benefits. To him, the possession was all. A view with which his world heartily agreed. But that was the one thing it was not in Isobel Leigh's nature to allow.

A gradual chill had come over the house in the crescent. Dinners and luncheons were given for his friends and associates, his mother and aunts came to tea, they went to the theatre and the opera and to Mass on Sundays, but it was all a performance. She played it perfectly, but that was what it was. Because the chill had spread inside her too and she knew it. It had seeded long before, after the death of her mother and, aware of the change, she had been troubled by it and at first resisted it. But in the loss of her father and the perilous position in which she'd been left, it had taken firmer root. In the wasteland of her mistaken marriage, the evolution had been completed. The slow shutting-off of herself. The locking of the door. The mystery.

'And then, out of nowhere, I *did* feel love,' said Isobel now. 'But for someone else. And my husband knew of it. But I belonged to Edwin Reed. Every instinct of his being told him so and the law told him too. So it was not to be borne. Not to be borne, you see. And something had to be done.'

Isobel paused. She leaned back in the rocking chair and closed her eyes for a moment. Frank said nothing, though his eyes never left her.

She'd been asleep, she said, in the bedroom into which she'd moved once all pretence of harmony had been abandoned. She slept then with the light of a single candle, as she had when she was a child and afraid of the dark. She was always careful to lock her door but, exhausted that night, she had forgotten. She never heard the cautious turning of the door handle or the hinge that creaked a little. It was the smell of him that first nudged her back into consciousness; a mix of alcohol, cologne and sweat. When she woke properly, he was already on top of her, his hands tearing at her nightdress, her breasts half bared. The lower part of the nightdress was being pushed upwards, the rings on his frantic fingers grazing her thigh. When she resisted, he began to shout at her. That he was her husband, that it was his right and not a judge in the land would gainsay him. She had denied him for nearly a year now, though giving herself gladly to that damnable fellow, that scum. Well, enough. He would take no more of it. She was his wife. His. And nobody else should have her. Out in the crescent, some drunken young gentlemen were singing songs from *The Mikado*.

For half a minute, no more, she had tried to fight him off. Then, she told Frank, she had lain there without moving, still as a statue, until the business was over. It had not taken long, though every second had seemed interminable. His violence, all the more shocking because of the contrast with his usual icy calm, that frigid essence of his character and the reason she could never love him.

'*A wanderin' minstrel I, a thing of shreds and patches...*'

It had been Hugh Pasco's favourite tune. He'd never stopped singing it.

Panting like a dog, his brow soaked in sweat and the brilliantine off his hair, the man she had married climbed off her and stood looking down. For a moment, there had been a glaze of triumph in his wild eyes, but then it changed to something else. Certainty had faded and been replaced by something else. Regret? Fear? Maybe even his own awakening from some sort of sleep. Suddenly, he'd grabbed hold of the bedpost and clung to it, as if the floor was shifting beneath him. She had stared back up at him and spoken for the only time.

'I loathe you, Edwin,' she'd whispered. 'I loathe you.'

He had let go of the bedpost, backed away from the carnage of the bed and stumbled from the room. For a while, Isobel had lain there staring up at the unlit chandelier. She began to count the small pendants of glass. There were sixty-eight. Eventually, she hauled herself up from the soiled sheets and went to sit at the mirror, at first unable to look at her reflection. The golden hair was spewed out across her naked shoulders, its matted tendrils like a curtain half-drawn across her face. Her bottom lip was swelling up where she'd bitten it to quench the pain. She saw the imprints of his fingers around her neck, when he'd held her down and she'd thought she might choke. One of her breasts hung out of the ripped nightgown, the nipple sore, reddish weals already rising in protest.

And there was the other red, too; that which came from between her legs. She'd felt its warm wetness, seen the lurid streaks of it on the nightdress before she dared to look beneath the fabric at the havoc he had made there too, the very worst of it. Her flesh still reeked with the smell of him – the cologne, the sweat, the other odours. Lips, neck, breasts, cunt; he had wanted to leave his mark on every part of her. Evidence of entitlement. An entitlement which most God-fearing folk would have granted him, even if they might have averted their eyes at the claiming of it. The marriage contract written in blood.

She had sat looking into the mirror for an hour or more, looking hard into her eyes to see what was left of her, how much remained of the woman she had been before. She was still looking when the candle guttered, flared for a second and then blew out.

Nearly forty years ago, she said to Frank now. And only yesterday.

Frank lay against the pillows, his face pale and expressionless beneath the light of a lamp. She waited for the realisation to come to him and for the question which would follow, as surely it must. Or then again, might it not? Might he flee from both question and answer? Which would be worse, she wondered. The giving of the answer or the not giving? Isobel waited. She saw the realisation come, then heard the question.

'Yes, Frank. You are the result of that night.'

He said nothing, just giving his nod.

'That is my story,' she said.

*

'I just wanted him to like me,' Frank said. 'That was it, I think.'

From time to time, since he had come to work in the garden, Isobel had asked him about his life above the butcher's shop in Tufnell Park. But the answers he'd given had been brief and cautious, like an obstacle being placed across a road. *Go no further*, the sign said.

But now he would. That was the agreement they had made and must each respect. He described the shop and the cheerless flat above it and his own little room up in the attic. He talked of the rancid odours of the meat, the saws and the cleavers, the blood on the aprons and the chopping-board and coagulated on the sawdust. He spoke of the Scottish couple and of the first son who lay in the cemetery and with whom he could never compete.

He told her of the harshness of the woman who he'd wanted to call mother until he learned never to do so.

All of this he told Isobel without apparent emotion, with a kind of detachment as if he were speaking of someone else's life and not his own. Isobel listened from the rocking chair, her face as pale and impassive as Frank's had been as she had told her own tale. Wiped clean of judgement in the quest to understand. Yet her knuckles were white as they gripped the arms of the chair. And then he noticed a great shiver run through her body from head to toe.

'You're cold,' he said once again.

'Yes.'

The heat from the stove had faded and it had turned cool in the old studio. Isobel went and put more logs on the fire. For a minute, they sat in silence, watching the dying flames grasp at the wood and roar up into new life. Something in the image gave Frank the strength he needed to go on talking, to speak of the worst of it. Now, as he'd done with Letty Blount earlier that day, he unbuttoned the cuffs of his shirt and held out his wrists towards Isobel. The light from the stove flickered onto the scars, making them look almost alive, writhing like worms on his skin.

'What?' she asked. 'What is this?'

But now Frank's courage teetered a little. He drew his eyes from her, gazing instead out of the window, the curtains still not drawn. For weeks now, a barn owl had made its nest in the stables and, after dark, came out to sit for hours on top of the clock. From where he lay on the divan, Frank could just make out its round white face, a second moon against the blackness.

'Behind the butcher's shop, there was a room,' he said. 'It was called the cold chamber. It was the place where I was punished.'

As he already had to Arthur and then to Letty, he now described to Isobel the scene of his torment. How frightened he had been. The cruelty of the troubled, drunken woman he had wanted for a mother. Her rejection of his very existence.

Frank paused there, still looking out through the window into the night. Some cruelty now must come from him, though he had no desire to inflict it. But it had to be expressed and that was that.

'I'd been rejected by a mother once before, hadn't I? Twice seemed like lousy luck.'

He made himself turn his gaze to her now and wished that he had not. Isobel's face was no longer a blank. Her head was twisted away, her eyes screwed tight shut, her hand over her mouth. Frank yearned to stop, but there was more he had to inflict upon her and it was going to be even more cruel. A thing he had never told anyone before. Not even Arthur. Out in the night, the barn owl suddenly screeched and flew away.

'So I turned to him instead. The butcher,' he said. 'Wanting to be his son. And he was usually kinder than the woman. Or so it seemed at first. He talked to me about football and cricket. He showed me how to use the saws and the cleavers, though I didn't much fancy any of that. He drank just like she did, though nothing like as much.'

Frank paused again. He didn't know how to go on. Maybe, he thought, if he'd been better educated, the words he needed to find now would have come more easily. Yet find them he must. It had never mattered more.

'But he was certainly drunk the first time it happened. Tottenham Hotspur had won some big match and he'd been to the tavern with his mates. When he got back, she was out. On Saturdays, she arranged the flowers in the Scottish church for the Sunday service. I must have been about twelve.'

Frank felt himself grow restless on the divan. Under the quilt, his legs started to move outside his control, even the one that was swollen and painful. He wanted to be able to walk around the room or take himself into a corner or stand beside the open doorway in case he needed to run. But that was impossible. Instead, he did what Isobel had done a moment ago: twist his head away and screw his eyes shut. Yet he knew that was pointless; the images were there already. And so, he turned back and looked her straight in the face as he told her.

That first time, he had been hauled into the cold chamber, but on the Saturdays that followed, the footsteps would come on the stairs that led up to his room in the attic. It had lasted three years, he said, until he had grown strong enough to resist.

In Isobel's features, he saw no sign of comprehension at first. She looked at him almost blankly. He wondered what to do. Damn it. He had not found the words he needed. As she had done in her own telling, he might have spoken of the blood, the sweat, the odours, the bruises and the weals. But then, suddenly, the right words came to him without bidding.

'I'd thought it was a sign of affection, you see,' he said. 'That he liked me after all. That I might be his son.'

He saw the truth lance into her. And for the second time that evening, Isobel Farrar threw back her head and screamed. But this time, more than once. Again and again, until her voice cracked and collapsed into a frantic gulping for air. It seemed to Frank that he would always hear those screams. He saw her try to move towards him, but she couldn't do it, only managing to reach out a hand.

Frank dragged himself across the floor from the divan to the rocking chair. He put his arms around her trembling knees and his head against her lap.

'I've sat in front of a mirror, too,' he said, 'looking into my eyes and wondering what was left of me.'

He reached up and traced her cheek with his fingertips.

'And that is why I understand you.'

35

In the old studio at Halcyon Hill, there hung several of what Sir Octavius Farrar had called his 'not quites'. Those paintings where he considered that his abilities had failed him. Not good enough for sale nor even for display in the covered court. Yet, like a bitch with the runt of her litter, he often retained a fondness for these 'not quites'. Among them, his favourite had always been a small watercolour of Isobel herself, painted just before their marriage. He'd just not caught her, he always said. What a bloody amateur he was. He might as well just give up. And so he'd exiled it from most eyes except his own, staring at it and cursing his mediocrity.

But now, in the small hours of the morning, as Isobel and Frank sat by the flickering flames of the stove, her gaze fell upon it and she decided that Octavius had been wrong. He had indeed caught her all those years ago; only not as he'd wanted her to be, but as she had been in reality. Still living a suspended life, still marked by everything that had happened, before Octavius himself had coaxed her back to some kind of joy. Now the sight of the watercolour, of her own desolation, spurred her to go on talking and to somehow make her lost child understand.

She said that she would go and make yet more tea.

'But you're tired,' he said.

'And so are you,' she replied, 'but we're not finished yet, are we?'

'No,' he said.

'Then we shall go on until we are done.'

*

Now that the screaming was over, the silence in the old studio seemed almost deeper than before. Even the soft sipping of the tea seemed absurdly loud.

Inside Isobel now, the knowledge of the life to which she had condemned her child lay heavily in the pit of her stomach. Still not truly digested. Something to be vomited up, though of course that was impossible. Yet it made what she must say now even more important; her case must be pleaded with even more passion. She knew that doing so might kill the fragile shoots of what had been slowly growing between them. Yet so many times, she had witnessed his reluctance to rip up anything and throw it away as hopeless, and now she must rely on that mercy being extended to herself. She took a long breath.

'When I found out I was carrying his child, I was horrified. It meant he was still inside me, his defilement never ending. I longed for him to be gone, so I longed for *you* to be gone. Do you think you can understand that, Frank?'

'I want to.'

'I couldn't imagine ever loving the child of that night. And I didn't want to bear a child I couldn't love. That would have been some kind of obscenity, something against every natural feeling. At that time, Alice Godsal was my only friend in the world and such situations were not uncommon in her profession. It would be quite simple, Alice said.'

Isobel got up from the rocking chair and paced around the room, coming to rest in front of Octavius's watercolour.

'But it wasn't simple, Frank dear, not simple at all. It stopped being simple at the moment of your birth. It wasn't simple when I first held you in my arms, nor when I first fed you from my body. It was never simple after that.'

'But you still did it,' said the voice on the divan, almost in a whisper. 'You still sent me away.'

'Because I believed it was the best thing for you. The world, Frank. Cruel and unforgiving. The world as it was then, and still is, for a woman on her own.'

Again, Isobel began to pace the cage of the little room, turning this way and that, going in circles around the divan.

'Shall I tell you what it was like? The day Alice took you away? Shall I? Do you want to hear?'

Frank didn't answer, so she asked the question again, almost shouting it as if he hadn't heard.

'You'd been lying in my arms asleep when I fell asleep too. And when I woke again, you'd been taken. So quietly, so gently, that I'd never felt a thing. But shall I tell you what I felt then, Frank? Do you have the courage to listen?'

She was panting, groping for the air to let her get the words out.

'You were the child of Edwin Reed, the child of a rape. But when you were taken, I wanted to die. Do you hear that, Frank? It was like a leg or an arm being ripped off my body, an absence of such dimensions that could never be filled. I've heard old soldiers who've lost a limb say how it feels as if it's still there. A ghostly arm or leg that still hurts, the nerves still sending out shocks to remind you that it once existed, that it once lived and breathed. It's just the same with a child, Frank. The life that you have carried in your body, feeling its heartbeat inside yours, separate from your own yet wholly and achingly dependent on it. Mother and child are never divisible, even when they are divided.'

Frank tried to rise from the divan to reach her but fell back on the pillows. But Isobel had backed away from him anyway, still talking, not ready to stop, her arms wrapped tightly around her body, as if afraid that she might somehow come apart.

'In my lifetime, I have lost my father and my mother. I have lost the two men who I loved. But none of those separations brought me the unspeakable grief that consumed me when I lost you. The broken heart they write about in poetry and sing about in songs. Every day of your life, Frank, you have been loved by the woman who gave you birth. I promise you that.'

She was shaking now, holding on to the rocking chair for support. Frank saw her draw herself up to say the simple words, the ultimate words.

'I'm sorry, Frank,' she said. 'I am so sorry.'

Isobel sat down and stared into the flames. All she wanted in this world was to hear his voice in reply.

'I brought something for you when I came this morning,' he said at last. 'Could you go and get it? It's by my coat in the cloakroom. A little package in brown paper.'

'What is it?' she asked when she returned. 'It's not my birthday.'

Inside the wrapping paper was a buff envelope. Inside the envelope was a photograph.

'You asked me to return it one day.'

And now, in her child's eyes, Isobel finally saw what she had yearned to see. That he finally understood their loss had been equal. Measured on the scales, it had been balanced to within the weight of a feather.

*

Yet on that long night in the old studio, not quite everything had been told. Sometimes, for the sake of human happiness, there are things which must be brought into the light of day. When, as Letty Blount had said to Frank, you must imitate the action of the tiger, confront it until it slinks away with its tail between its legs. But there are others which, in pursuit of that same happiness, must be kept in dark places. The wisdom lies in deciding which is which.

So, Frank Brodie would never mention the arches at Piccadilly Circus or the churchyards, the parks and the Underground stations. Nor would Isobel ever tell of the black night on the Embankment. There could be little catharsis in such revelations, little liberation from the tainted past. Regret and merciful silence must be enough. And the forgiveness of the self.

Suddenly, the stable clock chimed again. Three clean, clear chimes. How odd, Frank thought. For a while on this spring night, the present had been suspended to let the past be revisited and exorcised. But now time could move on again, the path to the future straight and clear. To the ears of Isobel Farrar and her lost son, no carillon of cathedral bells could have sounded more glorious.

'You should go to bed, Mum,' he said – that word never used until now.

'I'll stay here, if that's all right,' she replied. 'In case there's something you need in the night. I'll be quite warm in this old coat.'

So, in another time and in another place, Isobel and her boy slept again in the same room and kept watch over one another. As dawn came and a hesitant sun sneaked into the old studio, Frank opened his eyes and saw his mother dozing there beside the last faint glow of the logs. Sunset and sunrise.

36

There was no telephone at 74 Pitt Street, so the call was made to Arthur at the shop first thing in the morning. Frank, who never fussed, made a fuss about this. Arthur would've been worried last night when Frank hadn't come home. Arthur wasn't too well these days, he told Isobel.

When the doctor came, it wasn't their usual Doctor Palmer from the village, comfy and reassuring as an old slipper. That elderly aesthete was sketching frescoes in Umbria. Instead, a youngish man arrived at Halcyon Hill, brisk and business-like, whose name she didn't catch and who gave the impression that he didn't have much time to spare.

It was one of those spring mornings which delivers an unexpected mildness bordering on warmth. Isobel carried a cup of coffee down to the old oak tree and sat on the new bench that Frank had set there. The fat laurel bushes were now cut back, clearing the view down to the little river. Someone was rowing a boat; yet their arms moved so languorously, it scarcely seemed to move at all.

A languor not dissimilar filled Isobel's own body. She was tired after her night in the rocking chair, but it was a kindly tiredness, that which comes after something has been achieved. She'd woken up often in what had remained of that night, checking that the quilt had not fallen off him and that he wasn't distressed by his ankle. But he seemed to sleep as heavily as he had when a babe in arms. In the last light from the stove, she'd watched his face intently, seeing again the little things she had always remembered. The small mole on his left cheekbone, the slightest tilt at the end of his nose. When the cock crowed, she had slipped out of the room, leaving him to sleep on in what she prayed was some kind of peace.

After a time, the brisk doctor appeared by her side. The ankle would be perfectly fine, he said, after a few days bandaged and supported. Best if the patient could remain with the leg up for at least a few days.

'Mr Brodie is your son, I understand,' he said as if he found it slightly surprising. 'The resemblance is striking, but...'

'But?' she replied, deciding that she didn't like him. Snobbish and arrogant. A face, plain as a pikestaff, devoid of character.

'No matter,' he said. 'Apart from the ankle, I gave Mr Brodie a quick once-over. Heart, blood pressure, that sort of thing. I also examined his glands and found something rather interesting. Very interesting in fact. Tell me, Lady Farrar, is your son hard of hearing?'

'A little, I think, though he denies it, as you men do with such things. The shelling in the war. Did he deny it to *you*?'

'Yes, but I observed the signs of it.'

'Why do you ask the question?'

'Because I found another symptom which, in conjunction with some loss of hearing, indicates the possibility of a certain condition. A very unusual condition, rarely seen.'

'What symptom?' asked Isobel, a flutter of alarm passing through her.

'One of his armpits is filled with small nodules. Little lumps.'

Isobel's gaze froze onto the man's face.

'It's a condition called neurofibromatosis,' said the doctor. 'As I say, extremely rare.'

'Is it serious?'

'Not really, but possibly troublesome in years to come if it develops. So, it'll need to be kept an eye on.'

Isobel put down her coffee cup on the little garden table beside the bench.

'How is this condition acquired?' she asked. 'Some infection?'

'No, it's genetic. Runs in the male line. Passed on from father to son. Did Mr Brodie's father have similar symptoms?'

'Dear God,' said Isobel. She stood up quickly and turned away.

'Lady Farrar?'

'You're quite sure of this, doctor? That it is only passed directly from father to son? Is it possible the father could show no symptoms yet still pass it on? The skipping of a generation, so to speak.'

'No, the father would always show the symptoms. The nodules in the armpit, the loss of hearing.'

'There can be no mistake in this?' Isobel spun round to face the man. She saw slight irritation now. The sort who did not like being questioned.

'Most doctors never see a case in their professional lives, but I encountered it once in a field hospital during the war. Otherwise, I wouldn't have known what it was.'

Isobel's heart was racing. She didn't know what to do or say. Calm yourself, she whispered under her breath, calm yourself.

'Then I need to pay for a little more of your time,' she replied. 'Strangers as we are, I need to tell you of things I would rather keep private.'

'I am a doctor, Lady Farrar,' the man said, a slight smirk tightening his thin lips even more. How she longed for old Doctor Palmer, who by now would have gently taken her hand.

'Mr Brodie's father, my first husband, and I separated before I even knew I was carrying a child. It was an unhappy marriage. One of the reasons for its failure was that I had formed a close attachment to another gentleman.'

Isobel walked a few paces away from the man. Dear God, she said to herself again.

'The symptoms you describe were not possessed by my first husband. I am quite sure of that. But they were possessed by the other gentleman.'

When Isobel had stood up, the doctor had seated himself on the bench without invitation. Now he leaned forward towards her, his fingers locked together, his thumbs twiddling, a sudden sparkle in the small, piggy eyes.

'Then there is an obvious conclusion, Lady Farrar.'

'But that is not possible,' she replied, her voice rising in an arc of panic.

'Forgive me, but you were not intimate with the other gentleman?'

'We were extremely careful. Always, always. We wanted no such outcome until we were legally married, as we had soon hoped to be.'

'Careful? But this was when?' asked the doctor. 'Thirty-five, forty years ago? For me to give you a considered opinion, Lady Farrar, we would need to have the most personal of conversations. Are you willing to do that?'

Isobel looked out towards the little river. The rowing-boat was coming back now. How wonderful it would be to be gliding downstream on a morning like this, letting one's fingertips trail in the cool green-blue water. She turned back to the doctor and nodded. She answered the questions he asked about the long-lost intimacies. Exactly what these involved, down to the last detail. To remember them was not difficult because she had clung to them afterwards, forgetting nothing, keeping them sacrosanct. But to speak aloud of them, to share them with this cold inquisitor, was the hardest of things.

'I'm afraid to say that the stratagems employed by the gentleman were far from foolproof, Lady Farrar.'

'Then we were fools?'

'It was another time, Lady Farrar, when people were less educated in these matters.'

She told him then of Pelham Crescent. Her assumption that the very violence of her defilement had caused her subsequent condition. Again, the brisk doctor shook his head. That assumption had little basis in medicine. The bodies of women did not work that way. They were capricious, he said with a schoolboy smirk, just as the fairer sex were in every other way.

'Then I have been a fool twice over,' she said.

'It was another time, Lady Farrar,' the doctor said again, shaking his head as if to indicate sympathy. 'The dark ages, really.'

'You are quite convinced of this?' she asked, quite sharply, feeling an anger rise up inside her, though against whom she wasn't exactly sure. Against this smug young man? Against Hugh Pasco? Against herself? Or maybe just against the age in which she had been young. The age that had allowed her to be possessed, to be kept in ignorance of her own body, to be seen as somehow lesser.

'As soon as your son is walking again, I'll send him to a consultant who specialises in this area of medicine. It will of course be necessary for the consultant to tell Mr Brodie about his condition. It will be up to you whether or not you tell him anything more.'

When the doctor had gone, Isobel sat on the bench for a while looking at the view but not seeing it. Her coffee was cold now, though the sips of it felt good within the tightness of her throat.

The path down to the little river was a corkscrew that turned and twisted between an arching tunnel of pleached lime trees. She had always loved this path: the feeling of solitude that it brought her, though quite aware that she was far from alone, and was indeed being watched every step of the way. From burrows and hides, from nests in the treetops or under the bracken, their eyes were upon her.

She had read in some periodical that nature's creatures were infinitely happier than human beings. Their tiny brains were not designed to feel anxiety about either past or future. They lived entirely for the present moment and the little joys which that moment might bring them. A meal, a mating, a sleep. The feel of a thermal under their wings or the rough, knotty bark under their claws as they scaled a tree. How often Isobel had yearned for such simplicity of existence. All her life, the present had been elusive, the other two tenses by far the stronger. Regret and pain in the past, doubt and anxiety for the future. Now here were both again on this seemingly perfect morning, just hours after she'd thought some catharsis had happened, some freedom at last achieved from that past, some hope for a future without its shadows.

The tunnel of trees gave way and opened out onto the grassy bank of the little river. Scarcely broader than a tennis court, the river was always sluggish, even in stormy weather. Nothing much seemed to ruffle its never-ending journey from some unknown source to where it lost itself in a larger waterway. The banks were overhung with willows and thick with reeds, blurring the division between land and water. But at the foot of the path was a postage stamp of solid ground, where a big flat boulder did service as a seat. Octavius had loved it here too. Even when he had become frail, he would struggle down to this place. If you ever get bored with me, he'd said, just creep up from behind, shove me in and I'll float away, like poor Ophelia.

In her seventh decade now, Isobel Farrar had never known such a conflict within herself. The wild, overwhelming joy in her soul that Frank Brodie could be the son of Hugh Pasco; the sheer wonder of such a gift. But the horror that she had given that child away – the guilt and sorrow which for forty years had come of that act, now multiplied a hundredfold. And what she feared most was that her own conflict might be replicated in Frank. Which side of it would win in his heart? The growth of an even closer bond between them or that bond now broken forever?

Another boat passed her by. What a splendid day, called the rower. Isobel called back that indeed it was. Were they not lucky, the rower said? Perhaps it would be a glorious summer. She sat stock-still on the flat boulder watching the green-blue water. If she lived to be a hundred, she thought, no other morning would be as momentous as this. When the world eventually closed in on her, this would be one of the days she would take into the darkness, and she wanted to remember it with all the senses of her being. The sight of the translucent sky and the willows slumped above the water, the sounds of the larks and all the creatures of the woods, the smell of the grass, the cool touch of the old stone beneath her.

'Hugh!' she cried out suddenly, feeling a presence all around her.

The little river, quite uninterested, wound past her on its way. It had flowed here long before the house had been built on the hill and would do so long after it had fallen and crumbled into dust.

37

In the back of the taxi, she smiled. How extraordinary. Forty years on, the same phenomenon. As the cab climbed up the long hill from Swiss Cottage to Hampstead, the sun broke through the clouds. Just as it had always seemed to do when she and her lover had made it their trysting-place so long ago.

She looked through the window at the cobbled lanes of small houses in which they'd hoped one day to live. Among the writers and artists, the sculptors and musicians, the radicals and liberals. Our sort of place, Hugh had promised her. People like you and me can be happy here.

Frank was waiting for her outside the Underground station in his suit and tie. Johnnie Farrar never wore a suit and tie if he could possibly help it, but then the world of her second child was not the same as that of her first. The evening before, she had written to Johnnie in Canada, a task she'd been putting off. But it had been high time.

Frank now always kissed her cheek on meeting, though still shyly, as if half-expecting a rebuff. These days, he got Saturday afternoons off from the ironmongery in recognition of his long service. These were now his cycling hours, the garden still reserved for Sundays. But she had sent him a telegram just yesterday.

Please come to luncheon in Hampstead tomorrow.

They walked down the High Street and into Flask Walk. A friend who lived locally had told her the place was still there, though the name had long since changed. Inside the restaurant, everything else had changed too. When she and Hugh had come here, it had been Italian but was now French. The bad watercolour of Lake Como had gone, replaced by an equally poor one of Notre-Dame. There was no longer a table in the exact position as the one they'd always had. For a moment, she found this painful and thought she'd made a mistake in coming. But Frank seemed to like the place. She'd have to order for him, he said. He didn't know a word of French, apart from the curses he'd learned in the war.

'Thanks for sending me to that posh doctor,' he said. 'Honest to God, that room was like a palace. It was kind of you to pay.'

'Why would I not pay?' she asked. 'I'm your mother.'

'But thanks all the same,' he said, shy with her again, toying with the food on his plate.

'So the doctor thinks the problem isn't too serious?'

'That's what he said. Though I might need one of these new hearing gadgets in the future. Oh well, there are worse things.'

'Yes indeed.'

'A chance in a million, the doc said. Hereditary, he said.'

'I understand that's the case,' replied Isobel.

'So, I got my good looks from you' – Frank smiled – 'and this weird thing from...'

'It seems so,' she said. 'I'm sorry.'

They spoke of other matters. About the garden, of course. And about Arthur, who was poorly again today. A neighbour was looking in on him, Frank said, so he mustn't be too long away. And, if Isobel didn't mind, he might skip his usual Sunday this week. Just this once. He was worried about Arthur. Arthur wasn't getting any better. Isobel reached across the table and touched his hand and said that she was sorry for that too.

'Frank, dear,' she said, over the *meringue glacée*, 'I asked you to come all the way up here for a reason. I have to tell you something and I wanted it to be here. Silly really. An old woman's sentimentality.'

'In this restaurant?'

'No, but close by,' she said, a sudden urgency coming into her voice. 'Might we miss our coffee and go now, please?'

Unlike the restaurant in Flask Walk, the little chapel was quite unaltered, its pure white walls still dazzling in the sunlight against the sky and the soft pink of the cherry trees in the street. Inside, the simplicity of it struck her anew: a place stripped of fripperies and affectation, clear-headed in its essential purpose. Forty years on, the bare wooden cross still hung above the simple altar, before which she and Hugh Pasco had stood that day, saying nothing because nothing had needed to be said.

But something needed to be said right now. And still, as when sitting on the boulder by the little river, Isobel veered between the exhilaration of the telling and her fear of the question that might come in its wake. But tell she must. Of course, she was aware of having the option of not telling, of never telling, but that would be just another sin committed against this child of hers and there had already been too many. No, she would not do that.

As they walked slowly down the aisle, she slipped her arm through his. She had once done that on the slippery winter ground of the garden but had felt his arm tense against her own. It had taken time and patience for that tightness to release, but now she sensed that he liked it, that he felt he was caring for her as, so briefly, she had once cared for him.

Isobel tugged gently on his arm and steered him into a pew. And then she told him the truth that the posh doctor had just confirmed to her in a letter. That there was little doubt in the matter. That this strange condition made it overwhelmingly likely that Hugh Pasco was the father of the man called Frank Brodie. He stared back at her, his eyes wide. Looking at him then, her heart in her mouth, Isobel imagined she could see every pore of his skin, every hair of his head, every beat of the pulse in his temple. The child of whom she had fantasised throughout the long years had never seemed more real and alive.

He got up from the pew and walked up to the altar, standing there with his back to her.

'So I'm not the son of a cruel man,' he said over his shoulder. 'I'm not the child of a… of a wicked deed.'

'No, Frank.'

'I'm the son of a good man.'

'The best of men.'

'The man who built the house? Who first made the garden?'

'Yes, Frank.'

'That first time I came, when the place was all shut up and I still thought you might be dead, I stood there and wondered what such a man would have been like,' he said, his back still turned to her, 'and where he found it in himself to create such beauty. And I wished that even a fraction of that might be somewhere in myself, even if I never managed to find it. So often, as I've worked in the garden, I've thought of him and prayed that I was doing things he would approve of.'

'And you have, Frank dear.'

'And you're telling me he is my father?'

'Hugh was your father. *Is* your father.'

He turned to face her now. Isobel had stood up in the pew, holding on to the hard mahogany of the row in front. She waited for the question to come. Surely it could only be a matter of moments, half a minute at the most. And then she saw it in the sudden rapid blinking in the eyes, she saw the thought strike him and the question roll out along his tongue towards his lips. In her ears, she heard the words as if they had already been spoken.

'If you'd known...?'

'Would you have...?'

'Things might have been...'

But the lips did not move, the words never left them. She saw the blinking of his eyes slow down then stop. And she knew then that the question would not be asked. In some things, certainty was to be sought; in others it was not. Peace could come, deep happiness even, from uncertainty. Of questions and answers left unsaid. When she had asked herself the question and, in the past few days, she had done so until her head was spinning, she had come to the conclusion that she simply didn't know the answer. And no matter how long she thought about it, there never would be. But there was a fine mercy in that, and she knew it.

Mother and son stood looking at each other across a few yards of pale wooden floor. Then Isobel went to him and took his hand, guiding him gently towards the little altar.

'Your father stood here once. On this exact spot. And held my hand as you are doing now. Is that not quite wonderful?'

'Is it all right for me to love him, d'you think? It's not too late?'

'Of course, Frank. It's never too late.'

'And I love you too,' he replied.

And now for the first time since the brisk young doctor had come out to her under the old oak tree, Isobel Farrar abandoned herself entirely to the joy.

'Hugh,' she whispered up into the vaulted roof. 'Here is our son.'

38

In the small hours of the very day on which she and Frank were to travel to Dorset, the horror came for her again.

She knew she couldn't stop the thing that was about to happen. She knew that quite well, yet every time she tried again. It was to be the moment, after all, when the course of her life would change. One little moment. No more than the coming and going of a breath. From the warmth of love to the chill of loneliness. For fulfilment to desolation. Small wonder that, even just in a nightmare, she would try again.

And so, once more, she chased him into the mass of the crowd. Sometimes there were scarcely inches between them, the fingers of her lilac glove almost grasping the wings of his open overcoat as he flew along the street towards the great square. She would never catch him, of course. Yet in making one more attempt, some fleeting hope still came to her.

It didn't help that his overcoat was the same murky grey as the day itself. As always, she called out to him, but he did not, could not, hear. The rushing that filled his ears was not air but anger. Anger against the injustices of the world. Rage half-blinded him too, his vision filled by what that world might be if only people stood up and fought for it. And he would be one of those people.

His visions were always crystal clear. Doubt never assailed him, be it radical politics or the affairs of the heart. That blazing clarity had always been the leitmotif of their connection. From the moment their glances had locked together, they had each seen quite clearly what was going to happen. The proprieties they would offend, the boundaries they would cross. *Le Scandale.* Yet none of it had mattered. None of it. Because they'd had that vision, wondrous in its certainty, of what a life spent together might bring. And so they had hurried towards it, footsure and with eyes wide open. The sky blazing blue. The sun at its zenith. The path stretching before them, straight and true.

In the great square, the crowds grew denser. Shouting, obscenities, crudely made banners held up by grubby poles. Once or twice, she lost sight of the flying overcoat, then found it again. Still she shouted; still he didn't hear. The ground was wet after a thunderstorm, the hooves of the police horses unsure of their purchase.

Forty years on, in this nightmare of hers, she still heard the sudden whinny of the big black beast, rearing back from what was unavoidable. The shout of the rider. The bellowed warnings from the people nearest. Her own desperate cry, the last time she would speak his name in the hope that he might hear it. Forty years on, she still saw the havoc. The panicked animal, the rider fighting for control. The shouting fading away into hopeless silence. The faces crowding round, the banners lowered as if in mourning. All of them knowing that something unspeakable had collided with the happy fervour of their mission. And then she saw the coat flung wide across the cobbles, the body inside it twisted into an obscene shape, mocking the careless beauty she had come to worship. Above all, she saw his eyes, wide open, curious and disbelieving. The mouth agape too, a scarlet rivulet trickling down the chin onto the white shirt collar. All in a moment. In the coming and going of a breath. Bloody Sunday.

Forty years on, but still the nightmare came to her. Sometimes, it let her rest for months but then, just when she believed it had finally slunk away, ashamed of what it made an old woman suffer, it would return, its power undiminished by its absence. Whenever and wherever she woke from it, her forehead freckled with sweat, her hair rampant on the damp pillow, she gripped the edges of the mattress so that she could not be pulled back down into its depths. Waiting until her breathing had slowed back to normal, she would quietly resurface into her life.

Yet even in the merciful sunlight of such mornings, it would stay with her for hours, perhaps even a day or two. And she would wonder when, if ever, it would release her. Would it only be when she was claimed by her own ultimate sleep? Until then, it seemed she must go on hearing the shouts, the policeman's whistle, the pointless calls for a doctor. Until then, she must see the life trickling out from between his lips. Lips that still moved gently. Whispering, in that last second, her name.

But on that night before she was going, at long last, to the hillside in Dorset, the release for which she longed came to her. The nightmare resolved itself into a dream in which the flying coat tail was caught. In which she flung her arms around him and told him he had seeded their child within her. And that nothing else mattered. Not really. Not compared to the life that lay before the three of them. And then he wrapped her tight inside the wings of his coat and held her belly tightly against him. Then the great square somehow vanished and took the whole city with it. And they stood together on that path which stretched before them. The sky blazing blue. The sun at its zenith.

And when she awoke, Isobel no longer needed to grip the mattress or try to slow her heartbeat. As the first light crept between the edges of curtains, she lay there quite still, knowing that the nightmare would never return. Because Hugh Pasco was no longer dead. Within the body and soul of his son, he lived and breathed again.

*

They stood in the wind on a hillside overlooking the sea. They had not worn black. It was much too late for such obsequies. Besides, the journey was not to be a mournful one. Isobel didn't want that. It was to be a sort of reunion, she said, and surely those should be cheerful things. Instead, she wore dove-grey, with splashes of spring violet in her hat and gloves. Hugh had always liked her in dove-grey against her golden hair. Frank wore his suit, but his tie was dark blue.

Isobel had not known if this pilgrimage, to the place she had never felt able to visit, would bring comfort or pain and had come prepared for either. In the event, it was a mixture of the two which buffeted her in the churchyard perched high above the waves. In the corner where the Pascos lay crowded together, her handsome young architect, the great man to be, was squeezed in between a miner and a carpenter, though Hugh the radical would have liked that.

They laid their flowers and stood back a little from the grave. Frank took his cap off and bowed his head, but no prayers were said, at least aloud. What point when they had already been answered? Hugh Pasco, the wife of his heart and the child of his body were reunited and God was not needed.

'I wish he was at Halcyon,' said Frank.

'But he is,' she replied. 'You feel it, can't you? In the house? In the garden? I know that you do. He is everywhere.'

'D'you think that's why I felt at home there?' he asked. 'From that very first time I laid eyes on it? Did a part of me know his spirit was there? Do you believe that sort of mumbo-jumbo?'

'I do,' she replied.

Frank stepped back up to the grave and pressed his lips to the mossy stone. Then he crouched down and began to talk to the man who had been his father. He spoke in a whisper and Isobel couldn't hear the words, though she longed to. When he returned to her, he must have read that longing on her face.

'I just wanted to introduce myself,' said Frank, staring down at the cap in his hands. 'I told him my name and that I was his son. And that I loved him.'

At the lychgate, he stopped and looked back up the hillside.

'I don't want to be Frank Brodie anymore,' he said. 'I want to take my father's name. What d'you think?'

'I think that would be wonderful.'

And now the feelings she had kept in check all that day rose up inside her. She gripped his arm tightly, gazing up into those dark eyes just like her own.

'Dear Frank, you are the child of so much love. So much love.'

39

As summer reached its zenith over Halcyon Hill, Johnnie Farrar came home. Alone, because the Canadian wife had miscarried not long before and could not make the journey. She was doing well now, Johnnie had written, though she wouldn't be able to have any more. But she was young and strong, which was the main thing. Just jolly bad luck. Perhaps they might adopt a child sometime in the future.

Frank had been nervous about the meeting. As the house was dusted and polished, Johnnie's bed made up in his boyhood room and the fatted calf delivered to Letty's kitchen, Frank had spent most of the day in the garden, already stepping away.

Seeing it, Isobel had tried to hide the excitement she felt at the prospect of Johnnie's arrival but hadn't quite succeeded. The day before, she'd gone up to her hairdresser in Mayfair and returned with a large package from Molyneux. She had trotted in and out of Letty's kitchen, to discuss the fate of the fatted calf, the style of the potatoes, the meringues and the gooseberry fool. All of this she'd tried to do with some discretion, but it was the piano which gave her away, practising the same piece over again until Frank had asked her what it was and why she laboured so hard.

'An old favourite of Johnnie's,' she said without looking up from the keyboard, flushing a little.

'It's really nice,' he replied and disappeared outdoors again.

When the day came, she was up at dawn but took no break-fast beyond a cup of tea and a biscuit. Time and again, she went into Johnnie's bedroom, smoothed down the quilt, plumped up the pillows and rearranged the flowers she'd put on the chest of drawers. In the bathroom next door, she'd put new towels and a new toothbrush and flannel, in case he'd forgotten to pack his own. She sat at her dressing table and fussed over her hair, although it was immaculate and she'd paid a small fortune to make it so. She called Letty to help her into the new dress.

'Do you remember Johnnie, my dear?'

'He gave me my first kiss, even though I was a fair bit older than him. He'd have been about ten then. He'd come to the farm to watch a lamb being born. Maybe it was something to do with that.'

'It's just how he is. Always was. Quite free of the inhibitions that most of us have.'

'Well, he'll not want to kiss me now,' Letty laughed, but Isobel seized her wrist.

'Now stop that, do you hear me?' said Isobel, pulling the girl towards her and kissing the scarred cheek. 'I see your beauty, Letty, and I'm not the only one in this house, I think.'

As the hour approached, Isobel paced the lobby, peering out through the windows onto the drive. Today for once, the mistress of Halcyon Hill would open the door by herself.

Frank sat outside on the terrace, where Letty brought him tea without being asked for it.

'No thanks, I've been to the lav three times already this morning.'

'It'll be fine,' sighed Letty. 'Just fine. Why would it not be?'

'A hundred reasons. Can't you think of any?'

'Not a bloody one,' she said. 'Not one that's worth a light, anyway. Now get your arse inside and stand beside your mother.'

She raised her hand as if to cuff him, but he grasped it and held it close against him.

'Oh, you're a daft sod, Frank, you really are.'

But Frank only half obeyed her. He went as far as the covered court, then waited at the foot of the shallow steps up to the lobby. The moment had come. The arrival of the other son. The one who'd had everything. The one who'd not been sent away.

Isobel, sensing him there, turned and smiled.

'A big day for you,' he said.

'And for you,' she replied. 'I do see that, my dear. Please know that I do.'

A horn tooted. Isobel gave a little cry. The big oak door was thrown open and she was gone. Frank stood looking at the empty spot, wondering if what had so painstakingly restored might now be lost again, even just a little bit, even if only for a while. A car door slammed. Shouts and laughter. Then a sudden quiet. Out on the drive, words were being softly spoken. About him no doubt.

And then, framed in the doorway, Isobel behind him, stood Johnnie. Like six months before, at the counter in the ironmongery, Frank stared at a reflection of himself. For a few moments, Johnnie Farrar did the same, a smile corralled at the corners of his mouth as if he were afraid to release it. But then he did.

'Brother,' he said. 'My dear brother.'

He flung his arms wide, ran down the steps, wrapped Frank in a fierce embrace and kept him there. Then he stepped back and held Frank at arm's length.

'Bloody hell,' he said.

And now, Johnnie being Johnnie, the tears came.

'This is just wonderful, isn't it, Frank?' he said.

And Frank, being Frank, could only nod, the words unreachable. Isobel came and stood between them, taking each son's hand in hers.

'We're complete now, aren't we, Mum?' said Johnnie. 'I'd not known before that we weren't, but I know now that we are.'

When Letty appeared, she too was embraced and made a fuss of. Of course Johnnie remembered that first kiss. What man would forget, he said? Frank watched him with fascination, this other version of himself; younger, privileged, so confident of his place in the world that he could fling his arms wide open to whatever it might ask him to cope with. Joy or sorrow, pleasure or pain. Whichever it might be, Johnnie would ride out to engage it with banners flying. Johnnie would never, as Frank had learned to do, take cover behind the lines, making himself as small as possible so that the arrows might not strike him.

In the hours and days that followed, out on the terrace, across the gardens and in the nearest public house, Isobel Farrar's two sons exchanged the stories of their lives. Differently, of course. A gush from Johnnie, a trickle from Frank. Yet the trickle grew swiftly stronger. Johnnie had a way, which came from his father Octavius, of looking into the other person's eyes as if nothing was more important to him than understanding what went on behind those eyes. Into every corner of his half-brother's heart and soul, Johnnie marched fearlessly and conquered.

'Have they gone to the Feathers again?' Isobel asked Letty, early one evening on the terrace.

'Boys will be boys,' replied Letty. 'I'm holding supper back.'

'Come and sit by me, Letty, dear. I feel quite deserted.'

The invitation was often made these days, the demarcation between mistress and servant having slowly faded until it now meant very little. Though each still knew her place, a growing affection had brought a disinclination to stay within it. The shift had been accelerated by Isobel's silent observation of the parallel bonding of Letty and Frank and by her understanding of the good that it had brought him. Letty Blount, Isobel felt quite sure, now knew as much about Frank as she herself did, perhaps even more. And that was fine.

'I had a letter today,' said Letty, after they had sat for a while. 'From Germany.'

'Not bad news, I hope?'

'It's from the soldier who killed my fiancé. The man who shot my Ted.'

'Good heavens. How did he find you?'

'The letter was forwarded from Ted's old regiment. It seems the man has been searching for me for a long time. It turns out that he'd known the name of the man he killed. The famous Christmas truce, you remember that? When they'd come out of their holes and played football. He and Ted had shaken hands and introduced themselves. And then, a few days later, they came face to face again. And, well...'

'But what does he want?'

'He wants me to tell him it's all right,' said Letty. 'He's dying himself now, you see.'

'And will you tell him that?'

'Of course,' replied Letty, as if the question was absurd.

'I do admire you, Letty.'

'Why? I'd hated him for so long. This Hun monster with no name. Well, now I know the name is Gunther Schmidt. With a wife called Greta and a son, Helmut, who's eight. Before the war, he was a musician at the opera in Berlin. A man of peace. He's thirty-nine now, the same age as Frank, and he won't see forty.'

'And what will you say to him?'

'That it's been all right for a long time now. I'll just tell him that, I think. And tell him to lay down his guilt. We should go to our graves as lightly as possible, don't you think, Lady Farrar?'

When Letty had gone back to preparing the supper, Isobel sat for a long time on the terrace as the sun drifted down in the western sky above the little river. The stable clock struck half past seven. Soon, they would be back from the Feathers, smelling of beer and cigarettes. There would be happiness around the dining table. Johnnie boisterous and tipsy, telling schoolboy jokes and stories of the Rockies. Frank quieter as always, but perhaps persuaded into tales from the ironmongery – someone treading on the prongs of a rake, the handle flying up to hit them in the face, just like Charlie Chaplin at the pictures.

Could *she* have written to Gunther Schmidt that she bore him no ill will and wished him well on his journey? Or go to Brompton Cemetery, kneel down and tell her father that his nature had not been his fault? Above all, could she visit yet another grave, that grave on which the earth had scarcely settled, and tell Edwin Reed to rest in peace? Because more than anything, it had been that night forty years ago that had hardened the fatal tendency already seeded within the girl called Isobel Leigh. On that night, so much more had been taken from her than the sanctity of her body. She had been robbed too of the capacity for absolution. The blessing which, above all others, can heal us and make us whole again. The blessing which she had sought for herself from the child she had once sent away and which she had at last been given.

Yet she knew quite well that the worst damage had been the lack of mercy she had shown to herself. For the tragic mistake of the marriage a young woman had made for a safe roof above her head. For the rejection of her child, the unknown child of the love of her life, because she was a stupid woman who had been taught nothing of how her own body worked.

With cold clarity, it came to Isobel now that she was therefore not whole, never had been and never could be until she made that change in herself. And to struggle to do what seemed to come so easily to Letty Blount. Could she do it before it was too late, before her mind like her body would become arthritic, incapable of movement? She didn't know. She knew only that she must somehow try.

But perhaps the stars above Halcyon Hill were aligned in a kindly manner that evening and took pity on the elderly woman on the terrace. Because the next day, by the time the sun was high above the gardens, the change miraculously came.

She was standing at the great window, watching the brothers head down to Blount's Farm where Letty had said a foal was about to be born. Their heads were close together as they walked and talked, then Johnnie threw a careless arm around Frank's shoulders. She saw Frank go to raise his own arm towards Johnnie's back. But the movement was stiff and hesitant. The arm fell away before it reached Johnnie's shoulder and, up at the window, a shadow fell across their mother's heart. Yet it was to be the shadow of only a moment, for suddenly Frank's arm was lifted again and this time reached its destination.

And then, as the brothers were swallowed up by the coppice, something shifted inside Isobel Farrar. Some knot unravelled itself and the past, like a rowing-boat tied too loosely to a mooring, was caught by a fair wind and drifted out across the water until it became a speck of nothingness and vanished below the horizon. After half an eternity, all it had taken had been the awkward arm that had finally found its courage. And the unclouded joy of living, which Isobel had believed long lost, returned to her and she became herself again.

40

In the little house at 74 Pitt Street, there hadn't been such a party for years. The parlour was jammed and people spilled out into the hall.

In the kitchen, a fraction of the size of the one she was used to, Letty Blount prepared the sandwiches and sausage rolls. She'd come up and help at the wake, she'd said. Well, who else was going to do it? So that was that. Isobel handed round the plates and the cups of tea. From the silver tray at the window, Frank dispensed sherry to the ladies, whisky or beer to the men.

There had been far more at the church than Frank expected. People from Arthur's two lives: the first on the halls, the second in the shimmering shop. Neighbours too, of course, even the warring Italians through the wall. Everyone had liked Arthur and they'd queued up at the door of the church to tell Frank how much. That Frank was chief mourner seemed to be accepted by all. A status given in death that had never been articulated in life.

It wasn't hard to tell from which of Arthur's existences a particular person came. The oldest ones, those who'd once appeared on the same bill as the Camden Caruso, still paraded the faded airs of whom they once had been. The women wearing too much rouge, their hair unsubtly dyed. The men with florid faces and waistcoats not quite suitable for a funeral. One of these men, once an acrobat, had later turned himself into a solicitor to the less privileged classes and now whispered into Frank's ear that Arthur had of course left him the house. And Frank had gone out into the yard where, for a few minutes, he'd stood alone among his pots.

As the sherry and the beer took effect, the harmonium was opened and an elderly woman stood up to sing. This was one of Arthur's famous numbers, the woman announced. One of his tearjerkers. Never a dry eye in the house, she said. Yet what might have been embarrassing was not. The woman's voice, unlike her person, didn't seem to have aged. But the storm of applause was for Arthur not for her. That sound he had missed for so many years restored to him at last.

At the end of the song, the old soubrette broke down and had to be given another sherry. A few others got up and did a turn, then Frank asked Isobel if she would play. Expecting a piece from her usual repertoire, the music she chose was a surprise. Shyly, she told the gathering that she'd hadn't known Arthur long, but that he'd once sung her this song to cheer her up when she was low in spirits. And would everyone please join in, as she herself wasn't much of a singer? And they did. Louder and louder. Outside in Pitt Street, passers-by smiled and wondered what the occasion was.

'Pack up all my care and woe. Here I go, singing low. Bye bye blackbird.'

After a while, as the wake sailed on, Frank went upstairs and sat in the chair beside Arthur's bed. The chair where he'd sat on the evening Arthur had passed away, with Frank holding one of his hands and Isobel the other. All pain over, the merciful morphine cradling him in its arms. A moment before, Isobel had leaned in close to his ear.

'Thank you, Arthur,' she'd whispered. 'I'm so grateful to you.'

And Arthur had waved his hand dismissively, as if it had been nothing when of course it had been everything. Then he'd turned his eyes to Frank, given a soft sigh and left them.

Now, as the strains of the harmonium came up from the parlour, Frank sat silently in the room where the blinds were still half drawn.

'I wish he'd come out to Halcyon,' he said, seeing Isobel in the half-light of the doorway. 'I wanted him to see the garden. Even just once. I never understood that.'

'I think perhaps I did,' she replied.

The old bed sagged in the middle, the indentation suggesting that someone had just lain there. Frank stood for a moment, letting his fingers hover over the rose-patterned quilt. He remembered the comfort he had first been given in that old bed so very long ago and was grateful.

'I did have somebody who brought me up, you know,' he said.

'I know that and I'm glad of it,' she replied from the doorway. 'Yet something more than that, I think.'

'Yes, something more than that,' said Frank, turning and holding his mother's gaze.

'I'm glad of that too,' she said. And meant it.

*

He'd never known he had so much love in him.

He'd always been scared that he lacked the ability to love. As if it had seeped slowly out of him like blood from an unnoticed wound. Yet he'd known that he could at least care. He'd discovered that in the trenches, as he'd listened to the stories they'd told him and been caught up in the tentacles of their lives. He'd cared too when those lives had ended right in front of his eyes, and was baffled that he himself should have survived. He'd cared for Dora, the pretty chambermaid, until fate had ripped her from him, like an eagle snatching a lamb. And of course for Arthur. More, far more, than he'd ever done for another soul. For a long time, years even, he'd thought that was love, then slowly realised that it wasn't, not quite. That the waters of it were too muddied. By respect. By pity. Above all, by gratitude. So much gratitude; too much, perhaps.

But then love had finally come to him. When he was pushing forty. Better late than never. It had come that long night in the old studio at Halcyon Hill. And the love he'd so wanted to feel for the woman who had borne him at last suffused his whole heart. Until that moment, it too had been muddied water, its undercurrents far darker and harder to navigate than those in Pitt Street. But that was over with now. He had done what Letty Blount told him. He had faced down the past until it blinked and ran off. What Letty had called his heap of dung had shrivelled up, its foulness blown away on the wind.

And in the wake of that love for his mother, love of a different kind had followed. Creeping up so softly that he'd not at first recognised it for what it was. Before he asked Letty to marry him, he told her about Arthur, saying that he thought it was only fair she should know. He talked of that confusion in his desires, which he had no way of understanding. He told her all this with his heart in his mouth, expecting to see her run pell-mell back down the hill to the farm. But she said she'd always known, well, guessed at least. She made a joke about farmers' daughters having seen everything. And said that nothing in humanity offended her, if there was kindness to be found somewhere within it. That very same sentiment Hugh Pasco had once expressed to Isobel as they strolled on Hampstead Heath.

When Frank finally drew Letty into his arms, she blushed and confessed she'd taken a shine to him that first hot summer day when he'd stopped his bike at the farm. And later, from the farmhouse window, she'd glimpsed him weeping as he'd ped-alled away again. That had stayed with her, Letty said, and she couldn't stop wondering why he was distressed. She drew back from his embrace then and, taking his hands in hers, made a vow that she would do everything to make him happy, so that no more tears would be needed.

As the years passed, though she bossed him dreadfully and made him dry the dishes, she would keep her word. And one day, on an impulse, the dish cloth over his arm, he told her everything that he had once told his mother in the old studio. For a few minutes, they held each other by the kitchen sink, then quietly finished the washing-up.

Two children, when they came, were the icing on the cake. From the moments of their birth until the moment of his own last breath, everything Frank did would be in their service. He would labour all the hours that God sent to give them everything he'd never had. When, on a walk through the woods, one or other would reach up for his hand, his heart would ache, both with the joy of it and with the pain that no such hand had been there for himself.

He was too old a father, he sometimes said to Letty, but it wasn't true. For as his children had taken their first wobbling steps, Frank, as it were, had done so too. Into the reborn life that had come to him. With his mother holding him up on one side and his wife on the other, Frank Pasco slowly learned to walk and then to run. No longer did he shelter from the world, hiding in the trenches that a sad boy called Brodie had dug for himself. Now he strode out to greet it and to tell it who he was.

41

On the last day of May in 1937, Isobel Farrar sat under the oak tree below the terrace at Halcyon Hill. It was a glory of an afternoon. Tomorrow would mark the beginning of summer.

At her feet, Letty's dog snoozed among the buttercups. It had long been everybody's dog yet, for some unknown reason, it was still referred to as Letty's. Isobel and the dog had once been indifferent to each other but, with time, this had warmed into something like devotion. In dog years, the animal was even older than her and so they watched over each other, fellow travellers upon time's winged chariot as it sped ever faster.

She liked to sit here at this hour, waiting for the boys to return from school. She'd hear them from across the cornfield, the first far-off sounds of their high-pitched voices mixed into the birdsong. Emerging from the coppice, they'd see her beneath the tree and charge up the sloping lawns, bearing the tales of their day or the gift of some tiny woodland creature cupped preciously in their palms. She'd watch them coming, sad that she too could no longer run up a slope as she had once done without thinking, her body subservient to her command. Now, even walking around the lawns was a challenge. That infernal hip. Frank had bought a stick for her, a beautiful object of rosewood with a delicate silver handle. Yet she hated that stick, hated what it meant; that her time of sitting in this garden was no longer infinite. How many more summers?

Often, if the evening was warm, she would sit out here until long after dusk, catching the last of the western light, reluctant to go inside four walls. Sometimes, when the children had gone to bed and Letty was busy with her darning, Frank would come out and sit on the darkening grass beside her, his arm draped over her knees. Few words would be spoken between them as they listened to the last calls of the skylarks before the night took hold. And if there was a moon, they would stay there even longer, content to be among the ghosts with whom they shared the house on the hill.

The gardens now were as Frank had first planned them to be. More enchanting than ever before. Each July now, for three days, the gates were thrown open to anyone who wished to see them, a small fee charged in aid of charity. On the terrace, Letty served tea and cakes and glasses of barley water. And word of Frank's garden had spread. One day, without notice, a grand car purred up the drive. Miss Gertrude Jekyll had inspected every corner of the place, patted Letty's dog and expressed her approval, though not without a few constructive criticisms. When she'd gone, Frank had wept with joy.

Now, waiting for the children to come, Isobel smiled again at the memory of that afternoon. The last decade had brought such days in abundance. Eleven years ago, when she had returned to this house of many ghosts, it had been her fear that she herself might fade into one. Yet the very opposite had happened. In those eleven years, she had become more flesh and blood, her senses more vibrant, her soul more alive than they had ever been since the first time Hugh Pasco had taken her in his arms. The so-called mystery of Isobel Farrar was quite gone. The neighbours remarked on it to each other, though without putting it quite like that. Old Lady Farrar had changed, they said. Charming and courteous as ever, but somehow easier to talk to, almost jolly, even. A lot less of the goddess about her, sniffed the vicar's wife.

On the piano in the covered court, there were many more framed photographs alongside the one which had once been hidden in the jewel box. The marriage of Frank and Letty. The births of the two boys, Hugh and Arthur. The visits home of Johnnie and his Canadian wife. Johnnie and Frank rowing on the little river. Miss Maud Farrar, wizened now but still indomitable, at the opening of her new socialist bookshop, posed on the arm of her Greek companion. Isobel's seventieth birthday party. And, carefully placed in the warm beam of a Tiffany lamp, a young Arthur Collins in straw boater and striped blazer. A presence at last in the house he had never visited.

Other joys were less tangible. The success of Frank's business as a landscape gardener, started with the money from the sale of 74 Pitt Street. The respect in which people came to hold the work of Francis Pasco and the changes in him when he recognised that.

Isobel had watched from a distance as her son had found himself a father. Feeling his way into it, hesitant at first, unsure of how to show this form of love since he had never experienced it for himself. The eldest boy, nearly nine now, bore his grandfather's name. Little Hugh, she called him in her private thoughts. The resemblance which had bypassed Frank was in full bloom in the child. The Botticelli cheekbones, the sturdy build, the tousled hair. As Frank had been a simulacrum of herself, the child would surely grow into that of his grandfather. How she yearned to witness it. If she was allowed those summers.

From where she sat, she could see the ribbon of the little river far below, the path down to its banks now quite beyond her. Yet sometimes she could make out the sunlight glinting on an oar dripping with water, and that was enough. How clear the view was today, a warm breeze blowing away the haze that often blurred the landscape between their low hill and the far-off downs. Among the treetops, there were more chimneys than before, but people needed houses so houses must be built. Hugh had always preached that philosophy. It had been his dream not just to build homes for the wealthy of this world, but for all the classes. What plans he'd had for himself, what dreams about what small mark he might leave behind.

Isobel gazed up at the sky. It always seemed so vast at Halcyon Hill. *It puts you in your place, doesn't it?* Octavius had said the first time he'd brought her here. So true, she thought now, and she suddenly felt smaller than she ever had before. But how very beautiful it was. A flock of starlings wheeled across the arc of endless blue.

Yet it would not be long before the sky over the downs was filled with birds of a different feather. Flocks of dull grey metal, soaring and dipping. Their only song the roar and whine of engines. Their dying fall. The blood and bone on the good rich English earth. But Isobel Farrar was to be spared all that.

The old dog at her feet was being worried by a wasp. He woke, glared at it and swiped it with his paw. He turned his head to make sure Isobel was still there and thumped his tail when he saw that she was. Just the one thump. Tail-wagging took more effort now.

The stable clock struck half past three. The boys would be home by four, unless waylaid by some dubious diversion. Such scamps they were. She watched the breeze harry the rash of buttercups on the grass. On the little river, a canoe glided along the yawning water. She'd brought a book to read, but felt too sleepy to open it. She'd just close her eyes for a little, keeping her ears open to hear them coming across the cornfield.

The sun shone down on the silver casque that had once been golden and made heads turn in the grand drawing rooms of Victoria's England. A piece of thistledown floated on the breeze and settled on her hair like some gossamer jewel. But in her dozing, it was not the voices of the children which came to her from across the fat, green husks of the cornfield. It was a young man with tousled hair, and he was calling her name, calling her to come to him. In limbo, caught halfway between two worlds, she tried to rise from the seat but slumped back against it. The unopened book tumbled to the ground.

The old dog was startled. He dragged himself up and stared into her face, his head cocked to one side. He put a paw into her lap and licked the cool white hand that rested there. Then he took a few steps back, threw up his head and howled.

At this intrusion into their lazy afternoon, a flutter of dragon-flies rose from the reeds around the pond. Red and black against the sky, they hovered for a moment, looked down on the old woman under the oak tree, then turned and flew away towards the distant downs.

*

Into the garden the virgin ghost stole soundlessly and was made welcome by those already there.

Tomorrow. The first day of summer. A whiff of some new perfume among the jasmine and the honeysuckle.

Acknowledgements

To the late great author Sue Townsend, who, many years ago, first made me want to write this story.

To the team at Fairlight Books for their support and hard labour and with whom, once again, it has been a pleasure to work: Louise Boland, Laura Shanahan, Sarah Shaw, Mo Fillmore, Beccy Fish and Greer Claybrook.

To my agent Peter Buckman for his wisdom, his experience and, above all, his kindness.

About the Author

Alan Robert Clark was born and educated in Scotland. He briefly attended King's College London, before opting instead for a career as a copywriter and creative director with a number of leading advertising agencies. He has also worked as a freelance journalist, and has ghost-written and co-authored a number of biographies. He is the author of three previous novels, *Rory's Boys* (2011), *The Prince of Mirrors* (2018) and *Valhalla* (2020). *The Prince of Mirrors* was included on the Walter Scott Prize 'Academy Recommends' list in 2019.